Zero Tolerance

Zero Tolerance

By Heather Karn

Published: August 10, 2019

Cover Design by Nemo Designs

Dedication

To Jenny Bynum,

Thank you for being one of the strongest, bravest, kindest, and most determined people that I know. Raven could learn a lot from you...and so could the rest of us. Keep being that optimistic example of strength and perseverance!

Also By Heather Karn

<u>Standalones</u>

Phoenix Awakened

<u>The Weregal Chronicles</u>

Perfect Scents
Whitewash
Black Out
Redemption
Freedom
Unity

<u>Gargoyle Collection</u>

Gargoyle's Kiss
Gargoyle's Pixie

<u>Christmas Collection</u>

First Christmas
Cookie Christmas
Evergreen Christmas

<u>First Blood Series</u>

First Blood
Second Lineage
Third House (Coming Soon)

Contents

Chapter 1

If I was too late, they'd close the gate. If they closed the gate, I'd lose my one chance to help the world instead of hiding from it. I'd never have another opportunity like this.

So, I couldn't be late.

Heart racing, arms pumping, and feet slapping against the pavement, I forced resolve to strengthen my pace until the Elite base's gate came into view. Four soldiers manned the entrance, one with his hand on the fortified gate to pull it shut and lock it into place. One of the men heard the clatter of my feet and glanced toward me before calling to his companion to halt.

By the time I reached them, I was a shaky mess, and the man who'd first seen me chuckled as he shoved a water bottle into my hand. "Easy there, son. You made it, only by about thirty seconds, but you made it."

"Thanks," I gasped after chugging half the bottle, the chilled liquid quenching the burning ache in my throat. It wasn't as rejuvenating as blood would've been, but I'd never say that out of the blue to an Elite wolf shifter. He'd take it as a threat and have me cut down right here, before I even had a chance to prove I wasn't what they thought.

"No problem." He pointed toward a group of people standing outside a smaller building on the edge of the base. "I assume you're here for the Elite Interview."

"Yes, Sir."

"Then head over there and join the others. They'll be starting soon."

"Thank you."

He took the empty bottle from me, and I strode toward the group, my breathing evening out now that I wasn't racing time to make it here.

There were far more people present than I'd first estimated. I blamed the lack in my senses to the fact I hadn't drank enough blood before leaving home, and I only had two vials in the bag slung across my back. Those vials were from my brothers, and they were nearly as depleted in nutrients as I was, which meant their blood would do little to help me. That was what our race had succumbed to for not reaching out beyond the dark tunnels where we lived, hiding from the surface world. There was only so much blood we could share within our House before that blood held no nutrients at all. After that, it would be one slow, agonizing death after another.

A young, blond man hung back from the rest, studying the group as the other men and women spoke amongst themselves. He couldn't have been much older than me, and I was much too close before I could smell him. Shifter. Snow leopard. He noticed my approach as I shifted my attention to those around us.

"Hey, you're a little young for this group, aren't you?" he laughed, nodding his head toward the others, who were all easily in their mid-twenties to late thirties. At sixteen, I was likely the youngest person here. There hadn't been an age limit on the announcement for the Elite Interviews, and since most shifters and magic users were well trained by fifteen, they could easily join the Elite, at least those with battle skill. Schooling was another story.

"No age limit was listed." I shrugged my shoulders as his nose flared, trying to get a whiff of my species by scent. "I'm Raven."

"Avery. What are you?"

"Complicated."

The shifter grinned a wicked feline smile and shrugged, turning away from me. "I should push you on that, but I'm pretty sure those inside the building will do it for me."

Yeah, that was the part which worried me the most about this whole plan. Taking a steadying breath, I forced the anxiety out of my body, refusing to allow myself to feel it. Several of these people were shifters, and some could smell emotion. It would only drive them to dominate over me if they smelled any emotional weakness. My age was already a strike against me. I didn't need another.

"It's crazy, isn't it? That the humans know supernaturals exist." Avery sighed, still watching the group. "It's actually kind of a relief, don't you think?"

I shrugged. "I guess so."

"What's up with the sunglasses? With all the clouds, it's not even sunny out here."

"Sensitive eyes." I used a finger to push the sunglasses I wore further up my nose so there was no chance Avery, or anyone else, could see around them. They'd show off my weak magenta eyes, and if they knew anything of my kind and history, they'd know exactly what I was in a heartbeat. I may not even live long enough to make the gate. That was still a risk I took once I entered the building and was forced to remove the glasses and state my species.

"Species problem or personal problem?"

I grinned back at Avery, who was chuckling to himself. "You really want to know what I am, don't you?"

"You bet. I've never smelled anything quite like you before."

"And what do I smell like?"

"I don't know. It's a light scent. Maybe metallic."

Since I was so low on blood and nutrients, it made sense my scent was weak. Like several of the other races, we could scent what species most people belonged to. Shifters were easy to spot. They all smelled like animal, but with distinct differences. In the week it took me to arrive here, I'd learned what most smelled like and which ones to avoid. While I'd never gotten into a scuffle with any of them, I'd had to outrun and hide from several. Most were thugs looking for trouble. I hadn't dared an outright fight as I needed what strength and energy my blood had left for today. If I'd been smart, I would've drank one of my brother's blood vials before arriving, but I'd been too short on time as it was.

"You don't know what you smell like?" he asked, arching an eyebrow at me, and I shrugged, muttering my answer.

"My family doesn't socialize much." And not just my family, but my entire species.

Avery's mouth had just opened to reply to my statement when the front door to the building whipped open and a large man stepped out, inspecting those milling around. Anyone who I suspected had any military experience, well, experience in the old, human style military, stood to attention, some of them saluting the man. He saluted back and then took in the rest of us. His face was carefully blank, not allowing anyone but a telepath to know what he was thinking. It was frustrating.

"Ladies and Gentlemen, this is how today will work. You will form a line and four at a time will enter when I come for you. There will be interview questions that you each will answer and then you'll be asked to demonstrate your fighting skills, all of them. If you're a shifter, you will shift. Magic users will use their magic. Any Others will show their skills. Am I clear?"

A chorus of "Yes, Sir's" rang out while I gave a sharp nod. It took less than a minute for the group to line up, and when we were all in place, I was last, with Avery standing next to me. A tall, broad male and a female almost as large as him were the next two in front of us. If the numbers worked out perfectly, we'd be fighting them. Or I'd be fighting Avery and one of them, but seeing as the two were deep in conversation, if we were able to choose partners, I'd be with Avery.

"Please tell me whatever your species is can fight," Avery murmured, eyeing the pair over his shoulder.

Taking a deep breath, I fought not to groan. Lion shifters. The proudest of the cats, and they could be quite the bullies when they wanted to be. They were also at the top of the feline shifter hierarchy. I wasn't sure where snow leopards fell, but from Avery's grimace, it wasn't anywhere near the top.

"We're decent, although I'm a little weak right now."

"And what do you need to be stronger?"

I watched him without saying a word as the first four in line were taken into the building and the door shut behind them. Swallowing hard, I shook my head. Blood drinkers were the lowest of the supernaturals, looked down upon by all. I'd only make our position worse if I told him what I was.

"Not much at the moment." I shrugged and watched the lioness in front of Avery step out of line and count out the groups. When she got to us, she grinned wide, her sharp canines growing in her excitement.

"Well, look here Ross, my dear alpha brother, it's perfect," she stated, her r's rolling off her tongue. "We'll get to spar with the cubs."

"They're going to wish they stayed home today," the lion chuckled, stepping forward when the line moved to fill in the space of the four missing people at the front.

For the next two hours, the two lion shifters spent their time chatting, stretching, and goading us on. Well, mostly it was filled with taunts. They kept referring to me as a cub, which meant they either couldn't smell me or Avery's scent was too overpowering. Or they didn't care and only thought of me as a child, which technically was almost true.

All too soon, we four were the last standing outside the building. Avery and I hadn't spoken much, both of us trying to plan in our heads how this might go down since we didn't know one another or each other's strengths and weaknesses in a fight. I wasn't nearly ready when the door opened and the officer appeared, his lips twitching when he saw who Avery and I were up against.

"Come on in. Stand on the four taped off marks and wait your turn to be addressed. No speaking unless spoken to, and answer quickly and thoroughly."

He stepped aside to let us through. The lions entered first, followed by Avery, and I brought up the rear. I'd just stepped across the threshold when I was yanked to a halt when someone grabbed my backpack.

"No belongings allowed inside," the officer snapped.

And this was the other part I feared. "Sir, I walked here. I've been on the road for almost a week. It's just some clothes and other personal belongings. Can I leave it right here?"

The officer looked over my shoulder at someone further in the room. I peered in the same direction in time to see a man sitting behind a desk on the other side of the room give a sharp nod. Trying not to show the relief coursing through me all over my face, I slipped the backpack off my shoulders and left it sitting beside the door. I didn't even turn around when my ears picked up the sound of the zipper opening. There was nothing questionable in the bag, except maybe the kit I used to draw blood...and my brother's two vials. Oh well, it wasn't like I could keep this a secret much longer.

Once I reached my taped mark, the man behind the table addressed us, the scent of bear drifting off of him. He looked like one. Big, burly, and a growl in his voice. Grizzly. He had to be a grizzly.

"My name is General Davis. I'm the commander of this training center and Elite base. To be clear, you are all aware that you're here to Interview for trainee positions for the Elite, the government's most advanced and special unit, correct?"

This time I joined the others in the communal "Yes, Sir." He nodded.

"Good. Now, let's start over here."

He pointed toward the male lion shifter and started asking a series of questions. By the fifth, I wanted to run and puke. I wasn't going to even make the door at this rate. By the time General Davis reached me in his questioning, I was sure my skin tone was a sick green hue.

"It's a little dark in here for sunglasses, don't you think, kid?" His voice held cruel humor and the lion shifters and a few others in the room chuckled. I could smell at least three magic users. This wouldn't end well.

I swallowed hard. "Sensitive eyes, Sir."

"Has his voice even dropped?" one of the dozen or so people milling around the room's walls whispered far too loud. The general ignored them.

"Name."

"Raven Cartana." Silence followed. Obviously some people knew my last name. Great.

Even General Davis's eyes narrowed. "Category."

There was no more spit in my mouth, making swallowing impossible. "Blood drinker."

A few growls and hisses, both human and animal, echoed in the room until the general raised his hand, then all fell silent again.

"Species."

"Vamlure."

This time, even Avery's mouth fell open. "Well that explains the metallic scent," he muttered and shrugged.

General Davis turned his attention from the paper to lean his elbows on the desk to study me. "Not much is known about your kind. Besides that you drink blood. Why are you here?"

"To help keep people safe from the Threats," I explained before I was cut off by someone else's mutter.

"You are the threat." It was some female. From where her voice came from and the scent of magic, it had to be a witch who spoke.

"No, I'm not," I told her before removing my sunglasses and blinked profusely in the dim light in the room. "I'm not a threat. Vamlure are peaceful until provoked. We drink blood, yes, but only for its nutritional value. We don't crave it until our First Blood, and only when we've been without for too long. Even then we'd rather die than take from another who is unwilling." Staring at the general, I held eye contact. "I only drink from those who are willing to give to me."

He nodded, still in thought. "I heard vamlure's eyes are supposed to almost glow magenta, yet yours are so dim they're almost black."

"I'm lacking in nutrients, so I'm weaker." It wasn't something I wanted to admit, but he needed to know. All of this clicked in Avery's head and a tiny gasp escaped him.

"That's what you need, blood. Gosh, why didn't you just tell me?"

I stared at him like he'd grown another head. "There were too many ears out there listening for me just to announce I'm a blood drinker. As it is, I probably won't see tomorrow. No one likes blood drinkers."

He tilted his head at me. "So then why are you here?"

"So that I can prove vamlure aren't like vampires and other blood drinkers. We're civilized, not murderers. How can we prove that when we hide and slowly die?" I shook my head. "I'd rather die here and now while trying to give my people a chance than to watch myself and my people fade into nothing and slowly die."

General Davis cleared his throat, bringing our attention back to him. "All right, now that we've cleared that up. Age."

"Sixteen."

"Have you had any formal battle training?"

"Some. I wouldn't say I'm advanced by any means."

"Schooling?"

"Homeschooled. Haven't completed all the courses yet."

The general nodded and moved my paperwork to sit with the other three. "All right. You have five minutes to choose your partner and prepare for this sparring session. This isn't about winning and losing. It's about showing us your skills, all skills. Your time starts now."

Before I could even think past the thought that they were actually letting me Interview, Avery grabbed my arm and yanked me toward the back of the room where we'd entered. During his Interview, I'd found out he was twenty, the son of the local snow leopard pride alpha, and he'd already graduated from college. So, he was tough and smart. I couldn't even match him.

"Okay, what do you need me to do?" he asked when we'd reached the back of the room, and I only stared at him, my brain still reeling and trying to catch up. "Do you have to bite me? What? How do you want the blood?"

My eyebrows shot up. He was giving me his blood? Willingly? In front of everyone? Most everyone's attention was on us now, including the lions.

"Umm, I have a kit that draws it so I don't have to bite. We don't bite one another."

"You take blood from your own kind?" he asked, eyes darkening.

"Yes. It's complicated. Few people actually like to be bitten, so we each have a kit we use to draw blood from ourselves or someone else. Are you sure?"

Avery nodded. "How much do you need?"

"Very little, but it's still your blood."

"Hurry up and let's do this. We don't have much time."

In a matter of minutes, I had a tiny vial of Avery's blood in my hands. The warmth seeped through the glass and saliva filled my mouth. It'd been so long since I'd drank fresh blood that actually held a nutritional value.

"Thirty seconds to be on the mat," General Davis barked, even though he and everyone else in the room were still staring at me. "You going to drink that, kid?"

Nausea twisted my gut. I wanted to, but not in front of all these people. From what I understood, most of the world found drinking blood to be disgusting and taboo. What would they think of me if I tipped the vial back like a shot? Not that I was allowed to drink, but I'd seen television shows where it was referenced.

Avery moved to block everyone's view on one side. "Hurry up."

"Why do you even care?"

"Because I don't want to get beaten to a pulp by those two and you deserve as much of a chance to do this as the rest of us. You've been holding that vial of blood for a bit now, and you haven't gone all blood crazed. If anything, you're nervous to drink it. But you really need to drink it."

He nudged my shoulder, giving me that last needed courage to tip back the vial and allow the sweet liquid to cross my tongue and slide down my throat. I wanted more, lots more, but there wasn't time, and I couldn't risk weakening Avery. Plus, I knew what this was: blood deficiency. It occurred when we hadn't had blood in far too long. Often, those who'd allowed themselves to grow too weak took too much blood and ended up in a drunken state. Now was not the time for me to be blood drunk. I'd have to wait for this blood to spread into my body. If only we had a few more minutes, but time was up.

Avery and I made it to the mat as General Davis called time. The lions had already shifted, and Avery had stripped down to his boxers while he'd run to the mat. While I watched the lions, Avery's blood began to work its magic. My senses became clearer and less dull, strength returned to my muscles, and my eyes must have been brightening if the shocked stares from those across from me were any indication. The male lion snarled at me.

"You good?" Avery asked as the general walked up beside the large mat.

"Yup."

"All right," General Davis stated, "Don't kill one another. Try to keep this contained to the matted area, or close to it. Don't destroy the building. There will be no time limit. You will fight until I'm satisfied or you forfeit the fight. Once a participant has forfeited, they cannot rejoin the match, and the rest of you may not continue to attack them. Am I clear?"

The lions nodded as Avery and I gave the standard response. While the beasts across from us prowled from side to side, waiting for the fight to begin, a sour taste filled my mouth as my canine teeth elongated into fangs. Swallowing, I tried to clear my mouth of the venom my body was producing to counter their attack. Even the smallest bit could make them sick, and if I bit down too hard and pumped them full of the stuff, they'd be dead before they could reach a hospital.

General Davis stepped back and grinned. "Fight."

Chapter 2

The lioness wasted no time, but pounced at me, her front leg swiping out at mine. I leapt into the air, narrowly avoiding her long, sharp claws and powerful paw. She was ready for me when I landed, our faces inches apart until I swung out at her face, my fist connecting with her eye in a move faster than she expected. Speed and strength coursed through my body like it never had. Even when I'd drank my First Blood, I hadn't felt this amazing. The blood I'd drank then had still been weak. This was strong.

Snarls broke out beside us, but I didn't waste time or energy checking on Avery. Yet. If the snarls turned into cries, I'd check it out. The lioness was ready for retribution, and I was unarmed. I should've carried a weapon with me. A real weapon, not fangs and venom. Biting was certainly against the rules here, and there was still too much of the sour liquid in my mouth to attempt to bite and draw in her blood. Not that it would've been a good option since it'd leave me blood drunk.

The lioness glared at me, snarling and lunging, and again I barely moved out of the way before claws and teeth pierced my body. This was insane. I was a better fighter than this. Sure, I hadn't had much training, but even my teacher, Mr. Colinson, would've smacked me upside the head for this stupidity I was pulling with the lion shifter. I should've taken less time worrying about drinking blood and took more time to study my opponent, especially outside. Every scenario I could imagine then was null and void here.

Daring to take a peek at the pair sparring beside us, I found a shifted Avery with his teeth clamped down on the lion's muzzle. The two cats were fighting for dominance, using their front paws and claws to do as much damage as possible. It was becoming a bloody mess.

Turning back to my opponent, I grinned, letting my fangs grow. She narrowed her gaze on me, but I was gone before she could attack, leaping high over the fighting pair beside me so that when I landed, they stood between me and the lioness. Avery's eyes swung to me for a second before returning to the lion as I studied them. If we could take out the male, we could fight the female together.

I'd heard that my kind could create a shield over our skin, which was both offensive and defensive. It was like a coating that hardened our skin, making it impenetrable to piercing, but also made attacks that much more unforgiving. In all of my training, they'd never bothered to teach me, or any of my brothers how to do it. Our blood was too weak, too lacking, and it would've been a wasted effort. Now, though, I searched my body for the power, and when a purple shimmer exploded over my skin, I grinned even wider, sending my fist into the male's shoulder.

Bone crunched under my fist. The lion cried out, his muzzle still in Avery's hold, and he fought even harder to free himself while the female raced around behind him to join me. Not willing to engage her yet, I leapt over them again, this time using the lion's back to help me hurdle him. She returned to our original side in time to watch me send another brutal punch into the lion's other shoulder. He tried to shake off Avery again, but the snow leopard was now firmly clutching the lion's mane and neck with both sets of legs, making him impossible to throw off, and with the lion’s shoulders broken in several locations, his front legs were almost useless. If the lioness could free Avery from the male's face, they'd gain the upper hand again. I'd need to keep her occupied until I could launch another attack on the male, or he forfeited. That was an unlikely option, but one could hope.

I wasn't fast enough to avoid the next blow she dealt out since I'd been too busy with my own. Her paw smacked me across the chest, the momentum throwing me halfway across the room and completely off the mat. My ankle twisted from my crappy landing and I cried out, but kept my attention on her as she stalked me instead of helping the male. One track mind was going to be the end of that pair. Or maybe not. Avery and I weren't doing much better. At least the shield had saved me from a worse injury from the chest blow, but now the shield was gone. I was growing more exhausted, and I'd never trained with it. That would take much more practice, and a sparring session where I was going to get my butt kicked wasn't a good time for practicing.

"So, you don't like me messing with your friend? Or do you just not like me?" I taunted, taking several steps back, babying my injured foot. She knew that I'd injured myself, so there was no need to hide it. Not a bit, but I could always be a bit dramatic...

Stepping harder on the wounded ankle, I faked the best I could, grimacing, gasping, and dipping my leg a little like it wanted to buckle. The female grinned and advanced. Sweat broke out on my forehead. The wound wasn't fake, just the intensity of it, and the pain in it made my ankle throb. Breathing heavier, I brought up my fisted hands to protect my face. My only hope was if I could actually use the ankle.

The lioness pounced, aiming her jaw toward my injured ankle. Praying my leg would cooperate, I jumped into the air and kicked out with the injured leg, my foot connecting with the lionesses nose and muzzle, the force of my kick sending her backward as I landed on my knees, my breath escaping me in a hiss as the world spun and my vision went in and out of focus. Gulping down air and rising bile, I forced my attention back on the female. She'd recovered from my counterattack, blood leaking from her nose. Lips curled back from her teeth in a bloody snarl that chilled my blood. Whatever energy Avery's blood had given me was wearing thin, my body so depleted it was eating through it, just like when I'd first started to drink blood.

I didn't want to forfeit, not after everything I'd just gone through, but my body was shaking so bad I wasn't sure I'd be able to continue longer without losing life or limb to this raging female. Her battle experience far surpassed mine. Her strength was remarkable. She also had two hundred pounds of muscle on me. Even though I was almost six feet tall, with a few more years of growing left, I hadn't quite filled out yet, and I could stand to beef up a bit.

Raising my hands in front of my face again, I rose from my knees, my eyes never wavering as I kept most of my weight on my good leg. Sweat dripped down my back and across my temple, narrowly avoiding my eyes. If that sting caused a distraction, the lioness would be all over me.

She'd just crouched to take another lunge in my direction when a much smaller, spotted cat landed on her back, his sudden weight bringing her down. I didn't wait, I didn't even think. My body responded. I raced across the short distance between us, my injury forgotten as the lioness turned her head to try to take a chunk out of the snow leopard on her back. There was no way I'd let her have him. Instead, I wrapped my arms around her neck and flipped her onto her side, Avery clamping onto the back of her neck to hold a grip on her as she fell. His teeth barely missed my arms, but when our eyes met, the deep trust in his told me he'd made sure not to grab me.

With both of us pinning her neck to the ground, the female was stuck. Avery's weight on her body left her front legs useless, and she couldn't lift enough of her body for the back half to be of any help either. Not allowing myself to be too distracted, I lifted my gaze to find the male. The last thing we needed was to be attacked while our focus was on her.

I found him sitting against the wall, stark naked, holding his shoulder as a woman held a blue glowing hand to the opposite arm. So, he'd forfeited. That's what that meant, right?

Renewing my efforts, I found what little extra strength I could muster and tightened my grip on the female's neck. "Forfeit," I growled in her ear. She growled, and I clamped down harder, closing off more of her windpipe as an angry sound rumbled up Avery's throat and he tightened his hold. It took another five minutes for the female to realize she couldn't beat us in her position, and when she whined and the fight left her, both Avery and I released her.

Standing, I took a step back onto my injured foot. It gave out under my weight, sending me backward to the floor. A second before I hit the tile, arms grabbed me and pulled me back up and I adjusted my weight.

"You did good, kid," a tenor voice laughed, patting my shoulder after he released me from his hold. "You messed up quite a lot, and you were a smidge sloppy, but overall, you did well."

"Thank you," I murmured, my breathing heavy from the screaming pain in my ankle and from the exertion I'd given during the fight.

Looking around, I found the female already shifted and dressing, not a sight I wanted to see. I turned away to find my battle companion zipping his pants and searching for his shirt. Limping over, I picked it up and handed it to him.

"Thanks. And thank you for the assistance. I don't think I could've taken him without your help." Avery pulled the shirt over his head and I nodded.

"Honestly, I wouldn't have survived much longer if you hadn't come to my rescue. I would've been the one forfeiting."

"Your eyes, they're dim again. Is that from the fight?" Avery stared at my eyes rather than into them, like he couldn't even see me staring back.

"Yeah, and from still lacking nutrition. It'll take my body a while to stop absorbing the nutrients too quickly."

He nodded. "Interesting. Do you need more?"

Shaking my head, I took a bit more weight off my injured ankle. "No. If I do, I'll want too much right now and end up blood drunk."

"Blood drunk?" Avery chuckled. "That sounds interesting."

"Apparently it's our version of being intoxicated."

"And that's a bad thing?"

"It leaves us vulnerable." I jerked my head toward the man leaning against the front of his desk, watching us. "Time to go face this again."

Nodding, Avery followed me back to stand on our marks. Well, he made sure I didn't fall over. I didn't want to mention it to him that I was also depleted because my body was trying to heal itself and failing miserably. If I'd had my First Blood two weeks ago instead of two years, I'd be begging him for more blood since these injuries would likely kill me with my lack of good nutrition. Even still, I had my brothers' blood in my bag. For now, that would have to suffice. For an hour anyway. No reason to let myself drink too much, not until I found somewhere safe.

"Well, I have to say I never saw any of that coming," General Davis chuckled as the lion shifters joined us, still bleeding and broken, though not as bad off since the male had been healed of his shoulder wounds. Thus far, no one had bothered to ask me if I wanted my ankle healed, and it didn't surprise me. Magic Users and Blood Drinkers weren't friends, and that wouldn't change now. "How long have you boys known one another?"

Avery shrugged. "Since he showed up for the Interview, Sir."

The general nodded. "Interesting. All right, I want the four of you to head out this back door and join your comrades. We'll be out soon to announce who's staying and who isn't, and if you stay, who your commanders are for your training. Move."

There was no way I was not making it out of this building on my own strength, so I declined when Avery offered his assistance. Shaking my head, I followed after him and the lions at a slow limp that had sweat breaking out of my forehead before I'd even managed to make it halfway to the door. This was insane. I was not giving myself points in their eyes by showing such weakness, but I couldn't bear the pain that would allow me to walk with my usual stride from this building.

A soft grip halted me, as did the light, feminine voice that followed. "One moment, Blood Drinker. You forgot your bag."

My head fell forward, and I groaned. Whether it was more that I'd forgotten it in front of all these people or that I'd have to walk all the way back across the room to reach it before leaving, I wasn't sure. This day was not going as I'd planned, and my brain refused to think how it could have been much worse.

Her grip tightened on my shoulder as her other hand reached around me to place a cool hand against my burning cheek. "Telnar is retrieving your bag. Relax and let me work on that ankle."

"But I'm a vamlure," I argued, knowing she'd know the history between our people, the wars that they'd fought.

"I know. You're also a child who's hurt. Stop arguing and relax."

That she was calling me a child didn't bode well for my future, but I did as she asked, letting my muscles loosen and allow her power to work on my body as my pride crumbled. I shouldn't have done it. She was now in complete control of what happened to me and could cause as much harm as she could a healing. The tickling of her power entered my body and coursed through my blood. I quivered at her touch, hating the feel of her magic under my skin, but when it reached my ankle, the magic went to work.

By the time Telnar set the bag beside me on the floor, the throbbing had left the abused muscles, and stiffness remained. The witch released my shoulder and removed her hand from my face. Turning to her, it surprised me that we stood at the same height. I wasn't short by any means, and staring a witch in the eyes was almost unnerving.

"Thank you," I offered in true gratitude. She nodded, patted my cheek and turned to move back to her place against the wall beside a brute who glared at me like I'd just bitten him. One whiff of the air and I had my answer: warlock. Unlike the witch, he wasn't nearly as kind toward my species, or it was just that she was like some healers and couldn't bear to see the hurting, no matter who they were.

Grabbing my bag, I hustled after the others, remembering too late to take the sunglasses out of my backpack where I'd stashed them when I'd grabbed my blood kit. The sun beat into my eyes like a chisel and in seconds, tears were streaming down my cheeks, and I couldn't blink them away fast enough. I barely recognized Avery as he came over to me and led us off to one side.

"You okay? What happened? What did they do?"

The worry in his voice had me chuckling before I could stop it. "They didn't do a thing. In fact, the witch healed me a little."

"Then why are you crying?"

"I've spent my whole life in the dark. The sun and I don't get along much."

"Gotcha." The word had barely left his mouth before he was unzipping the bag on my back and handing me the dark sunglasses. "You should put those on anyway. The lion shifters aren't wasting any time letting everyone know there's a Blood Drinker among us."

Chapter 3

I'd known before we'd even entered the building that it wouldn't take the others long to find out about me. The fact that we'd beaten the two lion shifters only made their determination to spread the news faster that much more annoying to me. With my sunglasses in place, I turned my head so that I could see the others gossiping in a large group, the lions in the middle, gesturing toward me.

"If you value your reputation, you'd probably better step away," I muttered to Avery, angered heat rising from my gut to spread through my body. My fangs lengthened on their own, sensing my distress, and sourness filled my mouth. I needed to learn better control, and quick.

Avery laughed and walked toward a wooden picnic table and took a seat on the tabletop with his feet resting on the bench. "Honestly, I don't think my reputation will take too much of a hit."

"You're an alpha's son," I reminded him, walking nearer to him so our words wouldn't carry far, like to the group of supernaturals. "I'm sure he won't be happy to hear you've defended me, let alone gave me your blood."

"He wants me to succeed here, and I guarantee you're going to help me with that. You're sixteen and you saved our butts in there. You're the one who had us working as a team. That's instinctual. You either have that mind-set or you don't. Those lions didn't, and they lost because of it." Avery patted the tabletop beside him. "Come on, get up here. I want to interrogate you further, and there's a couple females over there I wouldn't mind having a clearer view of since you're blocking them."

I peered over my shoulder, seeing the females for the first time, or rather being aware of them for the first time. They had to be shifters, and that was likely the reason I hadn't noticed. My kind weren't drawn to them, but obviously Avery was, and he didn't hide it as he watched with open curiosity as they glared over at us. Well, all but one black haired beauty that even I knew was checking us out. She tugged on her lower lip with her teeth, resting her hands on her slender waist, drawing attention to her shapely curves. This was one shifter I wouldn't mind being attracted to, except that sly glimmer in her eyes had me more than a bit wary.

Turning my back on her and the others, I climbed up onto the table and sat beside my new friend. At least I was pretty sure we were friends since he didn't seem to mind my company like most everyone here. He hadn't told me to go fly a kite or get lost yet.

"Would your dad really be okay with you hanging out with a Blood Drinker?" I asked Avery when he'd been silent for several minutes. He'd said he wanted to check out the females, but with the way his eyes roved over the crowd, I assumed that was just his verbal excuse for wanting to keep an eye on the group.

"He'd deal with it. He's more of an alpha who's willing to change with the times. You had my blood in your hands and wouldn't drink it because of how you felt everyone else would react, even though I could sense you craved it. You also had plenty of opportunities to bite our opponents, but you didn't, even though it could've helped us in the fight. I think you've proved what kind of person you are by that alone."

We didn't talk after that, letting us both contemplate those words. I hadn't thought I'd find someone understanding in the world. From the stories my parents and others told of the outside world, it was a place to be feared, with so much hate and animosity I wouldn't survive a day on my own. Well, I'd already proven them wrong by surviving days, and I'd gone a step further and met Avery, who'd willingly given his blood to me. Me.

It was almost a half an hour later when the same man stepped outside who'd let us into the building in the first place.

"Listen up," he directed, crossing his arms as he stared at the large group and over at Avery and I. "You'll all enter in silence and cross to the far side of the room. Everyone's name will be called and you'll be notified if you're staying or leaving. If you're asked to leave, you'll exit out the way you first came in without any argument. If you argue, you'll be escorted off the premises by our warlock, and I can promise you, it won't be a pain free walk out. Line up."

We did as he asked, Avery and I reaching him first. My goal was to head straight for the other side of the room where I wouldn't have to be seen until it was my turn, and then I wouldn't have far to walk to make my way out the door when I was asked to leave. Trying to make my way through the group of supernaturals, with all eyes on me, would've been torture.

Once we were all gathered, the man led us inside, and I made my way to the furthest part of the room and rested my back against the wall, Avery right beside me. It wasn't long before our area was filled in and the pretty shifter from outside took the open space on my other side. She linked her arm in mine and bent close to whisper in my ear, her coyote scent swimming around us.

"I hear you like shifter blood. If you ever want some of mine, I'll be willing to share it...for a kiss."

I was certain those directly in front of us heard her, and even Avery covered his mouth to hide a grin and a laugh. The girl couldn't have been much older than me, if she even was older, but for a shifter, she was pretty. Maybe even gorgeous, but I couldn't allow myself to be distracted by anyone, not even her.

"If I become desperate, I'll let you know," I murmured so even fewer could hear me.

Her eyes widened and she stood straight, her gaze threatening to start me on fire. Avery choked and one of the men in front of us turned back to stare at me. It was only then I realized what I'd said in my attempt to decline the kiss. The girl's hand twitched, likely wanting to slap me, but controlling herself in this room full of soldiers and officers of the Elite.

"I'm sorry," I told her, meaning it. "I didn't mean that the way it sounded."

"You sure about that?" she growled, sticking her face in mine. "Because that sure sounded like a put down if I ever heard one."

"What I meant was that I don't want someone's blood in exchange for anything. I only want blood that is given freely and without price."

Another grin split her lips, and the anger dissipated so fast I was getting whiplash. "Not even for a little kiss?"

I swallowed hard when she licked her full lips, my eyes drawn toward them. It wasn't that I wanted that kiss, but I did want to know what one felt like before I died, which could be sooner than later. General Davis came to my rescue by addressing us, and even the she-coyote turned her attention on him in an instant, leaving me forgotten.

"Ladies and gentlemen, I believe you've already been given formal instruction as to what is about to happen. You'll be notified of your position in the order you entered and gave me your name." He rattled off the first name and informed the man he was not accepted. The man deflated, and a woman behind him patted his back before he turned and made his way to the door.

One name after another was called off, and to my surprise, most of those people were asked to leave, even some who appeared like they were former military. No one argued or made a scene. They just left.

"Jezzelle Coye," General Davis called, and the woman beside me stiffened. "Approved."

Another wide grin lifted her lips and before I could think or move, she reached over, grabbed my chin, and placed a hard kiss against my lips.

"I knew you'd be my good luck charm if I stayed close to you. Now I owe you some blood." She wagged her eyebrows at me as I stared in complete shock, not that I was turned on by the kiss, because I wasn't, but that she'd have the audacity to kiss me at all. Especially right here and right now.

The general ignored her celebration and continued while a few chuckles spread through the room. Even some on the edges of the room joined in, and my face flamed hot as I forced myself to focus back on the general. When he called out the male lion shifter's name, I held my breath.

"Ross Yates, excused." The lion glared back at Avery and I before stalking from the room. The female shot her own hateful stare at us. "Bethany Yates, follow your brother."

The female stared open mouthed at the general before finding her voice. "Excuse me? You're not choosing us because we lost to a pair of lucky, unprepared cubs, one of which is a Blood Drinker?"

The general glared at her over the sheet of paper he held in his hand. "I'm not choosing you because the two of you have poor attitudes. Now. Get. Out."

She gave me one last, fiery stare before stalking from the room. When it was my turn to be excused, I'd have to be cautious. I wouldn't put it past the lions to hide somewhere and jump me the first chance they got.

"Avery Clark." The leopard shifter beside me held his breath. "Approved."

My new friend released his breath and sagged against the wall with his eyes closed. I was relieved for him, but that meant there was only one more name to call, and all eyes were on me as General Davis lifted his from the paper. His face was still unreadable, which was killing me.

"Raven Cartana." He paused, making my nausea spike. "Approved."

I swallowed hard and heaved in a deep breath, closing my eyes and leaning back to mimic Avery. Like him, I needed the wall to hold me up. That was too intense.

My friend nudged me. "Hey, we made it. I told you my dad wouldn't mind me giving you blood, especially if it helped, and it looks like it did."

I didn't have time to respond as General Davis leaned back against his desk and called our attention back to him. There were no more than a dozen of us trainees left in the room. By scent, most were shifters with two warlocks and a woman with some form of elemental powers I didn't recognize.

"You all have been approved because you carry specific personality traits that we're looking for as well as fighting skills that are either admirable or trainable. As you've probably already heard whether from your time outside or in here, we do have a Blood Drinker with us. He is to be given the same respect you'd give anyone else in this room. That goes for you as well, Raven. If I hear that you've taken blood from an unwilling person or used any sort of threat or enticement to receive blood, you're out. Understood?"

I nodded. "Yes, Sir."

The general stared around the room again. "If anyone lies about him doing either of those things, you'll be out. Now, let's assign you to a team. Each person in here is the leader or a second in command of an Elite team. They'll be your trainers and you'll work with their team."

"What about housing and meals?" one of the shifters left in the room asked. Taking a deep breath, I winced. Fox.

General Davis looked at his sheet and then back at the shorter, ginger haired man. "Jonas Garhart?"

"Yes, Sir."

"Housing and meals are provided by the Elite. We'll feed you, house you, and give you a paycheck. It's up to you to buy personal items. Each team also has a slush fund, and it's from this fund that your weapons, uniforms, and any body armor you need will come from. Also, if your skills require you to have special items, we'll provide those as well, within reason."

Avery raised his hand and spoke when General Davis nodded. "What about blood, Sir? I'll give Raven what I can, but is there any way we can set something up for anyone willing to donate to do so?"

I wished he hadn't asked that. It would show one of my areas of liability. They'd see it as too much of a concern, or a weakness in battle or times of dire circumstances.

The lead man cocked his head at me. "How much blood do you need on a regular basis?"

My shoulders sunk. "To be honest, at first I'll need quite a bit to replenish the nutrients I'm missing. After that, if my body regulates itself as it should, I'll only need a few vials a month. If I'm injured or in an intense fight, I might need an extra one or two. I've never been fully hydrated with nutrients, so it's difficult to say for sure."

He nodded. "How old can the blood be?"

"If kept refrigerated, it can last a few months, and I only need a vial like the one I used with Avery earlier."

He nodded again and addressed the team leaders in the room. "Whoever he ends up with, whether you volunteer or I assign him, you'll work with your team and at least two others to provide him with the necessary blood he requires. This is not a hardship you have to take on. We allow our shifters time to shift as they need, and our water folk spend time in the pool and lake to keep them hydrated. This is the same and should be treated as such."

Why on Earth was this man helping me out like this? Was he like Avery and his father, willing to branch out and give me a try? Or was there some other reason, like a gut feeling? I'd never have the courage to ask, so I pushed the thoughts away. There was no use dwelling on them if I wasn't brave enough to inquire.

"Any other questions?" the general asked as he grabbed a clipboard from his desk and set the paper down on it. When the room was silent, he grinned. "Good. Let's assign you a team, then. Each team lead can choose who and how many of these new recruits they want. If there's more than one of you wanting a particular student, you'll either work it out together or I'll decide. If a recruit isn't chosen, I'll assign them. First up, Jonas Garhart."

Chapter 4

The warlock across the room raised his hand, and this time I took a better look at him. His hair was shoulder length with gray streaks mixed in with the dark browns of both his hair and neatly trimmed beard. He kept his hair combed back out of this face and behind his ear, giving a clear view of his face. Bushy eyebrows and a sharp nose made him appear hawk-like in appearance, and stern as he didn't seem to know what a smile was.

"Cole, he's all yours. Jonas, please go stand next to your team lead." While Jonas moved, General Davis moved onto his next victim, a jaguar shifter.

One by one he went down the list. Some of the team leaders didn't seem to care about what was happening as they stared around the room or conversed lightly with their neighbors. Either they weren't interested in any of us who were left, or they'd never been interested in being here in the first place. Those who showed interest raised their hands for recruits. Jezzelle ended up with the warlock, Cole, and when it came time for Avery to be chosen, I wished him luck.

"Avery Clark."

The warlock's hand lifted again. Was he collecting shifters or something? He already had four new recruits, all shifters. Another man had attempted to raise his hand but lowered it when Cole glowered at him.

"See you around," Avery grinned and headed across the room.

That left me standing alone. Maybe last in line hadn't been my wisest idea. It always seemed to put me on display for everyone to see. I'd rather enjoy mingling with others who were as nervous as I was.

"Raven Cartana."

Just like I'd figured, crickets. Nobody moved, and an eerie hush fell over the room as those in it waited to see who'd crack first, or if General Davis would have to choose someone for me. It was by far the most humiliating moment of my life, and I'd embarrassed myself back home on more than one occasion. Heat raced throughout my body and I fought not to let my gaze fall to the ground, but kept it pinned on the general and he stared around the room, waiting. His hard stare landed on a few team leaders, but they shook their heads with glares matching his. Whoever I would be assigned to wouldn't be happy, that was for certain.

"Last chance or I'm assigning him," General Davis growled to the group, and I felt my resolve slipping. If I was any less of a person, I would've bolted for the door and raced out and gone straight home, but I was so close, I couldn't give up now. Whoever I ended up with didn't matter, I'd prove my worth. They'd see.

With new resolve burning through me, I lifted my chin a little higher. They could humiliate me, but I wouldn't allow any one of them to break me. Not now. Not ever.

"I'll take him," a deep voice off to my left spoke and I nearly let my jaw drop when my gaze met that of my new trainer: Cole, the warlock.

"Good. Raven, join your group."

Swallowing what little spit I had left in my mouth, I crossed to them. At least I'd be with Avery and Jezzelle, but now I'd be under a warlock, a

Magic User who I was sure hated me and would likely make my life here a misery like I'd never known.

Well, he could do that, but I wouldn't give up. I'd hold to the promise I made myself.

"Does anyone have any final questions or concerns?" General Davis's voice boomed in the room as I found a place to stand beside Jonas and a team leader who hadn't chosen a single person. When no one spoke, General Davis grinned. "Good. Take your recruits to your base of command. We'll have Lieutenant Blockney and his team come by and work their magic to make sure they're prepared to start training. You'll be notified of the training schedule in the morning. Dismissed."

I'd done it. I'd actually succeeded in my plan. Thus far anyway. Now I needed to pass the training.

There was no time to celebrate as Cole led our group out of the building. We walked through the back door and he stalked across the parking lot to a large SUV. When he reached it, he turned to our group. There was me, Avery, Jezzelle, Jonas, and two other females I didn't know. While those I knew the names of were around my age, the other two females were much older, at least in their early thirties, and both appeared ready to crack some skulls. They were both bear shifters, and already I knew I wanted nothing to do with putting them on my bad side.

"Who in this group knows how to drive?"

Every hand raised but mine. Of course.

Cole eyed me with distaste, and it wouldn't have surprised me if he regretted his choice in choosing me and had rather let General Davis assign me to someone else who probably didn't already have a recruit, let alone five. Again, I refused to let my gaze drop to the ground. I couldn't, and I wouldn't, let anyone make me feel less than what I was.

"We don't have cars back home," I explained. "I've never even ridden in one."

When your home consists of underground tunnels and main rooms, you don't need a car, especially when you walk or run everywhere. Plus, the exhaust alone would kill us. Someone would also have to purchase the thing, which meant they'd have to leave and go out into the sun, which no one ever wanted to do. That, and there was always the risk of danger.

"All right, then we add earning a driver's license onto your list of training duties," Cole snapped, pulling a set of keys from his pocket and tossing them to Jezzelle. "You drive."

She grinned. "Just tell me where I'm going and I'll drive anywhere." Without another word, she rounded the SUV and climbed inside. The others made their way over to it while Cole climbed inside the front, but on my side of the car.

Not wanting to appear like an idiot, I followed. I knew how cars worked because of television, but the whole experience was new. It was louder than I imagined, and the smell... I didn't like it. The seat belt was restraining, but according to Jonas, it was illegal not to wear it.

Before escaping my parents' underground home, I'd never been allowed on the surface for any reason. It had been so frustrating. I'd always wanted to see and experience what movies showed of normal life for everyone else, even after the Great Reveal, the day the President of the United States revealed himself to be a lion shifter. My family had predicted total and utter chaos would ensue, but it hadn't. Sure, there were many problems and quite a bit of violence, but nothing like what had been expected. The most dangerous situation now were the Threats, the supernaturals whose only purpose was to harm those around them, werewolves and vampires being two of those races. Their damage was running rampant, hence the need for a supernatural military force that could stop them.

Now I was one of those soldiers. I'd do whatever it took to keep humans and supernaturals safe from those threats. It would also allow me to show that my race wasn't a threat like most thought.

"I hope you all are paying attention to where we're going," Cole stated in a warning tone. I'd been paying attention, but I was so lost from the start it did me no good to pay much more attention than what I was giving. I'd had to ask five different people for directions to the Interviews, and I was lucky I'd made it there at all.

"Sir?" Jonas asked, leaning forward in the seat to gain our leader's attention. "How exactly are we supposed to address you?"

"Call me 'Sir'. If you feel the need, call me Major Pike."

"Yes, Sir," Jonas responded with a grin. I wasn't sure what he found funny, but as a fox shifter, I likely didn't want to know.

Jezzelle followed Major Pike's directions and after a half an hour in the car, drove us straight into the parking lot of what appeared to be an abandoned five story hotel. Well, if there hadn't been a whole parking lot filled with cars it would've looked far more deserted or like it should've been condemned. When he directed Jezzelle to pull into a space, there were several groans, even from the bears in the back seat.

"I hope this place isn't a rat's nest or bug infested," one of them groaned.

The car turned off and Major Pike turned to face us before we could move. "No, this place is not bug infested. We need it to look the part, but it's renovated inside. Our floor is the top, number five. You'll have access to the whole floor, except the rooms that don't belong to you and your roommate. Yes, you'll be sharing a room with someone. I'll let you choose who that will be, but if there are any problems with this, I'll be the deciding factor, and you won't like it.

Avery reached around Jonas's back and tapped my shoulder. "I call dibs on rooming with you."

I nodded. "Sounds fine with me." I wasn't in the mood to share with a fox, and Jezzelle was way too forward with her advances. The bears would probably kill me in my sleep.

Pike called attention back to him as the bears claimed one another, leaving Jonas and Jezzelle together. Lucky pair.

"Also, I know most of you live in town. You'll have access to bus passes which will allow you to go home, pack a few bags, and be back here before the ten o'clock curfew." He looked directly at me. "When they leave, you and I will figure out how to manage your predicament."

My predicament. That wasn't quite a compliment. Everyone started climbing out of the SUV, and since I'd watched enough movies, I knew how to do this. There was likely going to be plenty ahead of me that I wouldn't have any idea how to handle, like navigating this city. Maybe they had a map inside that I could memorize or study.

Major Pike led the way inside, using a key card of some kind to enter through the door. A man in the same black, sleeveless uniform that I'd seen on everyone else, sat behind a desk in a large foyer. He caught sight of Pike, nodded, and took a look at the rest of us.

"New recruits, huh? You take them all?"

Pike rolled his eyes. "Not quite. If any of them knock to be let in if they leave, please let them in. No games."

The man's smile only grew, making him appear more like Jonas. Great, another fox. Just what we needed.

Straight ahead sat an elevator and Pike tapped the button going up. Smells of food wrapped around me and threatened to steal all of my attention as my stomach rumbled. I may have drank blood when I had to, but I still needed to eat regular food, and a crisp salad or juicy steak were calling to me. Heck, the barbeque scent reaching me was causing my stomach to cramp and growl like an angry she-wolf.

"Hungry?" Jezzelle teased, bumping me with her hip. "You men are always hungry."

"Meals are free, right?" Jonas snickered showing off his white teeth. "I hope they have an all you can eat buffet."

A sigh cut us all off as Major Pike shook his head. "Be reasonable. There is a buffet, but also a regular menu. Don't gorge yourselves sick. We don't need you gaining weight unless its muscle." He eyed me and my thin frame. "When was the last time you ate?"

Did I look that bad off? Okay, yes, I walked here, but that didn't mean I was destitute. Okay, I was, but I'd hoped not to look it, nor did I want to be singled out to receive their pity.

"I don't want to be treated different than anyone else," I told him, keeping eye contact. Until now, I hadn't realized that I was almost as tall as him, and according to Mom, I was still growing.

"You drink blood and I have to make sure it's supplied. Face it, you will be treated differently than everyone else, boy."

"In every other way," I explained, hoping he'd understand. The truth was, I hadn't eaten since last night, and it was some scraps I'd found in a restaurant dumpster. There was no way I wanted to admit any of that to those around me. It was bad enough that it'd happened.

"Fine," he growled as the elevator dinged and the doors opened. It was empty so we all crowded inside and one of the bears hit the number five. Up we went, never stopping on the way until the elevator slowed and the doors opened onto our floor.

I hadn't expected the place to look so nice, and from the smiles and gasps, neither had the others. We stepped out into a large lobby, complete with multiple TV's on different channels, mostly news, from local to international. A row of computers to one side of the room all had the Elite emblem on them, well all except the one being used by a tiny man who appeared to be checking his email. Taking a whiff, my eyes widened. Rabbit. They had a rabbit shifter on the team? They weren't known for their bravery or fighting skill, but maybe this one was different.

"This way," Major Pike ordered, leading us left down a long hall of doors. Each one had two names listed on a nameplate, telling who resided in each room. We stopped at the first door halfway down that didn't have a nameplate. "Corporal Hunt, are you coming?" Pike yelled down the hall, and a second later, the rabbit shifter was sprinting toward us with a clipboard.

"Sorry, Sir. General Davis just sent the information over for each recruit. I was printing it to give to you."

I placed a hand over my mouth to hide my smile while Jezzelle failed to stifle a snort of laughter. This rabbit shifter's last name was Hunt? Ironic didn't even begin to cover this, especially since he was surrounded by predator shifters. I was the only one not eyeing him as potential food, at least in human form. As a bunny, he'd taste great cooked over a fire with the right spices. Seeing him as a human did dampen that longing for cooked rabbit, but my stomach didn't get the memo as it growled once again. This time even Jonas cackled, or he did until Major Pike grabbed him by the back of the neck and forced his face into the fox shifter's so their noses almost touched.

"You will give Corporal Hunt your respect. He's an officer in this military where you're barely a recruit. He's the smartest intelligence officer that we have, and it's because of him that our unit runs far better than all the others. If you can't respect him, you can leave now."

"Yes, Sir," Jonas sputtered, eyes wide as the major set him down. I hadn't even realized that Jonas's feet had hovered a few inches off the ground. This warlock was scary, and he hadn't even started using his magic yet.

"This same warning goes for the rest of you." Pike glowered at the rest of us in turn, and I hugged my stomach with one arm, praying for it to just stop already. I'd eat my bed sheets if I had to so that it'd stop embarrassing me.

Corporal Hunt appeared unfazed by the exchange, probably because he'd gone through such moments all his life. "Who is rooming together?"

It took a few minutes for the rabbit shifter to write out temporary room plates and tape them to the door's frames. The first room belonged to the bears, and once their names were listed, they entered their room to investigate, after a warning from Corporal Hunt that the bus would be by in forty-five minutes and if we wanted to make it home tonight, we'd better not miss it.

Pike led the rest of us to the end of the hall to a pair of rooms opposite one another. Avery and I were rooming to the right, while Jezzelle and Jonas to the left.

"Here are your meal cards. You'll need to swipe these every time you enter the cafeteria. They're unlimited, so you can go down whenever you like." Hunt gave us each a plastic card with a black strip on the back. "You'll use these until your official ID's are made, and then you'll give them back to me. These should also gain you access to the building, but I know there were issues with it before, so they might not. If you have any special requests, please notify Lieutenant Gander. His office is on the other side of the elevator, second door on the left."

I knew better than to ask if Lieutenant Gander happened to be a goose shifter, and by the look I shared with Jonas, he did too, although we both wanted to grin. With our luck today, though, Gander would end up being a bull or a rhino shifter, or he'd end up being a she.

After receiving our swipe cards, Avery and I entered our room. We hadn't been given any room keys, which likely meant we couldn't lock the door. Either they weren't worried about theft or privacy, or they just didn't care. Me and Avery's room was still set up much like the original hotel room layout. A bathroom opened off to the right after we entered, and to the left sat two queen beds, both with white linens. I hated white. Across the room were two large windows with blinds on either side. If Avery was all right with it, those blinds would be closed more often than not since I still wore my sunglasses now.

"Home sweet home," Avery announced the moment the door closed. "I call shotty on the bed closest to the windows. You probably want the curtains closed."

He was astute. "Not if you want them open to see outside."

Avery shrugged, sitting on the bed he'd claimed. "This place has to have a gym. Care to wander around with me? After we go eat, of course."

"You have like a half hour until you need to go home and grab your belongings," I told him, but he was already shaking his head.

"Nope, I don't. My dad's going to bring some stuff by, or that was the plan this morning. You see, my dad is the pride alpha, but he's also a Colonel in the Elite forces and has an office at the Headquarters."

Chapter 5

I didn't say anything to that, just dropped my backpack onto the bed that was now mine, and opened it to pull out my blood kit. It needed cleaning after Avery's use, and I had to put my brother's blood in the mini fridge beside our single desk. He watched me stock our fridge with its first items when I paused.

"Is it okay if I put my blood in here?"

He grinned. "I don't see why not. Is it even still good? It hasn't been refrigerated, and I thought blood was supposed to be, but maybe I'm wrong."

"Vamlure blood can last longer than other species outside of refrigeration."

"I see." He was quiet for a moment as I walked back to my bag and stared blankly inside. "Does it bother you that my dad's an Elite officer?"

"No."

"Do you have enough clothes and personal items?"

I shrugged. Even if I didn't, we hadn't been paid yet, and I'd run out of money the third day out. Of course, I'd only started with about ten dollars, which I'd thought would get me farther than it had, which only showed me I was clueless about the normal human and supernatural world. I'd need to learn, and do it fast.

"They'll do until I can go to the store after we're paid." And I had no idea when that would happen.

"So, back to the original question," Avery stated, standing and stretching before he spoke again. "You want to take a tour and go eat something because I'm starving, and your stomach won't shut up." He walked over and nudged me toward the door just as a knock came from the other side. Since Avery was closer, he strode over and opened it to reveal Major Pike.

The warlock's attention moved past Avery to settle on me. "My office. Let's go."

What had I done already?

He didn't wait for me to reach the door, or even move for that matter, before he spun on his heel and headed back down the hall. Avery grimaced and stepped aside to hold the door open for me so I could race after Pike. There was no way I wanted to lose him and get into more trouble.

The man was quick, whether it was magic or just his fast pace, and I had to jog to catch up with him and speed walk to keep up. We crossed in front of the elevator, heading in the direction of Lieutenant Gander's office, which we passed. The door was closed so I couldn't smell inside, not that I'd have time to do so anyway. Pike took us all the way down the hall and into his office at the end. He ushered me inside and closed the door behind us with an order to take a seat.

"What did I do?" I asked while he rounded his desk to sit on the other side and I sat on a less than comfortable chair facing him.

"You haven't done anything, yet. I know you wish not to be treated differently than the rest of the team, and I respect that, which is why we're having this conversation in private." His eyes narrowed on me as he rested his elbows on the desk and clasped his hands in front of him. "You know the history between our species, the Magic Users and the Blood Drinkers, particularly the vamlure?"

My throat tightened. "Yes, Sir. I know about the wars, the ones between the vamlure and witches. It's why I was surprised you chose to take me after all."

He nodded. "I surprised myself with that as well. I can tell you, you were the last person I wanted to even be approved, but General Davis was adamant that he wanted you as an Elite, for whatever reason, and now you're on my team and I have to care for you. Know this: it's my job, and that's all."

"Yes, Sir." I hadn't expected anything more, and I'd never asked for it.

"Now, let's me and you have a civil conversation."

"Yes, Sir."

"Did you or did you not run away from home to come here?"

This wasn't going to be a good conversation, that was clear already. "I did, Sir."

"I thought so. What do you have with you?"

"My blood kit, a change of clothes, and my toothbrush. That's about it."

"I see. Do you have any money?"

"No."

Pike rubbed his jaw. "It'll be a few days before your uniforms will be ready."

"Is there laundry services in the building where I can wash my extra clothes?" I asked, fully intent on not being a hinderance.

"Yes, but I have a different idea. You'll need more than clean clothes. Come with me." He stood so suddenly I almost jumped.

"Where are we going?" I followed him toward the door, confusion slowing my thoughts.

"I'm taking you shopping. Before you think I'm treating you different, know this: I'd do it for anyone on my team. If any of them falls on hard times, I will do the same for them." I nodded and followed him out. He quirked a grin at me. "You might as well go grab your roommate and see if he wants to come along since he doesn't have to go home. I'll meet the two of you in the main lobby. Five minutes, don't you dare be late."

Five minutes. That was plenty of time. Sprinting down the hall, I entered my room to find not only Avery, but a man several inches taller, and twice as old. They stood speaking softly to one another in the middle of the room, and both grew silent when I entered, awkwardness creeping up my spine.

"Sorry," I muttered, ready to turn and run, but Avery called my name.

"Raven, wait. I want to introduce you to my dad. This is Andrew Clark, the snow leopard alpha and Elite Colonel."

Colonel Clark stepped forward and offered me his hand, which I shook. He smiled at me. "Avery told me about how your Interview went today. I have to say that I'm impressed the two of you took down two lion shifters. He also mentioned the blood he gave you, and I want to personally tell you that I don't mind what he did. It was his decision, and he went with his gut."

"It was a rough fight, Sir," I murmured. "He did a good job."

Avery snorted. "So did you." He narrowed his eyes on me. "So, what did Pike have to say?"

Crap, how much time had I just wasted?

"Want to go shopping with us?" I blurted, eyes wide. "I have to be downstairs in the lobby to meet him, and he said you could come, if you wanted. Since your dad is here, please don't feel like you have to come."

"Actually, I'm on my way out. I was dropping off Avery's belongings," Colonel Clark stated, motioning to several duffle bags on the other side of the room, beside Avery's dresser. "You boys go on. You don't want to leave Pike waiting. He's a stickler for his schedule. He's also a good man, so pay attention to what he tells you. You could learn a lot from him."

We both nodded and Avery followed me out of the room and kept pace when I booked it to the elevator and smacked the down button. It was taking forever and I could feel sweat breaking out across my skin, and I fought not to fidget.

"Would you quit," Avery directed. "You're making me nervous, and I don't know why I'm nervous."

"I can't be late to meet Major Pike," I warned him as the elevator doors opened and we scrambled inside. I wasted no time punching the L button, which I hoped was the lobby. The descent took forever, and when the doors opened, we found Pike standing in the center of the lobby, staring at his watch.

"That was close. You made it by five seconds," he quipped, spinning and heading from the building as we followed.

This time, he handed his keys to Avery, who didn't question him. Like before, I climbed into the second row seat as Pike sat in the passenger's seat beside Avery. All Pike had to do was tell the shifter the location to go and Avery was on his way, needing no directions at all. I was still lost.

"Is there a map I could study back at the building?" I asked Pike as we drove.

"I'm not sure. I'll find you something." He was quiet for a moment. "When will you need more blood? You were concerned about taking too much at once."

"I can drink some again now."

"Good, when we return, I'll give you some of mine."

I gulped, which both men seemed to hear because Avery stared back at me in the rear-view mirror and Pike stared over his shoulder. "I can't take blood from you, Sir."

"Why not?"

"You're a Magic User. A little blood, like from a bite, would make me sick, but a whole vial...that would kill me." I shuddered. We each received a tiny drop of magic blood six months after we had our First Blood to show us what would happen if we drank from a Magic User. That was one of the worst nights of my life.

"Umm, why would you bite him if you didn't want to drink from him?" Avery asked, and I searched for the words to explain, but Pike beat me to it, still studying me.

"Vamlure have venom."

Avery's eyebrows shot up into his blond hairline. "Like a snake?"

"Exactly like a snake. You do realize what you just told me, boy, right?" Pike stared at me, and I nodded. I'd just given him a key to destroying not only me, but my people if no one else knew the knowledge

I'd shared. "I won't bring it up to anyone, and I trust neither will you." Pike glared at Avery, who nodded.

"Yes, Sir."

"Good. Okay, well then, I'll let Avery give you some more tonight if he's willing. I'll ask the team in our meeting tomorrow morning for volunteers. We'll keep you stocked."

"Thank you, Sir."

There was little more talk on the way to the mall, and even less once we'd parked. Avery and I hit up the food court with Pike paying for our meals, and once we were seated, he disappeared to do his own shopping. He returned when we were finishing, a small bag in hand. I knew better than to be nosy, so I didn't bother trying to figure out what he had inside.

Pike let Avery and I do our shopping, well, Avery kept throwing clothes at me to try on since I didn't know what styles were apparently "in." We also picked up essential toiletries that I didn't have, or was low on, like toothpaste. Pike was always there to pay for my purchases, which I hated.

"I'll pay you back when I get paid," I told him when Avery disappeared to use the bathroom while Pike stared at a pair of combat boots.

"Don't worry about it. This is from the slush fund that General Davis mentioned."

"It's not right."

The major took a deep breath and let it out, not like he was mad, but like he was pondering his next words. "Raven, what are your future plans? Your goals?"

"To save people."

"Beyond that. You've become a recruit. Once you pass training and become a full Elite, you'll be able to start advancing up the ranks. Is that what you want, or do you want to be a low level soldier? Neither is wrong, but I want to know what you want."

I stared at the boots with him, not really seeing them as I contemplated his words. "To be honest, I haven't thought that far ahead. All I've planned for was to pass the Interview."

"You've done that. Now plan ahead, much farther ahead. When you've figured out what you want to do, let me know. I'll do my best to help you, just like I'll do what I can for the others. And don't worry, I'm not singling you out. I'll be having this talk with all of them. This seemed to be the perfect time for you as we're alone and you're at a crossroad."

Avery joined us a minute later, but didn't comment on my lack of chatter, not that either of us had been extremely chatty to begin with for this trip. In no time after that, we left the mall with bags in hand. Even Pike was forced to carry some of my purchases. On the way back, Avery asked him about a gym in the building.

"Yes, first floor, to the left of the lobby. It's small. Once you have your ID's, you can go to the gym at the headquarters. It's much larger and better equipped. We'll talk about recruit schedules in tomorrow morning's meeting. There's also a pool in our building, but it's not heated."

Avery and I managed to carry all of my bags up to our room without seeing any of the other recruits. He estimated they were still on their way back from picking up their belongings from home. We did see a few other officers and soldiers, but none paid us much attention as they were going about their own business.

After piling my new things on the bed, Avery and I worked to take another vial of blood from him. I debated drinking it tonight or waiting. In the end, I drank it, knowing that if I needed more in the morning, Jezzelle would be a willing donor. I didn't want to take from her, but I couldn't afford to be picky at this point. Plus, apparently, she owed me.

Chapter 6

I awoke before the sun had a chance to rise, and it was blissfully dark. Dark enough I didn't even have to wear my sunglasses, which had been one of the first purchases I'd made after leaving home. The ability to see without color distortion this morning was a blessing, but even I knew that I'd have to let my eyes adjust to the sunlight. Maybe I'd work on that today if the schedule allowed me a few minutes of free time.

Since it was still early, I changed into the work out gear Avery had chosen for me and strode toward the door.

"You better wait for me," Avery slurred as my hand gripped the door handle. He slid the covers off his body and stood, only to strip out of his boxers a second later. I stared wide-eyed at the move. Most people I'd grown up with didn't just strip in the middle of a room. Avery chuckled when I turned away to give him some privacy. "You'd better grow used to seeing some nudity, Raven. Shifters can't exactly shift with clothes on unless we want to shred our clothing. I'm sure Jezzelle is just waiting to shift in front of you for the first time."

That knowledge did little to settle me. I was sure she couldn't wait, but I sure could. "I don't like her like that."

"I know, and she does too, which is why she teases you so hard. For her it's a game." The next second, fur sprouted from his skin and his body contracted and contorted in the oddest fashion until a feline stood where a human had seconds before.

"Can you talk in that form?" I asked him, to which he shook his head. It made sense since his mouth was no longer human, but I'd heard of some supernaturals who could speak telepathically. Obviously, Avery wasn't in that group.

We walked the deserted hall to the elevator and climbed inside when it opened. I hadn't bothered to look at a clock before leaving the bedroom, but by my internal clock, we had about an hour before the cafeteria opened, and another after that before we were supposed to meet in the fifth floor lobby for a team meeting.

The gym wasn't large, much like Pike had told us, but it was big enough for the two of us. Avery scooted into the room before me and headed straight for a mat where he stood on one side and glared at me, his version of bossing me around and ordering me to spar with him. I didn't have a weapon, so this could be interesting.

My eyes stung as the room's lights brightened when they sensed our movement, and I wished I'd remembered to grab my sunglasses. Avery noticed the moisture in my eyes and grinned. I was doomed.

We both readied ourselves, him ready to pounce while I raised my hands in a defensive stance. I'd never faced off with a shifter before yesterday, so I had no idea if this was right or if I needed to handle him another way. I was about to find out.

Avery made the first move, diving at my legs instead of my face like I'd expected. I didn't have a chance to jump out of the way, and he threw me backward, my body flying away from the mat so I landed hard on the room's tile floor. Whoever decided to put tile in a gym instead of carpet needed their head examined.

A slow clapping announced we had company as Avery gave my face a quick lick with his rough, long tongue. I pushed him away as he chuffed a laugh, not wanting to know who'd seen me take flight, but also too curious not to know. My eyes landed on a woman who was far slender than most I'd met already who were more burly than slender, well, except for Jezzelle. This woman was much shorter, but also had a gleam in her eyes that warned she wasn't someone I'd want to mess with.

"That was quite the tackle," she chuckled to Avery, who gave a feline laugh in return while my cheeks heated and my eyes fell to the tile. "You've got quite a bit to learn, don't you, recruit?"

I couldn't face her. There was no way I could. I'd just had my butt handed to me on my first attack, and she'd witnessed the whole thing.

"I've never fought a shifter, well, except for yesterday. I'm not sure how I even did it then besides instinct and quite a bit of luck."

She snickered, crossing the room to stand beside me, staring at Avery. "Your instinct is obviously still asleep. Okay, first thing to remember is that a shifter may look like a regular animal, but they're not. They have a human's mind inside of them, so they can think complex thoughts and act far more different in a fight than an actual animal would. Second, they're much faster and much stronger. Also, their claws are generally sharper. The best way to win against them is to outwit them or to use your own skills against them. Also, learn what each species weaknesses are. If you know that, you're that much better off. Felines have the ability to jump high and far, but they know you know that, so they'll play you, like he did, and strike low and close. Watch for that."

I wasn't sure who this woman was, but for the next forty-five minutes, she and Avery teamed up to teach me how to fight a feline shifter. Her scent was unknown to me, and though I knew she could tell exactly what I was by my eyes, she wasn't cruel.

"All right, boys, it's time for you to go clean up and eat. You don't want to be late for your first team meeting." She made to leave, but I took her arm to stop her.

"I'm sorry, but who are you?" Avery watched her the same as I did, both of us expecting an answer.

She grinned and set her hand on my cheek. "I forget you newbies don't know me yet. My name is Kara. I'm the resident alchemist. My specialty is liquids, so I'm able to help in the medical clinic here to combine and separate different liquids. We make our own medicines, and right now we're also working on a program to separate poison from blood inside the human body to help save someone in the field."

"How?" I asked, wondering if maybe her focus would someday be on my venom. "How could you do that?"

Kara shrugged. "We're working on some antidotes, or that's what we're calling them since we don't have any other name for them." She set her hand on my cheek. "Don't worry about yourself. We're still far from the ability to separate a poison from blood, let alone a vamlure's venom. That's a whole other complicated animal. Hurry up. You don't want to be late."

Not a chance. We left Kara behind to work out on the weights and machines and made our way to the elevator. More Elite were out and about now, but none of them batted an eye at a snow leopard wandering the halls. In fact, a small feline I'd never seen before in my life passed us, waving its tail at Avery, who watched it walk past us and down the hall and he almost walked into a wall.

"I guess that was a female," I murmured with a laugh and he snorted at me. Definitely a female.

We took turns in the shower and made it to breakfast with plenty of time. This time I remembered my sunglasses, though I received several odd stares for wearing them inside. They had to come from those who didn't know what I was because most people started pointing and whispering the moment I walked into the cafeteria. I ignored them and noticed Jonas sitting at a table with Jezzelle on the far side of the room.

We joined them for a quick breakfast before heading upstairs. The coyote shifter was a bit more subdued this morning, likely because it was our first day, and she wasn't the only nervous one. Most of our food went uneaten.

The fifth floor lobby filled up quickly as more and more Elite gathered. Our team was much larger than I'd first realized, until I found out this was two teams meeting together. Apparently we worked closely with the team on the fourth floor. The woman who led that floor's team hadn't taken any recruits, and she glared at us where we stood together with the bear shifters, who I found out were cousins, against the wall to the left of the elevator. The other Elite watched us like we were oddities on display. At least I could claim that position as I made sure my sunglasses were securely in place.

Pike stood near the far wall across from the elevator, the one with a window behind it so I was glad I wore my sunglasses when looking at him. The sun was just starting to rise and the glare off the window's glass hurt even with the sunglasses in place.

"Good morning everyone. Welcome to our weekly meeting. Also, if you haven't noticed, we have some new recruits." Pike pointed in our direction. "We'll get to them in a minute. For now, let's go over our laundry list."

For the next ten minutes, Pike and Major Knight, the other team's lead, a Witch, asked for updates on various tasks assigned from last week's meeting. I paid extra attention, hoping to find out more about what we'd be assigned to do. The assignments had been everything from surveillance to watching for trends in police reports. Nothing too fancy, but all important.

"Now, before we hand out this week's assignments, we need to introduce the new recruits," Pike informed the bunch. "Each one will be assigned to a partnership. You and your partner will make sure that recruit is taught about the job you are to accomplish. However, you'll do that in a structured way. Every morning the recruits will have two hours of weapons training, followed by an hour of supernatural studies. They'll have an hour or two off midday for lunch and their own study time, unless you need them. For a minimum of three hours in the afternoon and evening, you'll train your recruit in field duty. After that, each trainee will write up a report on their day and log it into the system. Whatever time is left of their day will be their own to do with as they will. I suggest studying and working with other Elite in weapons training for the first few months.

"Also, we have a special case, much like our water adapted brothers and sisters. As I'm sure you've heard, we have a Blood Drinker on my team now." Murmurs filled the crowd and gazes landed on me, some confused and others hostile. "Enough. General Davis has personally vouched for this one. He's a vamlure, and as far as we've been able to witness, he's peaceful. I know you're probably thinking that it's insane to have a peaceful Blood Drinker, but he's had several instances where he could've gone postal, and he hasn't. What we need from you are volunteers, people who would be willing to share a small vial of your blood monthly. This is for shifters and non-magic users only. Corporal Hunt will take down names of volunteers, so raise your hand if you're willing."

The room stilled, and I swallowed hard. It wasn't like I'd expected to be welcomed with open arms, but I'd hoped for at least one person to volunteer. In the end, three did: Avery, Jezzelle, and Jonas. The three shifters raised their hands and stared down the rest of the group.

"Are you insane?" a short male asked, his words spitting from his mouth like venom. "He's a Blood Drinker. He could suck you dry."

Avery snorted. "He's drank my blood twice now. From a vial. He doesn't bite anyone. In fact, he has more control around blood than my mother has in the candy aisle at the store."

That received a few chuckles, and a few Elite nodded before raising their hands. Their names were also noted by Corporal Hunt. After an order for them to speak with me about how we'd handle the blood exchange, Pike looked to the tablet he carried to give us our assignments. After how everyone had already reacted, I was sure my partners wouldn't willingly accept me.

Jonas was assigned to a pair of wolf shifters who were looking into some suspicious disappearances. The cousins were divided between two pairs who were searching out Threats in the nearby areas. Drones were being used to spot Threats on the move, and they'd search the footage for anything suspicious. Jezzelle and Avery's pairs were assigned to assist a local police unit with any extreme cases they couldn't handle with the supernatural community. That left me, and the room held its breath waiting to see who the lucky pair would be to have me at their side.

"Raven, you'll be assisting Major Knight and I in our work," Major Pike announced, and I wasn't sure if I should be disappointed or relieved. Knight appeared anything but pleased, which didn't bode well for my future. "All right, take some time to discuss plans with your partner and get to know your new recruit if you've been assigned one. There should be no excuses for leaving them out."

The room erupted in noise as people moved around to stand beside their partner if they weren't already, and to draw in their recruit, whether with a wave or walking toward them. While everyone else moved around me, I made my way to the front, unsure what Pike and Knight would have me doing. Grabbing coffee for them? Checking the mail? Other office tasks? That wasn't what I'd joined the Elite for, but, like Corporal Hunt, someone had to do it, and if it helped in some small way, I wouldn't argue. I'd be the best gopher I could be under the circumstances.

"How're you doing?" Pike asked me when I finished my approach. Knight stood beside him, still glaring. I shouldn't have expected anything less from a Magic User. Pike was the oddball here, not her. Well, Pike had become the oddball ever since I'd met him downstairs to go shopping.

"Fair," I reported, going for honest.

"Thirsty?"

"Not exactly. The cravings aren't like that after your First Blood."

His eyes narrowed at me. "Explain please."

I sighed, noticing that I had the attention of nearby partnerships, some of which were those who volunteered to supply me with blood. "I crave nutrients. Those nutrients are in blood, but it's not the blood I crave. It's difficult to explain. The closest thing I can think of is that it's similar to when you crave a steak. You can control yourself from entering a restaurant and attacking the first person you see with a steak and eating it off their plate. You want it bad, but you'll wait until you order it and it's delivered to your table."

Pike nodded, and even Knight seemed to contemplate my words, like neither had ever understood this about vamlure before. They likely hadn't. Our histories were too intertwined with hate that rumors spread and grew out of control, spreading the wrong information about both sides. To most everyone else, we had the same lack of control around blood that vampires had.

A chuckle escaped Pike when he finished thinking about my explanation. "Then should I start asking you if you're craving a steak?"

More laughter from those around us made my lips twitch. It was the most accurate description to ask.

"If that's what you want, Sir." I gave a sharp nod and a shrug.

"Okay then, answer the question." His laughter died as he watched me, and I sensed the tingle in my throat that always came from focusing on my need for blood.

"Yeah, I could use a steak. Avery gave me some blood last night, but like I said yesterday, I'll need more. After I reach my peak, it'll plateau, and I won't need as much."

Pike's eyes narrowed. "You mentioned blood drunk to Avery. Would it be harmful to drink a lot of blood now and rejuvenate yourself faster? Or will that not work?"

I bit my lip and thought it through, ending in a shrug. "It might work, but I'd be useless for hours with the amount I'd need. I'm not sure what the ramifications of that process would be either. It might make it worse, or it could cause the plateau. I'll leave it up to you to decide, Sir."

He thought for a moment and turned to Knight. "Have any thoughts?"

"I say it's worth a try. I want to see what he's capable of when he's fully charged. I've heard stories and I want to see if they're true. What I saw yesterday proved one theory correct, and I want to know more."

She had to be talking about me shielding my skin. That would make sense. I was the most unique creature in this group, unique in that no one had any idea what it was that I was capable of, even me. I knew some things I was supposed to be able to do, but because of the lack of nutrition, I'd never experienced them, and I'd never seen anyone demonstrate. Even having enough venom to fight yesterday was shocking.

"Corporal Hunt, please meet with everyone on that list. Have them go straight to the conference room and we'll have the blood drawn. Have Kara come up to help. I want her drawing the blood and Raven drinking."

"You might need to have someone carry me to my room after you're finished with me and I'm drunk," I muttered. "There's no way I'll be able to walk."

Knight tipped her lips into a smile. "You'll be that intoxicated? What, you won't be able to walk straight?"

"I'll be passed out," I corrected. "The amount you're talking about will leave me way passed tipsy."

"Is it safe?" she asked, "giving you that much?"

"It won't kill me."

Knight nodded. "Then let's do this."

Was this my mission for the week? To plateau and let them study me? If so, I wasn't sure how much I liked it. Oh well, it wasn't like I had much of a choice. Taking a deep breath, I followed Pike to the conference room and awaited my vial shots of shifter blood.

Chapter 7

When I woke, I was in my room and the curtains were drawn, but no sunlight filtered in underneath them. It was night. It had to be. Listening, I picked up soft snores from the bed beside me. Avery was back...from wherever it was he'd ended up going yesterday.

After they'd started drawing blood, I'd waited until five vials were filled, and then I started drinking. Another three followed, and by the time I'd finished all eight, my head was swimmy and the moment I stood to go lay down, the world had gone black. I was sure Pike had been close and moved toward me when I fell, but I honestly wasn't sure if he'd caught me. My head didn't ache, so it hadn't hit anything, or I'd healed already. If that was the case, it was the fastest I'd ever healed.

Sitting up, I swung my legs over the bed. I still wore yesterday's clothes. I'd lost a whole day to being blood drunk. It was disorienting, and I didn't like it one little bit. Rubbing my head, I stumbled to the bathroom to wash my face and clean up. After coming back to bed and checking the clock, I knew sleep was hopeless. I'd slept all day and long into the night. There was only an hour left until it would be time to wake up and head to breakfast. Since we had weapons training first today, Avery and I had decided to skip our own training, which I was now thankful for.

Changing into clean clothes, I strode from the room with my key card. Maybe I'd be able to find some sort of vending machine. After a tiny breakfast and missing every meal after that, I was starving. I'd already been up and down our hallway and hadn't seen any type of vending machine, so I headed down to the main floor. Most of that floor had already been searched, so there was a chance that the area I hadn't checked held food. This was one of those times I wished I'd stashed food in my room.

The elevator doors opened when I reached the bottom floor and I was shocked to find Major Pike waiting for it. He took one look at me and stepped inside, blocking me from exiting when he pressed the number five so it lit up. He remained silent as we rode to the top floor. While I felt exhausted and still a bit fuzzy headed, he appeared well-rested and fresh.

"Your eyes are nice and bright. I take it that's how they're supposed to look instead of that dull purple and almost black look you had going on."

"Yeah, this is normal." I'd only ever seen one person with eyes this bright, and he was a vendor, a man who spent half his time on the surface and half underground. They were looked down on for putting our kind in danger, which was what I was now considered if I thought long and hard about it.

"Good. How do you feel?"

"Physically, never better. Except I'm hungry. For food," I qualified. "Real food. A hamburger. Even French fries."

Pike chuckled. "Good. I was almost worried you'd say steak."

The doors opened and I followed him off the elevator and down the hall toward his office. He didn't need to ask me to follow. Somehow, I already knew that's where he wanted me to go. When he opened the door and stepped aside to let me in, I was rewarded with the knowledge that I'd assumed correctly.

"May I ask a question?" I inquired the moment the door shut.

He sighed. "You want to know why you've been assigned to Major Knight and I instead of a regular team."

"Yes, Sir."

He sat down at his desk while I took a seat in the chair I'd used last time we were in this room together. "Two reasons. One, Major Knight wanted to make sure the teams were comfortable with your presence before we assigned you to one of them. The second is that the more time I spend with you and watch you, the more potential I see. I'm not sure why. In the back of my mind you're still the enemy, but I can't see it, especially not after your steak analogy yesterday. Anyway, with that potential, I want to train you personally. I can see you as an officer some day, and I want to teach you what I can about leading so that you have a better chance of reaching that potential. Does that make sense?"

I hadn't had a chance to think much more about what he'd said about planning for my future, but if I thought about it, being an officer would likely allow me to help people more than what I could do otherwise. I didn't want to be stuck in an office, though. I wanted a field position.

Pike nodded when I expressed this concern. "Don't worry, son. We're in a lull right now. You'll see action soon enough. We'll see enough to make you wish for lulls like this."

After a brief silence, I couldn't keep quiet any longer. "What would you and Major Knight like me to do today?"

Pike rubbed his face and turned on the laptop sitting atop his desk. "The governor makes regular trips around the state to the four Elite bases to check on our progress, like having him personally visit will be enough pressure to keep up the good work. Only, he doesn't understand that it puts more pressure on us in the wrong way. We have to worry about his safety for the four days he's here when we should be focusing on the Threats around us. He's scheduled to visit a month from today. We try not to have the meetings in the same location twice in a row so as not to draw attention to him, and we need to vet all the Elite guards who will be his personal escorts while he's present. That'll be the longest part. For the most part, we try to keep them the same, but we've had some transfers, so we'll need new ones assigned to him. It's a complicated process, and I want your help with it."

My eyebrows shot up. "I'm sixteen, been a recruit for one day, well, maybe two, but only one I can actually remember, and you want me to help protect the governor?"

Pike grinned. "Yes. He's going to be shocked and probably a bit worried that a Blood Drinker is helping protect him, but I have faith in you." He took a deep breath. "Also, his wife is coming with him this time, and we need to make sure she's protected as well. You and I will personally provide that protection."

Me? He wanted me to help provide protection for the governor's wife? He wasn't done explaining, though.

"You have something the rest of us don't. You have venom, and most enemies we deal with aren't used to fighting someone like you. I saw you fight. You're a natural. You just need a bit more training to help focus your scrappiness into actual fighting. Every day you'll have two extra hours in the evening of combat training with actual advanced Elite. Our teams here help to put out the small and larger issues, but the teams stationed at the headquarters bring down the major Threats. I've already gained permission for you and Avery to train with them. You start tonight. Be there at seven. Not a minute later."

The required weapons practice and supernatural studies were basic lessons that morning. Our weapon's teacher, Captain Smith, a gorilla shifter with more muscle in his biceps than I had in my entire body, had us running and learning strength building exercises for his two hours. Running I could do without a problem. Underground, when messages had to be delivered, the only way to deliver them was to walk or run. Most of the time I ran. Some of the exercises I knew, but most were foreign to me.

We were given a warning that tomorrow we'd start training with real weapons and begin learning yoga, to clear the mind and strengthen the body as well. Captain Smith also warned us to practice the strengthening exercises in our free time. I'd take that warning to heart, mostly because I had a family to protect in a month. I hadn't yet had a chance to tell Avery about it, but since he'd be joining me tonight, there was time to explain it. Likely he was coming to drive me.

The supernatural studies class was taught by a Witch. She took one sniff in my direction and squished her nose up in a dirty look. Could she smell me? I still wore my sunglasses, though I'd be trying to take them off more.

We met for this class in the conference room on our level, the one in which I'd drank way too much blood. At least my body was recovered from the effects of that much blood at once. Not only recovered, but stronger. I'd been able to do far more repetitions of our exercises last class, and when everyone else was heaving by the end of our run, I was lightly gasping with a sheen of sweat on my skin where their clothes were soaked through. Jezzelle had the nerve to glare at me for it, so I'd given her a shrug. It wasn't my fault.

"Who can tell me some of the Threats?" Corporal Misty Glamour, the Witch, asked the six of us recruits.

Sherri, one of the bear shifters raised her hand in an instant. "Vampires, Werewolves, Wights, and Ogres."

"That's right. Anyone else have any examples?" Corporal Glamour waited for us to respond. I'd heard about the ones already mentioned. The news was focused on those species, especially the Vampires and Werewolves.

"Poltergeist," Avery threw in. "Why exactly is an annoying ghost on the Threat list?"

Glamour crossed her arms and stared at him like the answer should be obvious. "They're on the list because some of them have become more than just an annoyance. They've decided to use their power of moving objects and biting, pinching, and other forms of annoying behavior to cause more harm than they previously have before. It's a trend that is catching on among the species as a whole."

She then listed off at least another dozen creatures that I'd never heard of or knew nothing about and started quizzing us on them. Sherri and her cousin were well informed about most of them, as was Avery, but Jonas, Jezzelle, and I were clueless.

"Every day we'll talk more in depth about these creatures. You'll need to know more about them as Elite because I can promise you'll be dealing with several of these species before your time is up."

Our time was up. I guess that could be anything from quitting, retiring, or death. Going up against some of these creatures, death was likely what she was thinking. When she glared at me, I could imagine she was wishing it was me who'd die out of anyone else in the room.

"Dismissed," she called, and one by one we left the room.

Jezzelle bumped me with her hip. "Ooo, someone doesn't like you."

"That's nothing new," I grumbled, walking with the others to the lobby of our floor. "So, what's everyone up to with their partners?"

Most of them shrugged.

"We have to go meet ours downstairs in half an hour," Sherri stated, motioning to her cousin, Bekka.

The coyote shifter still standing beside me wrapped an arm around my neck, cozying up to me to speak into my ear with a seductive tone that did little to affect me like she hoped. "I still owe you some blood. If you want, we can exchange that now, and I don't mind if you bite."

My eyes widened and met Avery's. He was already shaking his head. "Trust me, Jezzelle, you don't want Raven biting you."

She glared at him. "And why not?"

"I could kill you," I told her. "Trust me, it's not safe."

Jezzelle was ready to respond when the elevator door dinged and someone stepped off.

"Good, you're right here. I don't have to send someone to find you," Major Knight spoke, her gaze zeroed in on me and the coyote tucked into my side. "Let's begin, shall we? Meet me in Major Pike's office when you're done here. We have much to do." She turned on her heel with the same exactness Pike had and strode down the hall toward his office.

"If she hurts you, let us know," Jezzelle spoke into my ear, the same smooth, seductive tone in her voice. "Between us all, we can take her."

"I'll be fine." I stepped out of her hold and followed the Major down the hallway. She closed Pike's door before I even passed Gander's office. That door was closed again, so I still had no idea what he, or she, was. The curiosity was killing me, and I wasn't even a cat shifter of any sort. I grinned. I'd have to have Avery find out for me.

Knocking on the door, I waited for Pike to call for me to enter before opening it and walking in. The office was slightly different after my meeting with Pike earlier. To the right, which had previously been empty, sat a small table, two chairs, and a laptop. Knight already sat in one of the two chairs and motioned for me to take the other.

"You're mine today," she warned with a sly smirk.

I took the seat, and for the next few hours, Knight walked me through the Elite database to find information on the list of names up for consideration for security duty for the governor. She showed me what to look for and how to write the comments about each one beside their name on the spreadsheet. It was long, tedious work, but by the end, I had a good grasp on what she wanted me to look for, so much so that she sat back and let me do the last five names for the day solo. Since we were logged in under her account, she had to remain there to watch me, but she seemed pleased by my progress. I wasn't as pleased. We'd only managed to make it a third of the way down the list. I'd hoped to finish it today, but when I'd seen how slow we were working, I'd adjusted that goal to halfway. We hadn't made that either.

"Well, he learns quick," Knight grumbled to Pike, like she didn't want to have any excuse for giving me a compliment. She turned back to me. "You and the others will be receiving your ID's today and access to the database so you can research as necessary and write up reports. I'll work with the team in charge to give you a bit more access so you can do this on your own account. Just know, if you attempt to look up something you shouldn't, security will be notified and you'll be done. I mean it. Gone. There will be no second chances."

"Understood." I held her gaze, and she nodded.

"Good. This is the first batch of names. We'll receive the next ones in a day or two. I'd like to be finished with these before we receive those. Major Pike and I will choose the soldiers to assist in protection detail, but we'll need your notes to do it. Now go eat some lunch and be back here so we can start working out meeting location ideas and security details."

My eyebrows shot up. "You want me to help with that? This is my third day."

She sighed, shoulders slumping, showing a woman who was far more tired than she let on. "We don't have time to take this slow, not with you or any of the others. The Threats are growing far bolder, as are some of the less deadly, but still dangerous, supernaturals. The human law enforcement can't contain them all, and we're running thin. If we can get you all up to speed, we'll have a force to be reckoned with sooner than they'll expect. Off the record, the President should've seen this coming after his announcement and already had the Elite program built up more instead of waiting for the Threats and others to escalate their attacks. We're running behind and have to catch up. Allowing you to help will train you as well as give us further insight into possible ideas. The other recruits are being trained in much the same way, but in smaller, less public situations."

"And a lot of what we're doing is trial and error," Pike added with a grunt. "You're only the third batch of new recruits, and you're the largest group at that. Now, go eat lunch. Be back here in half an hour. Don't be late."

This man really liked his time schedule.

Racing from the room, I jogged down the hall to grab my key card to enter the cafeteria. I should've carried it in my back pocket, but I'd forgotten to put it back in my pocket after changing into workout clothes for weapons practice.

Avery joined me a minute after I entered the room. "How's it going?"

"Fine."

"I hear the two of us are receiving extra training at night. I'm not sure how I like this."

I shrugged, thinking about what Pike and Knight had just told me. "I think it'll help us a bit more than having one class on weapons, and learning with more advanced Elite can't hurt."

He huffed. "Oh, it'll hurt all right, I guarantee it."

Chapter 8

The afternoon wasn't as informative as the morning had been, and by the time I was changed to go to our practice at the Elite headquarters, I was ready to release some energy. We'd been instructed to take our new ID cards and a change of clothes for after the session since what we wore there could end up bloody, but definitely sweaty. For extra security on my part, I tucked a vial of blood into the thin bag we'd been given today and pulled the drawstrings tight and flipped it onto my back.

Avery sported the same bag, as well as the same athletic shorts and t-shirt with the Elite emblem embroidered on them. He jerked his head toward the door, and I followed him out. He'd been to the Elite headquarters before to visit his dad. Also, he knew the town, so he wouldn't become lost on the way over.

It took forty-five minutes to reach the same gate I'd passed through a few days ago, but different guards were on duty. We handed over our IDs and were waved inside. I tried to keep up with Avery's turns, but it didn't take long for me to become completely lost on this base. Pike still hadn't provided me with a city map. Maybe one was available on the Elite database.

We found a place to park the SUV and strode into the building, Avery leading the way. In minutes we stood just inside the gym doorway that Major Pike had mentioned for us to find, and I wanted to turn around and run back to the old hotel. These people weren't like those on either the fifth or fourth floors. They were worse. Battle seasoned and relentless as they warmed up, sparring with one another or stretching in ways I'd never be able to move. Some used weapons, and they moved with such deadly speed and accuracy I could already feel a knife slitting my throat.

"You have your will written out?" Avery asked in the softest whisper he could manage, and I was sure he heard my responding gulp.

"What do we have here?" a woman cackled behind us, and I turned to find a shorter, slender woman and a man her same size standing a foot away. I hadn't even heard them approach, and what they lacked in size, they made up for in muscle. Trying to be inconspicuous, I sniffed the air. Bobcats. More felines to avoid.

"Fresh meat is what it looks like," the man snickered, taking a step closer and openly sniffing us. "Hmm, feline and something else." His eyes darkened. "Blood Drinker."

"Major Pike sent us," I told them, hoping they'd back off knowing we'd been ordered to come here and join them by someone higher up in rank. At least I hoped Pike outranked these two.

"Fennel, Cage, leave the recruits alone. They're here to train with us," a familiar, baritone voice boomed inside the training room. If it was possible, I wanted to leave now more than I had before. Captain Smith, the gorilla from our morning training, was also going to be our evening trainer it appeared. I stifled a groan and faced where he stood on a mat on our half of the room. "Get over here, kids. Let's see how much work we have to do to catch you up to our speed. Avery, you first."

Avery and I set our bags down against the wall near the door and headed toward the mat. While I stopped at the mat's edge, he continued walking onto it until he faced the gorilla shifter, who gave him a wicked grin. Both took defensive stances, and I held my breath.

"Give me all you've got, and don't worry about hurting me," Smith warned. "I can take it."

I was positive he could, but I wasn't so sure about Avery. Without warning, my friend shifted and dove at Smith like he'd done to me yesterday morning, only Smith shifted just as fast, grabbed Avery right before his teeth could latch on, picked him up, and tossed him across the mat. Okay, tossed wasn't the right word. Chucked was more like it.

The snow leopard hit the ground hard, stunned, and took too long to recover, giving Smith the upper hand, allowing Avery to be chucked to the other side of the mat. That blow sparked something in Avery I hadn't seen yet, and he stood, turning bared teeth toward Smith. For the next ten minutes, the two exchanged blows. Avery was a much better fighter than I'd given him credit for during our Interview. I was likely our weakest link that day and he'd been making up my slack.

When he was satisfied, Smith shifted to his human self, a very naked human self, and ordered Avery to stand down. Both shifters' clothes had shredded upon shifting, which was another good reason for Avery to bring a second set. He limped over to his bag, but Smith stopped him halfway to it.

"Don't bother, kid. You'll be shifting again. In fact, I want you to work with Fennel and Cage for the next hour. Bobcats, don't kill him. We need him alive and learning."

The two cats were already shifted and now eyed the bigger cat approaching them. I would've guessed that Avery could take them since they were smaller, but the wicked grins they gave him didn't bode well for Avery's future. Neither did the wicked grin cast my way from Smith.

"Now, you're the one who interests me," he drawled. "I've never fought beside or against your kind, but I've heard stories."

I shrugged. "Sometimes stories are just that."

"We'll see. On the mat."

Following his order, I crossed to where he'd been standing when his spar with Avery had started. I wasn't sure how he'd fight me, so I lowered into a defensive stance, hands in front of my face. Smith's arms bulged and I could already feel my face aching from the hits I was sure to take. With a deep breath, I forced the fear of this fight from my mind and focused on my body instead.

Teeth lengthened and venom filled my mouth. Strength from the nutrient rich blood I'd received earlier filled my veins. Senses sharpened, alert for any movement from him or anyone else who would approach. This would be fun.

Smith's movements were rapid, shifting and lunging for me at the same time, his body mass doubling with power meant to break me. I grinned. He had no idea what he was going up against. Creating the shield over my skin took less than a thought, and when Smith's body crashed into me, I was prepared, shifting my weight, grabbing his body, and tossing him over my shoulder. He hit the ground with a grunt and raced to find his footing, but I was already there, my fist connecting to his jaw. His head slammed back, but his leg kicked out at the same time, a move I wasn't prepared for and missed until my legs were swiped out from underneath me. My back slammed against the hard wood floor and a growl ripped from my throat. Smith's foot flew toward my face, and I moved faster than I ever had, grabbing him by the ankle and again using his momentum to toss him. After a few more exchanges, Smith raised a hand and shifted, gasping for air from the exertion we'd both put forth in our fight.

"Enough." His eyes narrowed on me. "I thought you couldn't fight."

I shrugged, my sides heaving as I tried to speak without sounding like I was dying. "I've had some training back home, but I never had the strength and speed I do now. And I think some of this must be instinctual because I swear I don't know what I'm doing. I just do it."

I didn't mention that I'd had to stop myself from biting him a few times when he'd attacked and I'd panicked. The strike would've killed him, and I couldn't allow that. First, it would mean my death, and second, I was here to show my people could be trusted. Accidentally killing him could take us from a race to be feared straight up the list to a Threat. I wasn't willing to let that happen.

Smith nodded, a bloody grin lifting his split lips. "I think Pike made a good decision sending you boys here. Let's get this party started."

The next four weeks followed this same pattern, with the exception that we now had weapons to use in weapons training, and in the nightly training. Every day I worked through Elite names and searches on the database and helped Pike and Knight with their plans. I contributed very little, but my knowledge grew ten-fold or more. When I didn't understand why they made a certain decision, I asked, and they were patient enough to answer me. Knight still glowered whenever she first saw me, but she treated me with respect.

After the first week, I was given a laptop and used my spare time to continue searching for information on the list of names. When I finished the second list in a day, even Knight was impressed and assigned me the list she'd taken for herself. It was monotonous work, but it needed to be done, and I was ready to prove I could do it.

Nightly training was torture. We rotated between hand to hand training and weapons. The other Elite used this time to keep their skills sharp instead of learning, and once they warmed up to having Avery and I present, they started helping Smith with our lessons. The bobcats were as helpful as they wanted to be, but preferred to take cheap shots at us. It didn't take long to learn to keep my attention on the entire room instead of only those I worked with. In a way, it was amazing training that I needed to be constantly vigilant.

The day before the governor's visit, we met together again in the lobby as two teams for our weekly meeting. Excitement and anticipation buzzed in the air. We'd already chosen the replacement guards, and they'd been notified. Half were far advanced while the other half were Elite housed in this building. Two were from my team, and their teammates and the other team congratulated them on being chosen.

While I'd stayed teamed with the two Majors, the other recruits had been bounced around from one partnership to another. They'd been out in the field, but I didn't envy them. My experiences were ones that couldn't be created outside of Pike's office. The knowledge I'd received already was worth being benched, or that was how half the team referred to my situation. If this was being sidelined, I'd take another month of it so I could learn more before taking that knowledge and applying it to a field position.

"You all know why we're here and what we're discussing today," Pike warned everyone, silencing the room. "You were each required to report to me yesterday about your team's progress. Today's meeting will be short. Like usual, all those not chosen to be on duty to protect the governor are being assigned to patrol duty throughout the city. If there's trouble, the closest three teams will assist. You each should have your routes already emailed to you. If you haven't received your route, contact Corporal Hunt. Recruits will stay with the last pair they were assigned and their schedule will be changed this week only. No other classes or training will be required. We will do this in shifts so the city always has us guarding it. The other teams in the building are also helping patrol. We'll have the southeastern section, and if required, will help the others as needed. We're making this short and sweet today. Find your partner, discuss your patrol schedule and routes, and be ready. If any of you show up late, you'll hear from me. Dismissed."

The buzzing energy the room had before Pike spoke was now a dull hum. Avery snaked his arm around my shoulders and grinned. "So, you get to be with Pike on patrol?"

I hadn't been ordered not to say what I was doing, but in my gut, I knew it was probably for the best. "Something like that, I guess."

"Lucky you."

"Did you drink my blood last night?" Jezzelle asked, batting her eyelashes as the bears disappeared into the crowd, eager to find their partners.

I grinned at the coyote. Over the past few weeks she'd stopped becoming annoying. I'd had to remind myself over and over that I gave allowances to other shifters for their natural tendencies, and the flirtation and trouble were hers. I'd kept reminding her I wasn't interested, but she kept flirting.

"Yes, Jezzi, I drank your blood last night. I told you I would." The nickname had slipped off my tongue during a weapons practice that had left me too breathless to complete her name. It'd stuck. So had Rave, but everyone called me that now.

"How'd you like it?"

I shrugged. "It's shifter blood. It tastes okay. Less muddy than an elemental based person's blood."

She snorted. "That's not quite a compliment, Rave."

I shrugged again. "The only blood I love is my own kind. It's sweet. Shifters are bitter."

This news didn't make her happy by the disgusted expression she threw me, and when one of her partners called her name, she grinned. "I'll see you boys later." I'd expected her to run to the man beckoning her, not crush her lips against mine and then nip at my bottom lip before doing so. At least once a week the girl kissed me, and as long as she kept it to a kiss, I was fine with it. The nipping was new, and she and I would have to have a talk about that. It wasn't that she wasn't pretty, my kind just weren't drawn to shifters.

"I don't know why, out of all of us, she chose to make her advances on you," Jonas grumbled. "I can't even get her to notice me, and yet you don't want a thing to do with her, but she can't keep her hands off of you."

Pike was giving me a hard stare, so I shook my head and started moving away. "I don't know, Jonas. Maybe it's the whole hard to catch thing. I'll see you guys later."

"Girlfriend?" Pike asked when I made my way to him and Knight, who didn't look at all impressed either.

My snort caused their eyebrows to raise. "No. She likes to flirt, but I've made it clear I'm not interested."

"You sure about that?" Knight asked, eyeing Jezzelle.

"Is it against the rules?" I asked, having never heard a policy against it.

Knight shook her head. "No, but it's unwise to date a member of your team, in case it ends badly. We don't shift teams around because of drama."

That was understandable. "There's nothing there. I give you my word."

"Good. Let's go. We have a lot of work to do today without you waiting for a kiss."

Yup, Jezzi and I were going to have a long talk about her PDA. I didn't need any more attention, negative or positive. She gave me a brief wave as I followed the Majors toward the elevator.

Outside, a dark sedan waited for us beside the door. An Elite handed the keys off to Pike and stepped inside the building. Knight moved to take the passenger's seat, so I crawled into the back. As of yet, no one had given me a driving lesson, and I was sure now it wouldn't happen until after the governor's visit was complete.

Since Avery and I drove to the headquarters every night, I'd gotten to know the city a bit more. Avery had caught on quick that I was lost, so he started showing me around. We'd leave a little early and drive the streets so I could be more familiar with my surroundings. I'd also learned a few shortcuts to take if traffic was backed up, which had happened a few times, like today.

Pike wasn't deterred by it. He pulled off onto a street I'd never seen and managed to still make great time to the headquarters. The guards at the gate didn't even bother to ask him for his ID when we pulled up and Pike rolled his window down. One look at him and Major Knight and the man waved us in, not even checking on me in the back. They could've had a whole car full of illegal material and no one would be the wiser. Yet, the two Majors were two of the most trusted people to ever come on this base, so it made sense.

None other than Captain Smith waited for us just inside the front doors of the building. He gave me a lopsided grin, likely remembering the beating he'd given to me last night. I remembered, and still felt the bruises all over my body every time I moved. I'd gotten too cocky, and he'd put me back in my place. That beating alone proved I was unfit to hold any position near the governor and his wife during this visit. Venom or not, I was still too much of a rookie to have such a high position of defense.

"Are we ready here?" Pike asked Smith, who nodded.

"We've never been more prepared this far in advance. I'm not sure if that should make me nervous or relieved."

"Both," Knight grumbled before jerking her thumb in my direction. "Blame him. He's the one who worked overtime so we were able to have people in place early."

Smith's eyebrows shot up. "Over-achiever huh? I'll have to remember that." Then he chuckled. "Doing any extra strength training exercises?"

"Every day," I mumbled, wanting to be anywhere but here. "You told us to."

"I did, but I wasn't sure you'd actually listen. Anyway, let's get moving. There's still lots to do."

Pike had been staring at his phone since we entered, and the growl he gave now was far too human, but also far too livid for me to be comfortable with what it meant. "Well, we'd better hurry it up. Apparently the governor decided to come early. Must be to check our defenses and see how fast we can move. He'll be here in about an hour."

Chapter 9

Chaos. That was all it could be called. Those needing to be in place when the governor arrived were notified. Even I had a cell phone thrust into my hand and given a list of Elite to call. I'd had to have Pike or Knight confirm with the person that I was legit a few times. Once, Smith had snatched the phone from my hand when I'd been mid-argument with a soldier. That man had likely wet his pants after Smith was done with him.

"Come on, kid." Pike motioned for me to follow him back out to where Knight was standing beside a new vehicle, an SUV like the one we usually drove, only this license plate was different.

"Where are we going?" I asked the pair when I was comfortably sitting in the second seat.

"We're going to go pick up the precious cargo. If they want to pull this crap, then we're going to pull ours. Our security network just picked up chatter that the governor's convoy has been spotted just north of town." Pike sounded none too pleased, and Knight's huff confirmed it.

"Why in the world is he bringing a convoy? That makes him stick out like a sore thumb. Its only goal is to attract trouble."

Pike grunted. "Exactly. I'm telling you, he'd better not be reelected. He's playing with his own life and there's far more for him to do at the state capital. He doesn't need to keep traveling around doing nothing but making our lives harder." Major Pike stared at me in his rearview mirror as we approached the gate. "This all stays in the car, off the record."

"Yes, Sir. I wouldn't have told anyone, anyway."

"I didn't think so, but thought I'd mention it." Both of them had lost their tempers a few times during our planning sessions and had spouted off like this. I never opened my mouth about it, even to Avery. Some things weren't for sharing. Plus, I'd never been a fan of gossiping.

We drove through an unknown section of the city, and soon it was long behind us as the land opened up before us. Green, grassy fields took the place of buildings. I'd passed through fields such as this on my way to the city. They'd been beautiful, and the breeze swirling across them had been cooling when the sun had grown too hot. Underground was much cooler.

Pike took an exit further up the road and pulled into a gas station parking lot, but left the engine idling. Within ten minutes, a group of ten cars pulled into the lot, each one parking in the spaces surrounding us.

"He really did bring a convoy," Knight remarked in stunned amazement, but not a good amazement. More like she thought the man a complete idiot. I had to agree with her.

"Raven," Pike called my attention back to him, handing me back a ten dollar bill. "Go buy yourself something to eat and drink, and check inside the store for trouble. Take a walk, do anything. Be seen." Since I was wearing the Elite uniform, it wouldn't be hard for me to gain attention.

Climbing from the backseat, I strode toward the convenience store, my eyes taking in everything around me as I inhaled every scent around this place. Shifters, Magic Users, even a few Others and humans. They were all here, or nearby. I wasn't sure one little recruit would be enough to make them think twice about attacking the governor.

Inside the store, I meandered around the aisles. Those inside stared at me, first my uniform, and then my sunglasses. Last, they sniffed me. Some were confused and crinkled their noses at my odd scent. Others picked up on it and avoided me. I'd never smelled a vampire, but how close was my scent to one of them? At least they all knew not to mess with me.

After paying for my items, I took in the commotion near the convoy before opening the door. Men and women with weapons stood outside each vehicle, surveying the area as I did. They watched me walk back, my bag of jerky already open and I was nibling on my first piece.

That was when the scent hit me. I'd never scented anything like it before, so I had no idea what it was, but I knew where it was. Right above me, on top of the canopy above the gas pumps.

Pike was deep in conversation with another man, this one bald with a dark goatee. Knight was missing, likely somewhere in the throng of people surrounding a dark sedan three cars over from where we'd parked. Well, Pike had told me to look around, so that's what I'd do.

Setting my jerky and water bottle beside a gas pump, I strode back the way I'd come, searching for any means of climbing onto the store's roof. I found what I was looking for on the side of the building: a fenced section around two condensing units. The fence was easy to scale, and the roof was close to jump onto from there.

No one was around to notice me creeping across the shingled roof. The slope wasn't so bad that it made stepping across toward the pump's canopy dangerous. Thankfully, the canopy was also easy jumping distance from the roof's edge, but I found my target long before I reached the canopy. Swallowing, I took in his sallow complexion, sunken cheeks, and raspy breath. I'd seen pictures of this creature in supernatural studies, and as I stood on the verge of making the jump that would likely alert him of my presence, I tried to remember everything I could about Wights.

They were fast, hard to kill, strong. The best way to kill them was taking their heads off. Their hearts were tiny, making them difficult to kill by a blow to the chest. Yet, could my venom kill them? I didn't want to sink my teeth into something as gross as this creature, but if I had to, I would. Staying alive was a good reason to do it. Saving someone else would be too, though I'd likely be trying to save my own hide by the end of this.

Leaping onto the canopy as quietly as I could didn't work. I gained the creature's attention the moment I landed. He likely felt the vibrations or the sway of the canopy. His long, greasy black hair hung in thick strands around his head. In some places, his head was bald with patches of hair missing. No wonder these things were on the Threat list. I'd take Smith yelling at me on the phone over facing off against this creature any day. If I didn't soil myself in this fight, I'd be thanking Fate or any other forces at work today.

With a new target, the Wight made its way toward me in a crouched position, moving on the balls of its feet and knuckles of his hands. Taking a defensive stance, I brought my hands up and forced my teeth to lengthen. Venom filled my mouth, and this time, I accepted it, not bothering to swallow any of it. If I couldn't bite him, I could always spit on him. It wouldn't be as affective, but it would burn his skin where it touched. Or at least it burned most creatures. I didn't know enough about Wights, and I wasn't worried about testing theories now. All I wanted was to stay alive.

He raced at me, and I met him head on, ramming my knee into his face. His teeth embedded themselves into my skin and clamped down, taking me with him as he fell backward. We hit the canopy hard. Thankfully my elbow had saved my face from connecting first, but sheer pain shot up my arm.

The Wight released my leg and dove at my face. My hands shot out, gripping his neck in a tight grasp to hold him back, but it did nothing to stop the scent of death and deterioration that was carried to me on his breath. Bile rose in my stomach and up my throat, and holding my breath didn't help stop it. Kicking him in the groin, the creature bellowed a high-pitched scream before rolling away from me. While he held his manly bits, I lost every ounce of what I'd eaten today in a few solid heaves.

Shouting below announced that we'd been discovered, or at least heard. The Wight glared at me, having lost its prize, but I was still here and ready to be eaten. I wiped my mouth and dragged myself to my feet, a little lightheaded after throwing up and facing such noxious breath. Neither of us were concerned about being stealthy now that his presence was known.

He rushed me again, and this time I was smarter and more prepared. I shielded myself and didn't aim my counterattack so close to his mouth. My fist struck the side of his face, but it wasn't enough to stop his momentum, just his trajectory.

We flew backward...into open space. My back and head smacked against the pavement as the Wight's body slammed into mine. Screams erupted from civilians nearby as I shook my head clear. I'd managed to keep the shield up while we fell, but it had dissipated the moment I'd hit, but I'd been saved from the worst of the damage. The Wight had as well since I'd softened his landing.

He stared down at me and growled, his yellow, chipped teeth on full display. This time I knew better than to breathe, and I definitely didn't want to bite him, but as he dove for my face, it became my only option.

I shifted the slightest, allowing him to grab the side of my neck as I clamped onto his throat. Searing pain washed through my body at the bite, but my stifled cry was nothing compared to his, which made him release me and fight against my hold. My teeth refused to let go as I pumped more and more venom into his body.

The creature writhed in my grip, but I couldn't release him. Even when he stilled, I kept my grip on him, until someone grabbed my arm in a light hold.

"Easy, son, it's dead," Pike's familiar voice spoke. The fingers of his other hand trailed against my jaw. "Let it go."

I did as he said, and the taste of the creature assaulted my tongue and mouth. Rolling it off of me, I managed to twist away from it and Pike before I puked once again. A water bottle, my water bottle, appeared before me and I rinsed and spit several times before the gagging ceased. A soft cloth was pressed against my neck, causing the searing pain from the initial bite to flair again. My whimper was weak and pathetic, much like how I felt with all of these people watching me.

"Did it bite him?" Knight's voice asked, and of course it was Pike who responded.

"Yes, in the neck. I'm not sure about anywhere else. I didn't even sense this creature."

"Neither did I. That worries me, Cole. I was searching for Threats with my power, and I felt nothing."

Weightlessness took me as Pike lifted me into his arms. "Well, this young man found it. And killed it. Let's get the governor out of here. Obviously someone knows where we stopped. He rides with us. If you have to use force, do it. I'm tired of wasting time."

Pike carried me back to the SUV, sitting me in the passenger's seat and buckling me in. "Did he bite you anywhere else?"

"Knee," I managed to reply, the pain in both locations making it difficult to breathe.

"I see it. Don't worry, we'll have you back to Headquarters in no time. The Wight's mouth is a germy mess. You'll need to be put on antibiotics to stop infection." Pike growled. "Looks like I'll have to find someone to replace you the next few days."

"I'm sorry."

He patted my shoulder and chuckled. "Don't be. You saved lives today, I promise you. That creature would've come down on us, on the governor, without warning. How'd you know it was there?"

"I smelled it."

Pike's eyebrows drew low. "Our shifters didn't smell anything."

"I don't know how, but I did." Moaning, I let my head fall back. "I forgot to bring a blood vial."

"There will be plenty at Headquarters for you to drink from. I'll alert the med unit to have non-magic blood ready."

"Thanks."

After patting my shoulder again, Pike closed the door. More sounds bounced around outside, mostly yelling and people talking. When the doors opened, I jumped. Men and women filled the car and Pike climbed into the front seat and wasted no time backing out of the space, leaving the governor's convoy behind.

It was several tense minutes before anyone spoke, and it was Knight, leaning close so that her head was between the two front seats. "Raven, why didn't you alert someone?"

I didn't want to talk, didn't want to move, but I needed to answer her. All I wanted to do was relax into this seat and close my eyes against the pain, both from the bites and from my eyes. Somewhere out there I'd lost my sunglasses. I guess now was as good a time as any to let my eyes adjust to daylight.

"I didn't know what it was," I whimpered through the pain. "It was an odd scent I've never smelled, and I didn't know if it was friend or foe, or just some random smell I'd never been around. By the time I saw the creature, it was too late. He found me and you know what happened after that."

"I still don't understand how my shifters couldn't smell this thing and two Magic Users couldn't feel its presence," a man griped from the next row, next to Knight. His voice held an annoying whine, and I didn't have the energy to figure out his species. This had to be the governor. "But somehow, this child could smell it."

"And aren't you glad he could," Pike shot back, silencing the man's arguments. "It's strange too, I couldn't feel it after they fell and I knew it was there, even before Raven killed it."

"I couldn't smell it," a female from the far back, third seat announced. "Even after it was dead and they hauled it away, I couldn't smell it."

"This is odd," Pike murmured, a tinge of worry souring his voice. He patted my shoulder. "Rest, Raven. You have a long few days to recover. You did good, kid."

Chapter 10

The next hour was a blur. It didn't take long for everyone to find out what had happened at the gas station. In fact, more people knew once we reached Headquarters than I'd anticipated. The medics must've spread the word. I was taken to the med ward and instantly put on antibiotics and other medicines to stop infection. Pain meds were next, and in a blur, I was unconscious.

When I'd woken the first time, it was dark and I was alone. It wasn't until the second time I'd woken that I realized they'd made this room dark on purpose, for me. There were no windows, and someone had stuck a piece of tape over the light switch so no one would flip it on subconsciously. Whoever thought about that was my new best friend.

It wasn't until the third time that I woke up that someone was in the room. Avery sat curled up in a recliner in the corner, and even in the pitch black, my eyes, so accustomed to the dark, could tell there were dark circles under his eyes. Taking stock of my body instead of falling back to sleep, I found I was less stiff and the pain was gone, but some nausea remained. I wasn't sure if that was normal, but I didn't have the energy to speak.

Movement near the door drew my attention to someone stepping inside. Jezzi gave me a warm smile as she closed the door behind her, some light from the hallway filtering in with her. I turned my head away and closed my eyes, the light burning them.

"I'm sorry," she whispered, crossing to the other side of my bed where there were less tubes and wires hooked up to me. Avery didn't stir, letting me know he was exhausted. What had been going on out there? And how long had it been? I was still too tired to talk, and my heavy eyelids were growing heavier by the second. "Here, can you scoot over?"

I gave her a side-eye glance. Was she kidding? I couldn't even stay awake, or talk, and she wanted me to move? Sighing, I closed my eyes and relaxed into the pillow, already exhausted and I hadn't done a darn thing.

"Okay, fine, but don't blame me if this is a tight fit."

She kicked off her shoes as I managed to open one eye. I should've seen this coming, but I didn't. Jezzi sat on the bed, lifted her feet and spun so she was lying beside me. There was barely room, so she nestled into my side, resting her cheek on my shoulder, on the good side of my neck. Turning my head, I rested my cheek against her hair, needing her touch in that moment. It may have been a moment of weakness, but I needed it.

"They said you're going to be okay, that the Wight didn't cause too much damage," she whispered, her soft voice a lullaby. "You crazy fool. Next time warn someone before you go off on your own. I don't want to lose any of my friends yet." She curled in closer to me, wrapping one of her legs around mine. It was much too intimate, but I only had the energy to close my eyes and sigh. "Now I know you're out of it," Jezzi giggled. "You'd never let me get away with this if you were healthy."

She was right, so she'd better enjoy it while this time lasted. And she did, wrapping an arm around me and snuggling closer.

In total, I spent almost a week in the medical unit and then was confined to my bed at the old hotel for another two days. It was torture. By the end I was going stir crazy and Pike was threatening to have me leashed to keep me from going any further than the bathroom. He'd found me wandering the halls my first night back, my muscles stiff from not moving. I'd only wanted to loosen them, not cause problems, but he'd escorted me back to my room.

There were two more incidents while the governor was in town, and both were like the first: no one smelled the creatures before they attacked. Two warlocks had come to me yesterday to quiz me yet again about what I'd smelled, heard, and done to see if they could figure out exactly what was happening. I couldn't tell them any more than I'd already told Pike and Knight. I'd never even smelled a Wight before. Thankfully, both times no one was killed, though there were severe injuries.

Crawling out of bed, I dressed and headed downstairs to the gym. Since it was the middle of the night, I thought it would be empty, but it wasn't. I wanted to groan when I found Captain Smith bench pressing with enough weights that he could've lifted two of me instead. Ignoring him, I walked over to the treadmill. I'd start out slow and work myself up to a jog. If I could handle that, I'd try a full sprint.

The machine had just started and I'd stepped onto it when the bar was placed on the rack and Smith groaned as he sat up. Now that I was walking, I couldn't very well run from the room, so I was stuck when the gorilla came to lean on the treadmill's handlebar.

"I heard what you did."

Taking a deep breath, I turned to him. "I think everyone has, although they're mostly concerned that no one but me knew that creature was there."

He dropped his head to watch my feet, then reached over and adjusted the speed to go much faster than I'd planned this soon into my work out. Arguing would be useless, so I picked up my pace, jogging in time with the machine.

"Yeah, but I'm more concerned with the fact that you took on a full grown Wight and lived. So, I've talked to Pike." He paused for dramatic effect and grinned. "You're going to be mine to train for the next six months."

His words had the desired effect. Shock hit my brain with enough force to wash away every other thought, including running. Smith's belly laugh could have awakened the dead as I went flying off the back of the treadmill into a heap of tangled legs. This man was the complete opposite of Pike.

"So, what does that mean, exactly?" I asked Smith after I sat up and assessed my body for any further harm. There was none that I could find, thank goodness.

"It means that today you pack up your bags and move into the basement of Headquarters where my team stays. You'll be going out on our missions. I should also mention Avery is coming with us. He helped take down the Wight who tried to kill the governor's wife at the fancy dinner they insisted on having at an unsecure location."

Well, at least I wouldn't be subjected to Captain Smith by myself.

"What happens after six months?" I asked him, picking myself up off the floor as he slowed the treadmill back to a walk. Until he left, I wasn't stepping back on that thing.

He grinned at me. "Then, we evaluate where you're at and see if you qualify to become a full Elite, and an officer. Pike and I are both aiming for that, so you'd better be prepared. Between the two of us, we're going to be pushing you until you think you're going to break, and then we'll push you even harder."

That sounded miserable, but after all the talks with Pike, and after the incident with the Wight and the governor, I'd finally decided they were right. I wanted to be an officer, to have my own team. I wanted to make a difference in every way that I could.

"Should I start packing now?"

Smith snorted. "No. What you should do is go back to bed and sleep. It's going to be a long day and you of all people need your energy."

"I've been sleeping for a week straight."

"Then go climb in bed with that female who can't keep her hands off of you. She could probably get rid of some of that energy for you." He winked at me, then strode out of the room, leaving me groaning in his wake. Even he knew how I felt about Jezzi, but he'd started teasing me about it a few weeks back. Since landing in the hospital, and after that first night she'd stayed with me, Jezzelle had come to stay with me almost every night, at least until I'd moved to my room here. I'd put my foot down then. It wasn't like she'd been alone. Avery had taken over the recliner, and twice Jonas had shifted and slept at the end of my hospital bed, our little group giving me support in the only way they really could, given the circumstances.

"You still look like crap," Avery chuckled from where he sat on his bed when I walked in after a short run on the treadmill. "You should take it easy."

"Yes, Mother." I should've changed out of my sweaty clothes, but I was too tired to move. He was right, but I didn't want to admit it to him because then I'd have to admit it to myself. "Where are you going?"

"To find you. Pike will kill you if he finds you wandering the halls this late again."

"Don't worry, Smith found me first."

Avery groaned. "What'd he do?"

"He made me go flying off a treadmill. He also said we're moving into the lower levels of Headquarters to train under him. Did you know about that?"

The sigh coming from my best friend didn't sit well with me. "I found out two days ago. They ordered me not to tell you. I guess they thought it might stress you out too much. They must think you're ready for it now."

"I'm ready for them to stop treating me like a child."

With a soft stare, Avery looked over at me. "They aren't, Rave. You didn't see those bites. You didn't see what the fever did to you. They had to keep you heavily sedated so you wouldn't feel the pain from the wounds. It's no joke that Wights are so deadly. There's a reason those things are on the Threat list, and you not only let yourself be bitten once, but twice."

"It wasn't like it was on purpose." The second time I'd kind of let him bite me, but that was so I could end it. Just the thought of his breath and the taste of him on my tongue made my stomach turn over. "Let's not talk about him please."

Avery stood and came over to me, helping me out of my sweaty shirt before tucking me under the cool covers. "Call me mother all you want, but yours isn't around and you're still young. Someone has to take care of you, even if it's to save you from yourself."

Smith was right. The day was long, and by the end, I was more than exhausted. We'd woken up, started packing, met for the team meeting where Pike had announced Avery and I were leaving, and we'd finished packing. Jonas and Jezzelle helped us, neither happy we were leaving. Well, Jonas was hoping Jezzi would notice him now, but I found it unlikely. The she-coyote was quiet for most of her time helping, which was odd. When Avery and Jonas took the first of our bags down to the lobby, Jonas taking mine since they refused to let me carry them, I took Jezzelle's hand and pulled her down to sit next to me on the bed.

"What's up?" I asked her, wrapping my arm around her shoulders. It didn't take a genius to know what was wrong, but I wanted to hear it from her.

"You're leaving, you big idiot. What else would be wrong?" she asked, her voice cracking with the emotion she held inside.

"It's not like I'm leaving forever. I'm sure we'll still see one another."

"It won't be the same."

I laughed. "You mean because you won't be able to do this whenever you darn well want to?" I took her chin and turned her head, tilting it so I had easy access to her lips and pressed mine to hers. It was the first time I'd been the one to initiate a kiss, and it startled her for a second until she relaxed and kissed me back. When she nipped at my lip, I ended it.

"You sure you don't feel anything?" she asked, running her fingertips along my jaw.

"Nothing. I'm sorry Jezzi. I wish I did. You're an amazing woman, but there's nothing there. Traditionally my kind have only ever mated with humans or our kind...and on the rare occasion, a vampire, though don't say that too loud. It's disgusting. Most of the time that happens, it's not by choice."

"Oh," she breathed, and shook her head. "I won't say anything."

"Thanks. Now, let's finish this. Smith will be here any minute and he's almost as bad as Pike with his strict timeliness."

She kissed my cheek and breathed in my scent. "Then I guess we'd better hurry so you aren't late on your first day. And Rave, if you ever need anything, please don't hesitate to call. You have my number."

I did, in my cell phone, which I rarely used. "I'll call. I promise."

"Good."

It didn't take long to finish packing and we were on time in the lobby, waiting for Smith when he and Pike pulled up in a large truck. We loaded our things, said goodbye to our friends, and moved to climb inside. A heavy hand came down on my shoulder and spun me around before a set of keys was shoved in my face.

"Your turn, kid."

My eyes widened. "But I can't drive."

"You learn today."

Smith rounded the car while Pike chuckled, giving me a small wave as he strode inside. Swallowing hard, I climbed in behind the wheel while Smith went through the basics of where everything was located in the truck. After adjusting my seat and mirrors, I inserted the key into the ignition and turned the engine on.

It was the worst ride of my life. Even Avery was praying in the back as we made our way across town. The fact we even made it to Headquarters was a miracle. Even more of a miracle was that only three people had honked their horns at me. When the guard on duty saw me driving, he arched an eyebrow at Smith.

"How was the ride?"

Smith chuckled, far more at ease than myself and the third passenger in the truck. "Quite interesting, but he's catching on."

Once the car was parked, not so elegantly or straight, I turned it off and threw the key at Smith. "I'm done."

"You're done when I say you're done." He tossed the keys back at me. "When we're called out, you drive until you're comfortable with it. Until then, I'd take some extra time and practice while you have it. I'm sure our friend in the back-."

"Is going to throw up," Avery finished for Smith, diving out of the car to stand on solid ground. He managed to keep his breakfast down, but he kept swallowing to do it.

There wasn't even time to unpack. Smith ordered us to take our belongings down to our new room and then to head up to the gym to meet our new team. It surprised me that not everyone we trained with was on our team. Apparently some were regulars and came every day while some trained earlier in the day. Those people we'd never met. Also, not everyone we trained with at night were on our team. Three different teams preferred to train with Captain Smith in the evenings. Meeting yet more new people and knowing I was on the bottom of the food chain yet again left my stomach in knots.

"We'll be fine," Avery mumbled, throwing his duffle bag on the bed while his suitcase sat beside it. I had two duffle bags of clothes now, mostly uniforms, and both bags ended up on my bed. This room was similar to the one we'd left, but there were no windows. I couldn't be happier.

"We're going to be eaten for a snack," I told him. "Especially if Fennel and Cage are on our team."

"They are," he replied, stretching his arms above his head. "They mentioned they were on Smith's team once or twice while they beat the living crap out of me during one of our first trainings here."

That didn't bode well for us. I wasn't sure what we were supposed to wear, so we both stayed in our uniforms. We could always train in them. Avery would just have to remember to strip before he shifted.

The gym wasn't as full as most days we came to train. Usually a few dozen people filled the space. Today there were only a dozen, and all stood at attention in a line down the middle of the room facing Captain Smith. He looked over his shoulder as he heard us enter, and grinned.

"Welcome, kids. Please, take your place at the end of the line so we can start this shindig."

"Isn't a shindig a party?" I whispered to Avery, who closed his eyes and shook his head.

"Yes, and to him, this likely is one."

That was not comforting in the slightest.

"As you can see," Smith announced in his booming voice, "we have two new recruits. They may be new to us, but they've been in the program for over a month now. You're likely wondering why such wet behind the ears kids got moved to our team. Here's your answer: I requested it. I've been working with these two twice a day since they started, and I believe their progress can only improve by joining this team. Call it an experiment. If it works, they pass. If it doesn't, well, we have body bags in their sizes."

Chuckles followed that statement and I stifled a groan. Yeah, he had body bags in our sizes all right. I'd almost needed one of those a week ago.

Smith sobered, and the rest followed his example. "There's a few things you need to know about our recruits, specifically one. If you train in the evening, you know who I'm talking about, if not, well, hold on tight. Avery is a snow leopard shifter. His father is Colonel Andrew Clark. The other one is Raven. He's a vamlure, a Blood Drinker." A few gasps from those who never trained with me filled the space. "Don't get yourselves worked up. He's proven he can control himself. They had a good system worked out with his old team that we need to institute here. He only takes blood from someone willing, and to stay strong, he needs blood in his diet. We need donors. If you're willing to donate blood to him, please speak with him after this meeting. I expect no less than five of you to speak with him. He's a member of this team now. Also, no Magic Users may donate. Apparently your blood will kill him. That eliminates two of you. The rest, consider this and do something about it."

A woman halfway down the line raised her hand and spoke when Smith nodded at her. "How often will we need to donate?"

Smith turned to me to answer. "One person shouldn't need to donate more than once every other month if enough volunteer."

She nodded and turned back to the front. Smith asked for more questions, but the room was silent. That's when he ordered us to find a partner and spar. Most nights Smith trained me, but today it appeared someone else would be doing that, or sparring, so not necessarily training. I was so dead.

The female who'd asked about blood donations approached me and stuck out her hand. She was a tall female with the most brilliant red hair I'd ever seen. It only took one smell for me to know she was an elemental of some kind. Not a true elemental, but an offshoot of the earth magics. For some reason, those magics were safe to take from, their blood tasted horrible, but it was safe.

"Felix," she stated when I took her hand, her grasp tight and strong.

"Raven."

"Let's see what you're made of. Pick a weapon." She nodded toward the wall of swords, knives, and bows. I'd been trained in all of them, but I wasn't proficient in most yet, but I preferred knives, so that's what I grabbed.

Strapping a pair to my thighs and two more to my hips, I watched her do the same. "We won't use our other skills in this fight," she told me. "I want to see what you can do with a weapon alone since we can't always count on our skills to save us."

She was right about that.

Chapter 11

Felix was incredible. She was fast, elegant, and brutal. Most of all, she was an amazing teacher. Whenever I screwed up, and I did a lot, she was right there to correct me, of course it was after she attempted to skewer me. Her blades sliced into me several times, making this uniform my new one for training. It wouldn't be useable later. Not for official business anyway.

"You did good," she complimented when we put our weapons back on the rack. "Do you have your own?"

"My own what? Knives?" I asked, my face heating at my question. It was a dumb one, but I needed to know that's what she meant.

"Knives, sword, any of it. Do you have your own weapons?"

I shook my head, eyeing the amazing weapons available to train with. "No, I don't."

"Well that's stupid," she grumbled. "I'll mention it to Bruce and see what we can do for you and our other recruit."

"Bruce?"

She gave me a lopsided smile. "Captain Bruce Smith."

"Oh."

She grinned at me. "Next time we'll use our skills. I want to see if a vamlure can live up to the tales."

"I'm not sure I can," I confessed, but she placed her fingers over my mouth, silencing me.

"From the stories I heard about the Wight attack, at least some of the tales are true. Maybe-."

"Regroup!" Captain Smith bellowed, and the team went on alert, everyone running to reform the line, everyone but Avery and I until we figured out that was what we were supposed to do. Smith was holding his cell phone, his body tense. "I was hoping to let our recruits have an afternoon off, but we've got a problem. Northwest quadrant just reported a vampire coven attacking the mall. Apparently there's a pretty nice storm raging outside that we can't hear or see inside, making it dark as night and the creatures are a bit confused...and hungry."

"But we cleaned the vamps out of the northwestern quadrant last month," someone further down the line argued.

Smith glared at him. "Well either we didn't or they didn't get the memo not to return. Let's go inform them again. Grab your weapons, and don't forget something silver."

"Stupid Blood Drinkers," another person growled, and I stiffened. They may have meant vamps, but I was a member of the Category they chose to use in their description.

"Hey, watch it," someone informed the speaker, nodding toward me. Ignoring them both, I scanned the shelves for good weapons to take. Since I didn't have my own, these would have to do until I could return them.

Smith found me as I was strapping the knives back to my legs. "We'll get you geared up tomorrow. Be careful and stay with Felix. If you have to bite something, make sure it's fighting against us."

I had a sarcastic response ready for that comment, but I ignored him and raced after everyone else. Unlike Smith's warning that I'd be driving, the truth was, we were in too much of a hurry for me to drive today. Instead, I was shoved into the back of the team's SUV, the silver blade at my hip giving me little comfort. I knew about vampires, as did the team, but I was certain there were a few things about them that even the team didn't know. If need be, I'd educate them.

Whoever had given the report of vampires attacking in the middle of the day had been correct about the storm. Every streetlight around was on, not that any of us could see much with the curtain of rain cloaking everything and slamming into the windshield of the SUV so hard it was deafening. Relief hit me square in the chest that I wasn't driving in this. Felix sensed my body's responses and rested a hand on my shoulder, misunderstanding what was running through my head.

"We'll be fine. Just stay near me."

"I know." My teeth were already lengthening, and I ran my tongue over them. She saw me and her eyes widened. "Sorry."

"It's all right. Just keep those to yourself."

"I try to. In fact, that Wight was the first creature I've ever bitten. I don't want to make a habit of it if I can help it."

She nodded and stared ahead, prepping for what we'd find once we reached the mall. "Hey Bruce, exactly how are we going to draw these things in? Or are we planning to go store by store like the last time they hit up a place like this?"

"I'm still contemplating that," Smith called from the passenger's seat. "If anyone has any brilliant ideas, I'm open to hear them. We have a lot of people to rescue and we need to make sure that none of those creatures escape, with or without prisoners."

The car was quiet as I debated with myself whether I should speak up. Chewing my lip wasn't helping me decide. The closer we drew, the more I thought. If I was leading this mission, how would I handle it? And if a junior member of the team, a person not even an official Elite yet, spoke up, would I listen?

The answer was simple: yes.

Listening would be enough.

"Sir, I have a plan," I called toward the front of the SUV, and more than one head turned toward me.

"I'm listening," Smith responded, staring at me with a blank expression. I didn't realize I'd been holding my breath until I released it to speak.

"There isn't enough time to explain the full thing, but I need you to trust me."

"Not going to happen, kid. I need more than that."

I closed my eyes as the mall came into view and we turned into the parking lot. Thankfully the rain had let up for a minute. "I know a way to get them to come to us, but I need you to trust me. There isn't time to explain. They'll all come, and it'll happen fast, so the team needs to be hidden, everyone except me." I looked him square in the eyes. "It's a Blood Drinker thing."

We held eye contact until the driver pulled up in front of the food court entrance. This was it. It was now or never that he'd trust me, but I wouldn't back down. Too many lives were at stake, including mine.

"Fine. What do we do?"

"We'll do it here. Half the team stays outside in case any of the vamps try to escape this way when they're ambushed. The rest of the team will be able to handle what's inside. Vamp covens rarely exceed twenty, so we should be able to stop them, and they won't be in a hurry to leave. If we need help, we can always call in those outside. Any civilians can be hidden."

"You're sure about this?" Smith asked, and I gave a sharp nod. "Fine. Everyone be ready. I'm going to change this a little. I want four people outside. The rest come inside. Move out, people."

Doors opened and Elite piled out in a steady flow. Once we were all on the sidewalk, four were chosen to stay outside. While Smith chose them, I found Avery.

"You're the only person here who trusts me," I told him, "and I need you to trust me."

"You know I do," he countered.

"Thanks. Before tonight is over you'll need to trust me more."

His eyes narrowed on me. "You're scaring me."

I tried to smile, but failed. "I'm scared."

Smith led the way inside with the rest of us following. "Hide in here?" he asked me, and I nodded.

"Anywhere you can."

"They'll smell us."

"They won't. They'll be too focused on something else."

He eyed me with a narrowed gaze, but stopped as screams ignited throughout the mall. "Hurry. Hide where you can."

It took little time for the team to hide themselves behind counters, trashcans, and other walls that were used as decor and planters for random small trees and bushes. When I couldn't see anyone else moving, I pulled my silver blade. Though it wouldn't hurt me, I hated dealing with silver. My biology was too similar to a vamp that using silver was almost terrifying, yet my biology was just different enough to pull this off. I hoped.

Taking a deep breath, I moved to stand at the food court entrance and took another before dragging the blade down my left arm from elbow to wrist. It wasn't a deep cut, but it bled like a sieve. Steady streams of blood slipped down my arm and dripped from between my fingers to the tiled flooring. A few hisses from around me announced that some of my team had seen what I'd done.

It took almost a minute before the first vamp came into view, and he was followed close behind by four more, all eyes on me. My heartbeat tripled when another three entered the food court, and I slowly backed up, trying to keep an eye on what lay behind me as well as the vamps. If they thought they had the upper hand, they'd attack too soon.

"It's been a long time since I smelled such sweet blood," the closest vampire, the one leading the attack, hissed, her teeth lengthening so her fangs were even more pronounced. I let mine lengthen and pulled my lips back, but my fangs were laughable compared to hers, and laugh she did. "You pathetic child. We'll enjoy your precious blood and leave you for dead so the rest of your team can find you. You're too young and naive to know what your blood is to us."

Oh, I knew, which was why we were all standing here, all fifteen vamps. The screams from the rest of the mall had died down as the last vampire appeared, licking his lips as he threw a middle-aged woman's body away from him. He must've just finished draining her blood.

By now I was backed halfway through the food court and approaching the first of my hiding teammates. I couldn’t go much further without anyone being discovered, and blood loss was already affecting my senses. The room swam, and I almost lost my balance, but a table was close enough that I could lean on it.

The moment my eyes left the vampire, she screeched and raced at me. My reaction time was too slow and I couldn't lift my knife to defend myself in time, but a knife sunk into her chest anyway, and the Elite who'd hidden near me tossed her over our heads before focusing on the next target.

The room was filled with screams and cries as one by one, vampires were taken down. In the mess, I caught sight of one of them grabbing Fennel by her hair and pinning her to him. He searched close around him for danger and made to sprint away with the bobcat, but I had other plans. The silver knife was too large for me to throw accurately with my ever weakening body, so I dug out one of my smaller hip blades and dragged the blade and handle through my blood and let the knife sail through the air. I didn't aim it. I didn't have to. It flew straight past the vampire, the scent of my blood reminding him why he'd come here in the first place.

Too bad it also alerted another two vamps along the way so they lost interest in their fight to stalk me. The one holding Fennel threw her so hard into the wall she didn't move when she slid to the ground. Hoping she was alive, I gripped my silver blade in a shaky hand.

To my gratitude, none of the three vampires reached me. Each was taken down by an Elite when the vampire became distracted by my blood. The four Elite waiting outside joined us to finish off the remaining vamps and all went still...until I collapsed to my knees.

Avery appeared at my side first, his eyes fixated on me. "You need blood."

"Yeah, after I stop the bleeding I'm doing or it won't help."

"Give me that arm," one of the senior members of the team ordered as he dropped a small black bag onto the ground beside us. In a matter of seconds, he had everything out that he'd need to stitch my arm up. Swallowing hard, I turned away, especially when he gave me the warning that he didn't have anything to numb the pain.

Gritting my teeth, I bore through the sheer agony of having one stitch after another sewn into my arm without anything to dull the pain. Biting my lip didn't help, and when tears started to spill from my eyes, I ducked my head. I didn't want any of them to see me like this. I'd experienced pain before, but not like this.

"You're all right," Avery murmured in my ear when he wrapped his arms around my shoulders. "You're brave and you can do this."

"No, this is pathetic," I cried between small gasps.

"You cut your own arm. I don't think this is pathetic at all. Plus, you aren't even flinching or trying to pull out of Jared's hold. That's pretty impressive."

"You're telling me," Jared muttered. "Usually they move around a lot. He's not moved an inch."

It took another few minutes to finish the stitching, and when he did, Jared wrapped my arm and placed it in a sling. It still ached, but I was no longer bleeding. That left me with the task at hand or I'd pass out any minute.

"Do you trust me?" I whispered to my best friend, who nodded.

"With my life."

I turned to Jared. "I need a drink. Anything." He nodded and left, returning a minute later with a cheap paper cup of water. Taking it from him, I managed to spill half of it on the ground and myself before it reached my lips. The first few mouthfuls I swallowed, the third I spit out onto the ground, clearing my mouth of as much venom as I could.

"If you still have venom in there, is it going to kill me?" Avery asked, sounding a bit panicked with his voice raised an octave.

Shaking my head, I noticed the men and women standing around watching us for the first time. "No, it'll make you feel nauseous, but there isn't enough there to even come close to killing you." I ducked my head. "I wish I could do this in private. People already hate what I am."

Not questioning what he needed to do, Avery bared his neck to me, and a few whispered gasps followed. "Then show them you're not the same as the creatures we just killed. Show them you can control yourself. How many swallows do you think you need?"

"I won't take more than three."

"Then have Jared count. He'll be our witness."

"Got it." Jared moved closer so he could watch my throat.

Pressing my lips to Avery's throat, I swallowed when the scent of his blood seeped through his skin and the pulsing of it vibrated against my lips. Not wasting any more time, I opened my mouth and dug my teeth into his skin far enough that I could drag out the blood I needed, but not so far as to tear apart his flesh. Pulling them out, I latched on like a leech and sucked, swallowing three times. The blood was bitter, but still amazing and warm, and not enough to stave off all of the side effects of what I'd lost, but I wouldn't take more than I'd told him I'd take. There was more blood back at Headquarters in my mini fridge.

Leaning back, I grabbed a napkin from the table beside us and pressed it to Avery's open wound. "I'm sorry."

Jared snorted and stood. "Did you hear that, Bruce? The kid's sorry for biting someone. I guess not all Blood Drinkers are cold and heartless."

Captain Smith strode to us and stared down at me. "Next time, tell me the plan so I can tell you you're crazy." Though his words were a bit harsh, his tone was soft. "But good job. Mind telling me what this was all about?"

I nodded. "I will, but not here if you don't mind."

"Understood. Jared, check on Fennel. Felix, call for Knight's team to clean this place up and then call in a medical team. The rest of you, go find survivors and take them to the bookstore across the way. Tell them to stay in one location." Smith stared down at me and grinned. "I hope you can stand because this is going to be a long night and you're not going to get out of it because you lost a bit of blood."

Chapter 12

The next morning, I could barely move. Every muscle in my body ached, including my head. My arm was next on the list of pain, and it was all I could do not to throw up, and I was yet again thankful that we didn't have a window to let in sunlight. Climbing from the bed, I limped to the fridge where I dropped to my knees and grabbed the first vial that met my fingers. The taste was a bit muddy, so it likely belonged to Felix. Nothing against the woman, but her blood tasted terrible. It did manage to settle my stomach, though, so I wouldn't complain to anyone but myself about it.

"You planning to overdose today?" Avery mumbled into his pillow. "I wouldn't blame you if you did."

"Smith wouldn't appreciate it, though."

"No, but after what you did last night, I'm sure he'd understand. Dude, you sliced your own arm to attract those things." Yeah, I'd done that and then had to help carry dead vampire bodies to the van that would take them away to the local crematory to dispose of them. All I could say was that lifeless vampires were the epitome of dead weight.

A light knock sounded against the door and I winced. Even that slight noise was enough to make me want to be blood drunk. Avery pulled himself out of bed and crossed the room to unlock the deadbolt. At least this room had a lock.

"He up?" Smith questioned Avery and I fell back on the bed...in slow motion. "I'll take that as a yes," he chuckled when the mattress groaned beneath me.

"Don't turn the light on," Avery warned him, crossing back to his bed and crawling under the covers before he turned away from us.

Smith continued to chuckle as he pulled the desk chair across the room to settle it between the two beds. "For him or for you?"

"Both."

"So." Smith slapped my knee in an effort to gain my undivided attention. "I'm waiting for you to explain what happened yesterday."

"We can't do this later?"

"Nope. I'm busy later."

Rolling back up into a sitting position, I rubbed my face. "It's a little known fact that while vampires and vamlure are similar in that we drink blood, we're not exactly friendly toward one another. Some vamlure and vampires mate because they want to, but it's rare, and most won't run the risk of harming their mate. All it takes is the scent of our blood to make them lose their minds. It's their favorite meal and draws them in faster than anything else."

"Noticed that," Smith commented dryly, though he appeared interested, resting his chin on his arms across the back of the chair. "It was an interesting trick. Next time a little warning would've been nice."

"You trusted me," I murmured, still shocked that he had.

"I followed my gut. So, if a vamlure and vampire mated pair are cooking together, if the vamlure cuts themselves, the vampire is going to suck them dry?"

I shrugged. "That depends on the vampire's willpower and how much they love one another. If it's a new relationship and a younger vamp, the vamlure will die if they can't fend off the vamp."

He grunted. "That's one way to end a relationship."

"Yes, Sir."

"I should yell at you for what you did, but I'm not going to, not when you're apparently still recovering. Just know that I'm not going to be pleased if you injure yourself again like that. Next time, have someone punch you in the nose. A bloody nose stops bleeding much faster than a slice to the arm."

"That's true, but it wouldn't have been enough. I had to appear weak as well."

Silence permeated the room as Smith, and possibly Avery, thought about this new information. It wasn't long before Avery's soft snores filled the space and Smith sighed, setting his forehead against his arms. I wasn't sure what he was thinking about, and I wasn't sure after yesterday that I wanted to know.

"You boys take the morning off," he finally stated, standing up to take the chair back to the desk. "You've earned it."

"With all due respect, Sir," I countered, standing up and swaying until I caught my balance. "I don't want to take the morning off. I want to pull my weight."

Smith crossed the room to set his hands on my shoulders, staring me in the eye. "You're a good soldier, kid, but you're still young and learning. I appreciate your need to not be a burden or be treated differently than everyone else, and I respect it as well. That arm is healing, so don't overdo it. However, in the meantime, if you want to be useful, do two things: call home and tell them you're all right, and then go find General Davis and offer your services as his gofer today. His assistant is quarantined in her room with the flu, and nobody else wants it. The general will keep you busy. In fact, you may regret your willingness to be of help."

After Captain Smith left, I didn't bother going back to sleep. It would take me much longer to clean up today with my arm still stitched and bandaged, so I took my time with a shower and dressing. My hair would need cut soon, but I dried it as best as I could and ran my fingers through the longer strands. Their darkness made my magenta irises appear even brighter. It was still odd seeing my eyes so bright, like they glowed, after years of seeing them nearly black.

Avery was awake and sitting up on his bed, his blond hair standing up in every direction. He rubbed his eyes and didn't even bother with another morning greeting before closing himself into the bathroom. Still low on energy from last night, I opened the fridge and picked out a blood vial. When I read the name on it, I had to grin, and I sent a quick text to Jezzi after I swallowed and cleaned the vial, letting her know I'd drank her blood. She always had a good laugh over that.

My uniform was in place and I was ready for the day when Avery finished in the bathroom. "You going to breakfast?"

"I'm going to swing by and grab a muffin or bagel and go straight to General Davis's office. I'm not that hungry."

He cocked an eyebrow at me. "I thought you were also supposed to call your family."

"Not yet. That conversation needs to wait until I feel less like death and more like myself."

"It's not going to go well?"

I glared at my ID before tucking it into my back pocket. "If by not well you mean they're going to disown me, then yeah, it's not going to go well. I've been putting it off."

Avery whistled and crossed the room to his dresser as I left him to finish his morning routine. It was still early, so not many Elite were up and around, and if they were, they were in the gyms working out and training. Few occupied the cafeteria, and those that did were deep in conversation. It always surprised me how many morning people had joined the Elite.

Muffin in hand, I left before anyone I knew noticed me and felt like chatting, making my way to the elevator and up to Davis's office. It wasn't hard to find. All of the high level officers had their offices on the top floor, and knowing that, all I had to do was walk down hallway after hallway until I came upon a door with his name plaque beside it. The door was open, leading to an outer office where a petite blonde woman sat behind a desk, frantically typing on a keyboard. If this was Davis's assistant, she appeared quite healthy for battling a case of the flu. That meant Smith had lied to me. Or I was in the wrong office.

She finally noticed me standing in the doorway and jumped. "Oh, I'm sorry. I didn't see you standing there. Can I help you?"

"I think I'm supposed to come up here to meet with General Davis. Captain Smith sent me."

"Oh, you must be Raven, correct?"

Her light, tinkling voice gave her away before her scent did: Fairy. I'd heard they could hide their wings and grow to full sized people, but most hated it. They'd rather be as tiny as bugs and sparkle around in the woods at night acting like fireflies. She either needed the money for her family or she felt as strongly about the Elite cause as I did.

"Yes, I'm Raven."

She nodded and pressed a button on her phone. "Raven Cartana is here to see you, Sir."

"Send him in," Davis's voice spoke from the phone, and the fairy waved me toward the door.

"Good luck," she giggled before turning back to her computer, her fingers once again punching the keyboard keys in rapid succession.

Wiping my sweaty palms on my pants, I reached for the next office door and strode inside. The scent of bear was strong in here. General Davis sat behind an older, wooden desk that had papers scattered across it. He didn't look up when I entered, so I settled for closing the door and standing beside it. Taking a seat without being invited in formally seemed too inappropriate, like I was interrupting him.

"Come sit down, Raven. I'll be with you in a second."

He motioned toward a set of worn chairs without looking up at me. While he finished reading and signing the paperwork, I sat down, trying not to trip over my feet. There was something intimidating about this man.

Setting the papers aside, Davis lifted his eyes to me. "I heard about last night."

It was a fight not to drop my gaze from him, a fight I lost as my stare drifted to his desk instead of those piercing blue eyes that I was sure could see straight through me. "I know, I messed up by not giving Captain Smith the whole plan and doing something stupid. He already spoke with me about it."

Davis snorted. "He and I both agree you should've been straight forward with him, but you thought quick on your feet and came up with a pretty decent plan that saved lives. Was it perfect? Not even close, but we don't expect perfection, only results."

Lifting my eyes to his, I narrowed my gaze. "So, if I'm not in trouble, why did you want to see me?"

Clasping his hands in front of him, the general studied me. "I have an assignment for you. There are others working on it as well, but I'm curious to see if you get to the bottom of this before they do."

"Assignment, Sir?" I asked him, unsure if I should be excited or concerned. The butterflies swarming in my stomach were also confused as they dive bombed and fluttered around making me giddy and apprehensive. "What assignment?"

He grinned, and if I couldn't smell him to know for certain he was a bear, I would've thought him a wolf shifter with the predatory lift of his lips. "I want you to find out who's behind the attacks on the governor. You were there. You smelled that Wight when no one else smelled or sensed it. Something is behind that attack, as well as the two following attacks. Like I said, we already have a full two teams working on this, but I'm curious what you can do."

I couldn't stop myself form staring at him like he was insane. He had teams looking into this and then he wanted me to find something they couldn't? How would that happen?

"I'm sorry, Sir, but I think you have the wrong person," I confessed, shifting in my seat under his stare. "I wouldn't even know where to start."

Standing, Davis strode around his desk and passed me on the way to the door. "Then I guess it's a good thing I have an idea. Come on. We're taking a field trip."

"I think I've had enough field trips for one month," I muttered behind his back, earning me a chuckle as he opened the door and held it for me to exit. "Fay, I'll be out for a few hours. Don't forward any calls to my cell phone. I don't want to be interrupted until I come back."

"Yes, General." Fay smiled at me and winked. "Have fun out there."

Every time I left with an officer, I came back bloody. Fun was not the first word I would use to describe any of that. Neither was lucky. Ticking time bomb was more like it.

I wasn't sure what type of vehicle General Davis preferred to drive, but I wasn't expecting the little red sports car that he led me to in the garage. It didn't surprise me that he wouldn't let me drive like Smith had made me do. Had that been yesterday? That was the longest day of my life.

The ride was far smoother than the trucks and SUV's I'd ridden in since that first day. We made excellent time reaching the main gate since Davis didn't appear to abide by the listed speed limits, and the guards on duty didn't even bother stopping him. One look at his car and they opened the gate. They didn't even make us roll down our tinted windows.

"Do they ever stop you?" I asked, watching the guard station disappear in the side mirror.

"No."

"Maybe they should." He eyed me, and I shrugged. "If we get attacked out here and your car drives up to the gate, we've just let in some enemy who could cause major problems."

Smirking, Davis gunned the engine until we were going twice the speed limit through the city. "You're insinuating that some enemy is going to attack and kill me."

"You aren't invincible. I hate to be the one to break that news to you." I gave him a smirk when he chuckled at my remark, but he didn't respond. "Can I ask where we're going?"

His grin fell a little. "We're going to pay Luke Coye a visit."

"Coye?"

"Yes, he's your girlfriend's father."

I bristled at the title for Jezzelle. We were close, but we weren't that close. "She's not my girlfriend."

"Friends with benefits? Doesn't matter to me. I don't judge."

"It's not like that. Anyway, we're going to see her father. Why?"

Davis turned his head to eye me, but I wished he hadn't. We were speeding too fast down the road for him to take his eyes away from it for one second. That was all it would take for us to wind up in an accident. Then again, riding in a vehicle was still so new to me, maybe we were traveling at a safe speed and I was the one who was panicking for no reason.

He grinned and turned back to the road, obviously amused by the tension racing through my body. "Her father is the alpha of the local coyote pack. You may not know this, so I'll explain. The coyotes are the world's largest organized crime families. Most high level gangsters are either some coyote relation or they're in league with the coyotes. If anyone can help us with information, it'll be Luke Coye."

"And why would he want to help us?"

"He owes me a favor, and I'm here to collect." His grin grew into a wide smile as he turned to me again. "Plus, his daughter's boyfriend is with me. That has to count for something."

The coyote pack's headquarters was one of the largest homes I'd ever seen. Set back in the middle of the forest, it was completely hidden from the outside world. Only someone who knew its location would easily find it. Even the detached garage was jaw dropping. Davis didn't even blink at the buildings, which likely meant he'd been here before. Or he'd seen better. Living underground my whole life, houses were still new concepts to me.

"Jezzelle's family lives here?"

"Jezzelle grew up here. Come on. He doesn't like to be kept waiting."

I followed General Davis across the front lawn to the house's main entrance. A tall, dark haired man waited for us near the door, and when we were a few feet away, he stepped outside. I recognized him immediately, even though I'd never met him before. Jezzelle was the female equivalent of this man from her height to facial features.

"Connor, you're early," the man laughed. "The sun hasn't even risen yet."

Davis jerked his thumb toward me, and the man's eyebrows rose, like he'd just noticed I was present. "I believe your daughter has likely mentioned to you about this one. His eyesight is better in the dark, and we have a lot to do today, so we might as well have an early start."

"Yes, she mentioned a vamlure was accepted into the Elite program. I'm shocked, actually. You've become quite trusting, Connor."

"I'll trust him until he gives me a reason not to, and thus far, I don't think he'll misbehave. Can we come in and speak with you?"

"Of course. Follow me." The man led us inside. General Davis had said his name was Luke. I knew better than to address him that way yet. He'd be Mr. Coye until directed to address him another way.

Mr. Coye led us further into the house, past a large sitting room, a massive kitchen, and into an office that was three times the size of my bedroom at Headquarters. Large, leather couches and chairs formed a horseshoe around a stone fireplace with a large coffee table stretched in the center.

"Please, sit." Mr. Coye sat on one end of a couch while Davis and I sat across from him. "What do you need this early in the morning, Connor? It sounded important."

"It is." Davis sat forward on the couch, interlocking his fingers. "Have you heard about the attacks on the governor?"

"Why of course. Everyone heard about them. Why?"

"Did you hear about how the creatures had no scent and our Magic Users couldn't sense them?"

Mr. Coye's eyebrows furrowed. "No, that part I wasn't aware of. How is that possible?"

"We don't know. Yet."

Chapter 13

Mr. Coye leaned forward, his eyes wide and eager. "Tell me what you know."

"What I know," Davis murmured, "is that two out of the three attacks were almost successful in killing the governor and his wife. The first attack failed because one person could smell the Wight. We still don't know how or why it was only one, but the fact remains that it happened. The attack landed him in the hospital, so he wasn't around for the second or third attacks for us to test if he could still smell the creatures."

"Who was this?"

Davis didn't bother responding aloud, but pointed a finger right at me. The other man grinned, and it reminded me so much of Jezzi that she might as well have been in the room with us.

"Jezzelle mentions you every time she calls. You're a good friend to my daughter." He turned back to Davis and rubbed his chin. "Let me guess, you want me to put out some feelers to see what I can find, the stuff no one will speak to you about."

"If you would, that would be so kind."

"You know I can't work directly through you. That would be obvious, and those I work with monitor me like I monitor them. It'd be suicide."

With a grin like a coyote's, Davis leaned even further forward. "Could you work with your daughter's boyfriend?"

I wanted to die. Right then if the earth swallowed me whole, I'd welcome it. It was hard enough stifling the rumors within the Elite ranks, and each time I made sure I was clear that nothing was happening between us. But for Davis to tell her father I was Jezzi's boyfriend...death couldn't come on swifter wings. When Mr. Coye's eyes locked on me, I groaned and rubbed my face.

"It's not like that," I moaned. "I told you it's not like that."

Davis chuckled and patted my back. "Okay, so maybe you aren't her boyfriend, but the world doesn't know that, and the rumors going throughout the Elite ranks would support it. That would give Luke the needed cover to work with you. Luke, I've put my young recruit here on the assignment to find out how this is possible. You'll call him with any news."

Mr. Coye grinned wider, catching on. "And if it can't be said over the phone, have Jezzelle bring him over for a family meal. Yes, this could work out perfectly."

Needing to clear the air, I sighed. "Mr. Coye-."

"Luke."

"Okay, Luke, I'm really not Jezzi's boyfriend. She's a close friend, but that's all."

He nodded, a twinkle in his eye. "She's always been forward, especially with males. I know my daughter, so don't worry. You mean a great deal to her, so even if you're only friends, I'm warning you not to hurt her."

"I'd rather die, Sir." I meant it. Before I hurt her, physically or emotionally, I'd rather die. That went for Avery and Jonas as well.

General Davis laughed and stood. "Let's hope it doesn't come to anyone dying. That would be a pity." He shook hands with Luke across the table as the coyote alpha stood, and I followed their example. "Take care, my friend. Be careful. We don't know who or what is able to do this, but they won't like anyone snooping around in their business."

"Trust me, I'll be fine." Luke winked at me. "It's our young friend here who has to worry. Imagine what will happen when word gets out that a coyote is dating a vamlure. The supernatural headlines will explode with the drama."

"Please, no," I begged. "Can we please not let it get that far." Damage control was already too much, and it didn't work.

"He's right about that," Davis warned. "Let's not get too public with this. It's an excuse for him to be near you, not to draw attention your way."

"Yes, yes, I know. I was just riling the kid up." Luke led us back to the main entrance and yawned. "Now, if you don't mind, I'm going back to bed. It's pathetic when I'm awake before the rest of the household."

Chuckling, Davis pulled the car keys from his pocket. "Sorry for disturbing your beauty sleep."

"It was worth it to meet my girl's latest flame."

Burning cheeks and all, I didn't even bother denying this statement in the open where anyone might hear, so I turned and headed toward the car. It was a silent ride back to Headquarters, but this time when the gate opened for us, Davis rolled his window down. The guard on duty appeared perplexed and was at the open window in seconds.

"Is something wrong, Sir?" he asked the general, who shook his head.

"Nope. Just allowing you to verify it's me driving."

"Yes, Sir. Have a good day."

We drove past him toward Headquarters where Davis parked his car, but didn't get out. I followed his example and stayed put. There was something he wanted to say, but why'd he wait until now to say it?

"Luke is a good friend, and he'll help us in any way he can. Be careful. He has enemies. He's also likely to draw attention to himself by asking around. If or when he calls you to his house, don't go in uniform. Change into everyday clothes and for all that is holy in this world you'd better act the part of that girl's boyfriend. Understood?"

I arched an eyebrow at him as one side of my mouth lifted. "So, in other words, kiss her back?"

He snorted and opened the car door. "Yeah, that'll help."

"What do you want me to do now?" I asked, following him inside the building. "Captain Smith said I had the morning off, but I don't want to be useless."

"I want you to figure out a game plan, and I want you to choose members of your team," he said after the elevator doors closed behind us. "Raven, you are now unofficially a team leader. The other officers you've been working with, and I, all agreed this should be your assignment. Choose your team and bring me the list. I want there to be five of them, so choose more than is needed so that way if I take names off, there will be enough."

"Who can I choose?"

"Anyone you feel you'll need. And I mean anyone."

Anyone.

I'd spent the whole rest of the morning in the Headquarters library agonizing over this list. I still wasn't familiar with most of the Elite, and even fewer I knew by name. And if I didn't know a name, I couldn't even guess strengths and weaknesses, let alone if there would be a personality conflict. One thing was certain: I needed to choose a far more experienced team member as a mentor. Sure, I'd lead this team, my team, but I needed someone to bounce ideas off. There was only one person who I desperately hoped this could be. Just in case, I'd added my second option. If both were denied, I'd beg.

My phone rang as I was folding the sheet of paper I'd written the names on. "Hey, Avery. What's up?"

"Umm, what's up is that you're late for practice," Avery murmured through the cell phone. "You need to get here pronto."

I'd been planning to take this list to General Davis now, but a glance at the clock on the phone let me know I'd have to wait. It was one minute after noon, and I'd only been given the morning off. Stitches didn't seem to be a good enough excuse not to participate in the afternoon training, although with my speedier healing, I wouldn't have stitches for long. I'd just need more blood.

And more blood right now would be perfect, if I had some with me. I'd need to figure out how to safely keep a few vials on me, and keep them cooler. That was something I'd need to discuss with one of the officers, I just wasn't sure which one. Maybe that would depend on who made my list of teammates.

"Okay, I'll be right there."

"Hurry."

I didn't bother ending the call, knowing Avery would do it. Instead, I raced from the room, the librarian glaring at me as I accidentally kicked a chair on the way. I guessed the movies were accurate about librarians, or it was just this one who played the part well.

The team was already lined up when I entered the gym, and every eye landed on me, including Captain Smith. I wasn't sure if the look he gave me was supposed to be a glower or a pained smile. He likely knew what I'd been doing, and for whom, so he wasn't truly mad. Or maybe he had a guess at where I'd been.

"I know Major Pike has drilled into you the need for timeliness," he barked with little malice, "I expected better. Do you have an excuse?"

Standing next to Cage at the end of the line, I shook my head. "No, Sir. It won't happen again."

"I should hope not. For being late, you'll run five miles at the end of this training. If you think that'll be a piece of cake, I should warn you I'll be working you hard for the next few hours. Be prepared to wish for death, recruit. Maybe next time you'll be here early." Smith's satisfied smirk made my stomach roll, and for the next three hours he pushed me harder than he ever had before.

My body hit the mat with so much force time and time again that I thought it would leave a dent in the flooring. It was good my stitches were nearly ready to come out because I had to use my arm to defend myself from strong blows. When we finally moved to weapons, I could barely grip the sword in my hand I was shaking so badly. Even then, the captain never let up on me, and I almost lost several body parts more than once.

When he called an end to practice, Smith smirked. "You ready for those laps?"

Sweat drenched my entire body, and I barely had enough energy to nod, let alone answer him. Today I'd proven to myself that I was by far the worst choice as team leader for the mission Davis had planned. They'd all see it in time. I just hoped it wouldn't be too late.

By the time I finished my run, every inch of my body was trembling, and when Smith called out I was finished, I collapsed on the floor. That's what I got for skipping meals, and that included blood. If this was going to work, I needed to start planning ahead. These people were brutal.

"Learn your lesson?" the captain asked, crouching beside me as I gasped on the ground.

"Yeah," I stammered.

"Good. Now you'd better get up and stretch or you'll be in more pain later when you stiffen. Trust me."

"Can't move."

"Maybe this will help," Avery's voice stated. His footsteps echoed in the room as he crossed to us. A small popping sound proceeded the scent of blood in the air, making my throat tingle. Yes, that would help.

Finding some extra strength, I pushed myself to my knees. The vial found its way into my hand and I tossed it back, letting the red liquid of life flow past my tongue. Within seconds, energy fueled my body, and I was able to stand and start stretching like Smith had directed. I knew I needed to stretch, but I hadn't had the strength.

"You should carry some of that stuff with you," Captain Smith noted, and I nodded.

"I've been thinking about that all day. I need to find a way to keep it cool and protected."

He nodded, staring at the vial in my hand. "I'll find someone to work on that. By the way, you have a meeting with General Davis in an hour. Don't be late." Without a backward glance, Smith strode from the room, leaving me alone with Avery.

"Yeah, by the way, how'd helping Davis go this morning?" Avery laughed when I glowered at him. "That good?"

"Don't ask. Seriously, don't. I can't say much."

"Jezzelle called me and asked why her boyfriend wasn't answering her calls. Since when have you two been an item?" Avery's smile grew wider. I rubbed my temples. There was definitely a headache forming that no amount of blood could fix.

"Since this morning. I'll explain later. For now, I need to eat and then go to that meeting. I don't even want to think about what Davis will do to me if I'm late."

Avery gave me a once over before adding, "You might want to shower and change first, too."

He was right. My sweaty, dirty self couldn't go up to Davis's office like this. I'd need to clean up first, and then eat if there was time. If yesterday was long, today was even longer. No wonder the officers were always working. Did they even see their families? Did they even have families?

"Showering is a must," I commented, following Avery from the room. He punched the elevator button to go down and watched me. "What?"

"I don't know what's going on, but promise me you'll be careful."

"I'll be as careful as I can."

"Good. You're not a cat shifter. You don't have nine lives."

"And you do?" I arched a brow at him, never believing the saying about cats having nine lives.

He snorted. "No, but with the way you're blowing through your luck, you don't have nine either. Quit bleeding. Also, I'll go to the cafeteria and grab you something to eat while you go clean up. I think they have some pizza on the menu."

"Thanks. I'm glad you're my friend, Avery."

With a sigh, he slung an arm over my shoulders. "Someone has to watch out for you. You may be impressive for your age in most things they've thrown at you, but you're still young."

"So I should keep calling you Mother?"

Avery's hand moved from my shoulder to slap me upside the head in a second flat, leaving no time to react. "Call me that again and I'll make sure my revenge is sweet." The elevator arrived, and he jerked his thumb at it. "Clean up. You stink."

Chapter 14

Fay was gone for the day when I entered General Davis's office, and the inner door was open, giving me a clear view of him. When he caught sight of me, Davis turned his full attention on me from whatever he'd been staring at on his computer. Beckoning me in, he stood up and rounded the desk to sit in one of the two office chairs, which were now facing one another.

"Please close the door. Let's have a talk. You have your list of names with you, correct?"

I did as directed and handed him the list, and sat, waiting for his scrutiny. He rubbed his chin, which was showing a thick five o'clock shadow this late in the evening. There was a bit of gray in it, just like his short cropped hair. As he read, he didn't give away any emotion. He was good at that, and I'd never be anywhere near that composed.

"This is a good list. Who do you want most?"

"The top five, Sir."

He tilted his head as he studied the paper some more. "That makes it easy then. Hmm. Kara, the alchemist. Why her? What can she do to help you?" His attention lifted to my face to watch me as I spoke.

"We're assuming that the person behind this is an Other who has power we haven't seen before. Well, what if it's not? What if it's some sort of chemical being used or a genetic mutation in some of the Threats that someone has found and is using to their advantage. We can't assume anything, and if it's chemical, Kara's alchemy ability will be of use to the team. If that's not the case and it is a strange Other, she might be able to help us figure out a way to detect these creatures without using our natural skills."

Davis was quiet as his gaze dropped back to the paper, his eyes unfocused. He saw the list, but his thoughts were far from it. It took him several minutes to think through what I said, and when he came back to the present, he nodded.

"That's a decent theory. You've thought about this a bit. Okay, you can have Kara. Avery was an obvious choice. The two of you seem to play off one another, and he's always got your back. Jezzelle...explain that one."

I'd thought that one would be the most obvious. Apparently I was wrong.

"She's supposed to be my girlfriend, and if Luke finds something, she'll need to take me to him. It would be best if she was involved so that she could be in the meeting as well. If I misunderstand something or miss a detail, she could catch it for me."

His lips thinned, but he nodded. "I don't particularly like that two out of your five are new recruits, mostly because you make three and that's half the team, but you've backed up your choices well thus far. Now, Felix. How is a woman with earth elemental abilities going to help you?"

"Uh, have you seen that woman fight? Kara may be our intellectual component, but Felix is our brute strength. Give her a sword, a pound of gravel, or her fists and you'd better find a shield. Plus, she's willing to donate blood, just like the others. Well, I'm not sure about Kara. I don't think that would be a good choice since I'm not sure if her magic is elemental or true magic."

"It's true magic."

"Then I can't drink from her." Just the thought of accidentally taking blood from the alchemist was nauseating. It would be an accidental suicide as her magic blood would kill me within an hour, and it wouldn't be painless.

"Now, this last name...I'm not sure about this one or the next." He eyed me again, waiting for me to explain.

I shrugged. "I'm sixteen, almost seventeen, and I've never led anything, let alone an Elite team. I've only been on teams for a month and a half. There's so many rules and regulations that I don't know, techniques in the field I would never think about, and just knowledge overall that I don't have. They could give it to me." I shrugged. "Unless you know someone better who it wouldn't be as much of a pain or demotion to have to work under me. I never thought about that. It'd be a slap in the face for them. Never mind." I dropped my head, my face heating. How had I even considered adding Pike and Smith to my list? He'd said anyone, but I hadn't thought within reason.

"No, actually it could work. Cole Pike has been wanting a change. This could be good for him, and for your team. Good job, kid. Your team is complete. I'll reach out to all of them tonight and we'll have a meeting here tomorrow morning at eight o'clock. Don't mention what it's about to Avery."

"Yes, Sir."

"Good. Now, tonight figure out what your next step is going to be. Part of being the leader is thinking ahead. Not too far, but enough."

"How do you know it's enough?"

"Follow your gut for now. Even if that plan is to sit down and make sure everyone is up to speed, it's still a plan. Now get out of here. I've got to make those calls and get home before my wife comes looking for me. And Raven, good job."

I should've spent more time planning and thinking ahead last night, but after the craziness of my life in the last few days alone, exhaustion took me the moment my head hit the pillow. It wasn't often anymore that my alarm woke me, so when it went off, I wanted to smack it off my nightstand. Avery grumbled as well. It hadn't taken me long to find out that at his core, the snow leopard wasn't a morning person. He also switched between sleeping in skin and sleeping in fur. Last night had been a fur night as the temperature in our room had dipped a little cooler than normal. We'd need to mention it to maintenance to have them check for a problem.

"I'll shower first. We can't be late," I grumbled, grabbing clean clothes and heading to the shower.

Avery had cornered me as soon as I'd stepped into the bedroom last night, asking what this meeting was about. He hadn't been happy when

I'd told him I wasn't allowed to say and that he'd have to wait. We'd dealt with an awkward silence until he'd apologized for being grumpy.

After we were both cleaned up, we grabbed a quick bite to eat, then headed upstairs. I refused to be late. For one thing, Major Pike would be there. He'd take it as a personal insult. The second reason was because as the new team leader, I needed to set a good example for my team. Showing up late to our first meeting was unacceptable. Avery grumbled about having to be there ten minutes early, but he also didn't wait behind in the cafeteria.

Fay was already in the office when I arrived, and she grinned at me. "Welcome back, Raven. Who's this?"

"Avery Clark." Avery stuck out his hand as he introduced himself, his eyes almost glowing as he took in the blonde female. She clasped his hand while giving him a cheeky grin.

"I like that name. Maybe we can discuss more about you over dinner sometime."

And she was far more forward than I'd ever be. In some ways, she reminded me of Jezzi. Avery didn't seem to mind as his smile widened.

"That would be fun. I'll let you know when I'm free and we can work something out."

They were about to exchange phone numbers when General Davis's door opened and he stepped out. One look at the situation and he glowered at Fay, who ducked her head.

"You were supposed to tell me the moment Raven arrived."

She nodded, appearing thoroughly chastened even though Davis hadn't raised his voice with her in the slightest. "I'm sorry, Sir."

"Come on in, Raven. I want to talk with you a little while everyone else arrives."

"Everyone else?" Avery asked me as I made my way toward Davis's office.

"You'll understand soon, and try not to flirt too much while I'm gone." Smirking at my best friend, I entered the office and closed the door behind me.

My eyes widened when I found Pike sitting in my usual chair in this office. He stood and smiled wide, looking me up and down. It seemed like years since I'd last seen him instead of days.

"I see Captain Smith hasn't done too much damage yet," Pike laughed, shaking my hand. "It's good to see you, Raven."

"You as well, Sir."

He motioned for us to sit, and we did so, with Davis at his desk. "I have to say, I was a little surprised that you wanted me on your team."

"You've taught me so much already, and I'm going to need a lot more teaching before this is through. I know it's going to be like a demotion having to work with me as the team lead, so I hope that's not too embarrassing...if you even want to be on my team at all."

Pike chuckled and leaned back in his chair, studying me. "Never in a million years would I ever have thought I'd want to work with a Blood Drinker. Your kind has always been perceived as vile and dangerous. I'm glad to be proven wrong, at least thus far. And I have no problems working under you. It'll be a breath of fresh air, if you really want to know."

This warlock was like no one else I'd ever met. Who considered working under the direction of a sixteen-year-old Blood Drinker a breath of fresh air? I'd look the person in charge in the face and ask them what they were thinking because this was idiotic. I was going to get them all killed, I was sure of it.

"I hope I don't screw up too bad and make you regret your choice," I murmured, taking a deep breath.

"Raven, I want to give you a few tips before we're joined by everyone else," Pike told me, folding his hands in his lap. "First, there are going to be a lot of people who are angry with this decision. We can't please everyone, and what most everyone wants is a promotion. They'll see you as a young, new recruit, and jealous won't even begin to cover the animosity they'll show you. Everywhere you turn, someone will treat you like crap because of it.

"Second, they may treat you that way, but you hold your head high. You've earned this, whether you think you have or not. We've all seen something in you that has pointed to this moment in your journey, even if you are the most junior recruit we've ever accepted. If you don't make people respect you, and if you don't have respect for and faith in yourself, you won't succeed in this position.

"Third, trust your team. When you don't know the answers, turn to your team. They may not know them either, but if you don't ask and you sink, your whole team will sink with you. You all fail. If you work together and you still fail, at least you tried and failed as a unit. That's about all the words of advice I have for you at the moment. I'm sure we'll be able to talk more later."

His words sunk into my heart as the two men were silent, letting me digest what I'd heard. Pike had no idea how much I needed to hear those words. I'd figured I'd receive a lot of flack for being young and in such a higher level position. It wasn't like I'd asked for it. If anything, I wanted Pike to lead this team and I'd gladly assist under him. However, this was my reality, and nothing I could do would change it, or at least not for the better.

"Are you ready to face your team?" Davis chuckled, standing to open the door.

Releasing a deep breath, I stood and strode to his side of the desk. When I leaned against the wall behind it, he arched and eyebrow at me.

"Yes, I'm ready. I'd rather do this standing, if you don't mind."

"As you wish."

Without further comment, Davis opened the door and stepped out. While he addressed those waiting in the outer office, I took a steadying breath and then watched each file in. Kara sat in the seat I'd left while the others found open places to stand, including Captain Smith. My eyebrows shot up as his eyes met mine, and he chuckled.

"Didn't expect me, did you? I wasn't going to miss this little announcement." He rounded the room to stand next to me while my friends and colleagues looked on with interest. Apparently only Pike and Smith had been read into the plans.

Kara leaned across her chair, closing the gap between her and Pike. "I take it this is big."

"Huge," he responded, smirking at me while Kara leaned back and watched as Davis took his seat behind the desk once again.

"You're probably all wondering why you've been called to my office first thing this morning. It's simple. We're putting a new type of unit together. It's a beta team, and we're testing out several different ideas and missions with it.

"The first is that you'll be assisting in the determination of what is happening with these creatures we can't sense or smell. I learned this morning that there were four attacks by such creatures on our bases across the continent last night. Five Elite are dead, but so are the creatures, with no more answers than what we had." Everyone perked up, even me. He'd failed to mention this information to me earlier when he had the chance. Why wait? He had to have a good reason.

"The second difference is that you'll be living in off base housing. Your team leader will choose a new location for your team, likely in a suburban neighborhood. It'll decrease the response time to reach troubled areas since it takes a minimum of ten minutes to leave our grounds, and that's once you pull out of the parking garage.

"And the third, most unique difference to this team, is the team leader is a new recruit that has shown promise in the areas of ingenuity and who can smell these odd creatures. Yes, Raven is now the head of your team, and your boss. You will all report to him, and he'll report to me. Everyone except Bruce Smith. He's here as a witness."

Most everyone who didn't already know what was happening reacted when Davis made his announcement. There were a couple gasps and mouths popping open as jaws hit the floor. Avery's wide eyes watched me, and I wanted to duck my head from their stares, but Pike's words came back to me. I had to be strong, act strong, and make people respect me. I wasn't sure how to do that yet, but dropping my gaze in uncertainty wasn't the way. Instead, I stared each one of them in the eyes for a few seconds before moving on to the next person. It wasn't easy, but I did it anyway. I wouldn't back down from this.

"What exactly is Captain Smith witnessing besides the formation of this team, which doesn't seem like it needs to be witnessed..." Kara stated, trailing off with the raising of her eyebrow at the gorilla shifter, who chuckled at her tenacity.

"Funny you should mention that," Smith said after composing himself, though a large grin still covered his face. "This whole idea has several of the other Elite bases questioning our sanity, but we believe we're doing the right thing. I'm here because General Connor Davis needs a witness to his making Raven Cartana an Elite officer. You see, only an officer can be a team leader."

My eyebrows shot up as my head swiveled between the three officers in the room. They'd purposefully not told me this. Why? Did it even matter? I was going to lead this team anyway, but the sudden shock made my stomach turn. The statement that Pike should be the one leading this team was on the tip of my tongue, but Davis stood, his chair grinding into the floor as he did so.

I wasn't sure how to tell an Elite's rank. Most, even these men, didn't wear stripes or pins of any kind to reveal it. The ones I knew were officers I only knew because they'd been introduced to me and I'd heard the rank. Until this point in time, I hadn't cared too much to know how to tell them apart. It wasn't like we were as formal as the other military branches. Most of the time we didn't even salute an officer.

In his hands, Davis held out what looked like a bracelet or some unique band. It was black, with a silver stripe down the middle. For the first time, I noticed that the officers in the room wore bands on their wrists. There were slight differences in the bands around me that the officers wore. Smith's was silver while Pike's was a dark burgundy, and Davis's was gold.

"It's my privilege to promote you from trainee to the office of a Captain in the Elite Guard, Raven Cartana." Major Davis motioned me to give him my hand, so I did, and he slipped the band on my wrist. Without him doing anything, the band tightened to a comfortable fit. Magic.

"Captain?" I squeaked, looking over my shoulder at Captain Smith. "Same as you. When you said officer, I was thinking a corporal."

Smith chuckled, folding his arms over his chest, reminding me yet again of how large he was with the amount of space he took up. "We decided if we were going to do this, we were going to do it right. Honestly, we've been planning this for months. We just had to find the right candidate." He turned to the others, his smile fading as his lips turned down and a hard edge set around his jaw and eyes. "I want you all to know we support this decision. If you don't want to be on this team, fine. You don't have to be, but you should know that Raven personally chose you. Each and every one of you. He didn't ask for this, and he's going to need all of your help."

"And I won't take it personally if you don't want to be on the team," I added onto the end of Smith's statement. "I know being led by a Blood Drinker isn't something most people would want, especially when I'm the youngest and most inexperienced person on the team. But, I promise you, I'll do my best."

Jezzi smirked at me. "I'd follow you anywhere, boy."

And this was why everyone thought she was my girlfriend. Looked like that little lie was going to work in our favor, especially with her spouting off comments like that. Shaking my head, I met the eyes of Kara and Felix.

"You don't have to be on my team, but I'd feel honored if you'd consider it."

Felix's eyes narrowed as she studied me. "I'll say yes on one condition."

"Name it and I'll see what I can do."

"I want to help pick the house."

"Done."

"Ooo, can I help too?" Jezzi asked, excitement bursting from her. She stared at Felix, her eyes pleading. "I have great taste, if I do say so myself."

Felix grinned back. "The more the merrier."

Maybe I'd live to regret this choice, but only time would tell. "I have one condition ladies."

"Better be good," Kara snickered. "I'm in on house shopping too. What would you like? A pool? Jacuzzi?"

"A basement. No windows."

Jezzi snorted and shook her head as she leaned further into the wall. "He wants a cave. Don't you like the sun now that you're out in it?"

"If it didn't give me headaches all the time, I'd enjoy it." I'd made the decision last night to absolutely give up my sunglasses for good, except on rare occasions. They were a crutch, a way to protect my eyes from the sun's rays, but also a way to hide who I was from those around me. Now that I was leading a team, I had to step up and be a man, not a boy. I couldn't let years of prejudice decide who I'd be and how people saw me.

"Pft, you know you love the sun. I'll make it my job to convince you of that. Have you ever been sunbathing at the beach?"

Rolling my eyes at Jezzi, I readdressed the room at large. "We have a lot of work to do, and I trust you all to do your best. I mean this: if I do something you think is wrong or there's a better way, please correct me. I'm not perfect, and I never will be, but I can't do this alone."

"We won't let you fail, because then we will too," Avery announced, his deep voice creating a solemn tone in the room. "If we fail, people will die."

"I won't have that," I growled. "Not if I can help it."

Davis cut into our conversation before anyone else could speak. "Which brings us to our next order of business...or rather, yours. Raven, please take your team to the conference room across the hall and start planning where you'll start with your overall mission. Next, find a house. Ladies, Raven has the final say. Raven, don't be a pushover. These may be friends and colleagues, but you're still in charge. I want that house chosen within the week. Lastly, I'm going to give two police departments your cell phone number, Raven. When they find a situation they can't handle, they'll call you. If it turns out you need help, you'll call in another team. Right now we only have larger teams here on the base and in other locations. I'll give you a list of phone numbers and their locations. This starts today, so be prepared for anything."

Pike led the way from the room, and the rest followed. I was going to join them when Smith placed a hand on my shoulder. "I want your team to continue practicing with mine, but I'll leave it up to you on when that will be, if you want it to happen at all. Remember, we're equals now, at least in rank. You make those decisions for your team."

Snorting, I rolled my eyes and stared at him over my shoulder. "Most, if not all, of my team can beat me up. I'm pretty sure that I'm the one who needs to train with you."

"So be it. I hope to see you around. Good luck." He patted my shoulder and gave it a light shove, letting me be on my way to join my team again.

My team. I sure hoped I didn't get them all killed.

Chapter 15

Everyone was seated in the conference room when I joined them. The oval, dark wood laminate table was in stark contrast to the bright white walls which made the room almost glow. My eyes watered the second I entered, but I took a breath and closed the door. I would not let my eyes be my weakness, not now, not ever. I'd work through this. I would not be weak.

"Okay, ladies and gentlemen, I'm sure this is a shock." I stood at the head of the table, gaining their attention. "It was for me as well. Are there any questions not related to our case that you'd like to ask before we start on that?"

"Can I move over here now since I'm part of your team?" Jezzelle asked, almost cutting me off in her anxiousness to know my answer.

"Um, I guess so."

"So, where do I sleep?" She pursed her lips and gave me a once over with her eyes. "If there's no room, I'm sure your bed is big enough for two."

It was, but there was no way I was cuddling in it, especially with her. I didn't even need to ask if she could keep her hands to herself. She couldn't keep her lips off me. Giving her access to more of my body, especially in the dark, was asking for trouble.

"So is Avery's." The panic that spread over my best friend's face was almost too much not to laugh at, but I managed.

"I have a spare bed," Felix announced, giving me a wink. Jezzi caught it and narrowed her eyes on the unsuspecting female. Jealousy issues weren't what I wanted on the team.

"Okay, Jezzi will move in with Felix. Behave you two." My warning fell on deaf ears. Either they'd kill one another or they'd become best friends. I wasn't sure which was worse. "Any other questions?"

The room was silent.

"Good. Okay, like General Davis said, our big mission is to find out what we can about these weird creatures and who's behind the attacks. There are other teams working on this, but they haven't been able to crack the case yet. I'd say I hope it's us, but I honestly hope someone does. I don't care who. They've all taken the angle that this is an Other who has some ability to mask the senses. I'd like to take the angle that it's some chemical, a genetic mutation, or something like it."

"What makes you think that?" Kara asked, leaning forward in her chair. I'd guessed this would intrigue her, and I'd been right. When this meeting was over, I'd gloat. Now wasn't the time.

"Because it didn't work on everyone. Like me. My guess would be that if this was an Other, their ability to limit who was affected wouldn't be so precise. Whoever's behind this knows that Blood Drinkers aren't in the Elite, or they weren't until I showed up. I don't think they were prepared for their creature to meet me."

"Probably not," Pike muttered, swinging side to side in his swivel chair as he thought. "It's a good new angle. It may be completely wrong, but it's worth figuring out. Now, how do we prove it?"

"I want a look at those creatures they killed last night if one's close, or if we happen to still have the ones that attacked the governor. And their clothes."

Pike nodded. "I can see what I can do here, but I'm not sure I can help with the other bases. You may have to work with Connor to make that happen."

And I had nothing to write with to make a note of that.

"Got your back," Kara stated with a grin, pulling a notepad out from the small bag she carried. "I never go anywhere without it in case I come up with new ideas for liquids to separate or a hypothesis on my current works."

"Yeah, sorry for taking you from those."

She shrugged. "This is more fun. I needed a break to rejuvenate my creativity."

At least she was staying positive. While Kara made the note for me to speak with General Davis, I took a seat and studied the laminate wood pattern.

"Does anyone else have any ideas?"

"Well," Avery stated after a few seconds, "It can't hurt to read the reports from everyone involved with each incident. Maybe there was something in them that could lead us in a different direction, or confirm our current theory."

"I like that," Kara stated, writing this new task in her notebook.

"It can't hurt." Folding my arms, I leaned on them and nodded. "Okay, these are good places to start. Oh, crap..." There was one other thing I'd forgotten about. Running a hand through my hair, I ignored Pike's grin that he covered with a hand. "I forgot. We have a little more help. I had a visit with Luke Coye yesterday, or rather General Davis did and he had me tag along."

"You went to see my dad?" Jezzelle sounded shocked. I couldn't believe her dad hadn't mentioned I'd been over to see him, and I'd thought she'd known when she told Avery her boyfriend wasn't answering his phone.

The thought made me snort and shake my head, which wasn't the response she was looking for as she glared at me. "You mean your dad didn't tell you that your boyfriend stopped in?"

Her eyebrows shot up while Avery choked and coughed while Felix released a belly laugh that almost had her rolling out of her chair.

"My boyfriend?" Jezzi stared at me before a sly grin lifted one side of her mouth. "And just who might this boyfriend be, hmm?"

"Me."

"Rawr," Jezzi purred, staring at me with a sensual smile as her eyes once again did a once over, likely picturing what was under my clothes this time. If she didn't do it every time.

"Stop," I warned, trying not to squirm under her attention. "It's not like that. General Davis asked Luke to ask around and keep his ears open. If he hears something, he'll invite you over for dinner, and you'll bring me, your boyfriend. It'll be a nice little family dinner. Our 'relationship' doesn't go beyond that, okay?"

"Party pooper," she muttered. "You know, that could get my dad killed."

"We warned him, and he had a chance not to do it, but he agreed to help. Honestly, he's in as much danger as we are from this person. When the Elite are destroyed by these Threats, what's to stop the creatures from tearing down the packs? Killing shifters? Going after the Magic User covens? Nothing. This is preventing that from happening."

She shrugged. "I'm still not a fan of it."

"Even if you get to date me?"

"So, tell me again why I can't sleep in your bed, then?" Her eyes glittered with amusement as I squirmed.

Avery snorted and leaned his head back. "I'll tell you why, because he's my roommate and I'm not moving out. There's no way I want to hear what would happen over there."

"Nothing." I cut in before Jezzi could make an inappropriate comment that I knew was coming. "Nothing would happen, and nothing will because she's staying with Felix."

While Jezzi pouted, I had Kara go over our to-do list again before dismissing them. The females raced from the room, eager to find a computer and start house shopping. They'd make it a good one. As long as it had a large basement, I didn't care what the rest of it looked like.

Taking out my phone, I added everyone to a group text and sent a message telling them we'd be meeting Captain Smith's team for training that evening, and not to be late. It wasn't that most of them needed the training, but I wanted to see what Pike and Kara could do since I hadn't seen them fight yet. In fact, I hadn't seen Pike use his magic yet either. He was a warlock after all...

"Major Pike-."

"Cole," he corrected. "As long as we're on the same team, Captain," he smirked, "then I want you to call me Cole."

"Yes, Sir." We both chuckled as Avery shook his head. He hadn't left yet, likely waiting for me to leave too.

"Okay, what did you need?" Pike, Cole, asked, leaning forward to rest his elbows on the tabletop.

"What does your magic do? Is it a specialty or can you do anything with it?"

"I knew you'd get around to asking me that eventually." He shrugged. "I decided to specialize. My family's magic is defensive, mostly, though we have dabbled in war magic. We're not nearly as good at that as we are with defense. Anyway, I can create magical shields of various types, wards, and magical alarms."

I perked up as he spoke, already planning a way to use his magic. "Could you ward and shield our house?"

"I was already planning on it, but thank you for asking. Now, I need to go see if I can arrange a meeting for us with the bodies of those Wights, if they're still around and not burned already. You should talk to Connor and see if he can help you now before he becomes busy with other tasks today. Also, make sure he has Kay enter your promotion into the system. Then you can give our friend here," he jerked his thumb at Avery, "permission to read through all the reports coming in."

"Why is it the girls get to house shop and I'm stuck reading reports? Next time I keep my mouth shut." Avery stood, grumbling as he rounded the table to smack my shoulder. "Come on, Captain. Let's go start this boring day."

He wasn't wrong. After stopping in to speak with General Davis, Avery and I spent what was left of the morning reading through reports. I couldn't leave him to do it alone. Pike, or Cole as he'd asked me to call him, joined us an hour into our torture. He had further access than we currently did since my promotion was still being added into the system, so he searched the files from one of the other attacks.

Hours later, we made our way downstairs to the gym where the girls were already waiting. When Captain Smith's team lined up, I swallowed hard. This was unfamiliar territory. When Cole nudged my shoulder, I turned to him.

"What do you want us to do, Sir?" he asked, his use of the word 'Sir' was shocking, but his tone was respectful, not sarcastic or snide.

"I guess line up beside the others, but leave a little space between you and them."

"Yes, Sir."

While my team moved to stand beside the other team, I walked over to Smith. He may have been my equal in rank now, but it was odd to treat him the same, especially when Cole outranked me and treated me like a superior. It would take time to figure this out in my head.

"How's the first day?" Smith chuckled when I approached him. His voice was soft, only reaching the two of us. For now, I was grateful no one else knew, but after this, word would spread like wildfire.

"I'm still getting used to Cole calling me 'Sir' if that's any indication."

"It is. It'll take some time to become used to it, especially at your age. Now, let's make a little announcement and then start this. We need to make sure we're all up to speed." He lifted two fingers to his lips and released a shrill whistle. "Okay, ladies and gents, we have a short announcement, and then we'll start this training session. As of this morning, my young friend here is now known as Captain Cartana. You'll show him respect or you're out of here. These five off to the side are his team. They're a beta unit we're testing. If you have any concerns or complaints, don't take them up with Raven, but take them to myself and I'll escalate the issues, though you should be warned that complaints won't change anything. Raven is a captain, and that's how it'll remain. Now, pair off and spar."

There had been a few murmurs, and some had outright glared, glowered, and looked me up and down like they were trying to figure out what made me worthy to be promoted beyond them. I didn't have an answer for them since I was still trying to figure it out myself. That didn't matter. I'd prove to them I was worthy.

It ended up that it didn't matter if I was now a Captain or not, the gorilla shifter I'd come to think of as a friend still found new ways to catch me off guard and land a solid punch. Half the time I was too busy worrying about retaliating with a bite that I missed my chance to offer a counterattack and defend myself against a follow up hit. The bruising to my ribs was just one more reason I was inadequate for this job. It would only be a matter of time before the other officers realized it.

"What's up, kid?" Smith asked after a particularly painful blow to the back of my skull. "You're distracted."

"I...I don't want to bite you."

"Oh." The shock in Smith's voice was clear. He hadn't thought about that while we fought, and now that he did, would he refuse to train with me? I closed my eyes, waiting for the words to flow from his mouth. "Okay, I suppose this is good practice in not biting your friends and colleagues. Now, get over it and get your head back in this fight before I rip your teeth out, how's that?"

Shocked, I lifted my head to the smiling gorilla shifter. He rarely fought shifted with me anymore since he often stopped us to point out what I was doing wrong. Was he seriously finding this funny?

"Fight."

His fist flew at my face with blinding speed. Instinct kicked in and I caught his hand in mine, the force almost pushing me over, but I adjusted my weight. Another strike was aimed at my chest, but with bruising force, I smacked my hand against his, redirecting the blow's trajectory. In seconds I had Smith on his back, gasping for air that wouldn't come as my fingers closed around his throat.

Chapter 16

"Well, I have some bad news for you," Davis announced after I sat in my usual chair, holding an ice pack to the side of my face. Nothing could be as bad as the nurse telling me my skull was cracked. I'd never seen Cole Pike's blow coming, and he hadn't even touched me. His stupid ward that he created around Smith had blown me halfway across the room where I'd slammed into the floor with such force, I hadn't been able to slow the impact. A twisted wrist wasn't nearly as painful as it should've been with an achy skull, and I'd been given the equivalent of two vials of shifter blood to help me heal faster.

"What is it?" I mumbled so that my voice wouldn't hurt my head any more than it did.

"I can't get you a body to examine. The bases close to us have either cremated the creatures remains or there wasn't enough left to examine after their shifters got a hold of them. Not that you'd find anything on those bodies anyway. Any others are too far away to be worth examining. By the time you'd reach them, or they'd arrive here, it's likely the bodies wouldn't be in good shape and anything you needed would've been compromised, if it already hasn't been. I've warned all of their base commanders to be careful with the next batch should an attack happen. That goes for us as well. I hope this is the end of the attacks, but I fear if they're becoming bolder, we're just seeing the beginning of what they can do."

We both knew he was right, so I gave a slight nod. He chuckled to himself and sifted through papers on his desk. It was likely a dismissal, but I couldn't move yet. The room was spinning in a sickening way that had my stomach turning. Any sudden movement now and I'd be seeing my barely digested dinner again, no matter how little I'd eaten.

"I take it training could've gone better..."

A small groan echoed in my throat. "Cole packs a punch."

"Yes, yes he does. By the way, I hear you haven't called your family since you arrived. Why not?"

He wanted to talk about this when my face was breaking into a million pieces? "Dad would order me to come back, and if I don't, he'll disown me. It's best if I don't call and save us both the heartache that would cause."

"You know," Davis stated, leaning forward to rest his elbows on the desk, "I have three sons and one daughter, and I love them each dearly. Some of them have made some crazy, stupid decisions that make me wonder how many brain cells they were using when they made those decisions. However, I still love them, and if one of them ever ran off, I'd be worried sick. I'm not sure if your family would disown you or not, but being angry you left has got to be better than thinking you're lying dead in some street somewhere. Call them. Put their minds at ease, and let them know you're doing well. They may surprise you, or they may not. You'll never know until you do."

He was right. I'd known for days I needed to call home, but I couldn't make myself do it knowing it would be the last time I'd speak to my family. Davis was also right, though. My mom would be freaking out. Dad likely didn't care besides the fact that I was dragging our family image through the dirt. As the leading family of our House, one of the five vamlure Houses, our movements were watched with great scrutiny. When word reached the rest of the House, and the other two existing Houses, my family would be scorned unless they disowned me and I was forgotten. They'd likely disown me before word spread, making sure they weren't looked down upon, but seen as heroes for keeping their House secure. But Mom would still worry, and I owed her so much.

"I'll call in the morning," I murmured.

"You'll call tonight." The general's voice was hard, but he didn't yell. "I hear what happens when you say you'll call later. You never get around to it. Call them, and then tell me it's done or you'll spend the rest of the night in a holding cell, and I can promise you, those don't smell good and there's nowhere to lay down, so they're a bit uncomfortable. In fact, I might keep you locked in one until you actually do call."

His threats were never empty. I could tell by his tone and from what little I knew of him from the past few months.

"Fine. I'll call."

"Good. You can use the conference room."

At this time of night, there was certainly nobody using it. I was surprised Davis stayed as late as he did every night with how early he arrived every morning. For having a family, he must never see them. Or their relationships worked better by not seeing one another as often.

This time when I entered the conference room, the lights were off, plunging the room into nearly complete darkness except for the small window across the room allowing in a taste of moonlight. The silver glow was by far more than enough for me to see by, so I closed the door without even contemplating turning on the lights. This phone call would be torture enough on my emotions. I didn't need to add physical torture to that list.

It took a solid five minutes of staring at my phone while I sat in the same seat as earlier that morning before I punched in a familiar phone number and listened to the phone ring. There was a chance since the number wasn't familiar that she wouldn't answer, but I prayed she would. I wasn't sure that I was strong enough to leave a message, especially one that asked for a call back.

"Hello?" a timid voice asked just before the call went to voicemail. My breath caught in my throat, making it impossible to speak, let alone breathe right. "Hello?"

"Hailey," I managed to choke, my heart squeezing at the sound of her name on my lips. Those lips. I'd almost kissed those lips when I'd promised not to leave, only hours later breaking that promise by sneaking away from our home.

"Raven?"

"Hailey."

"You jerk," she spat, and I could almost see the fire in her dim eyes as they sparked with the rage drowning her words. "You lying, stupid idiot. Do you have any idea the mayhem you've caused us?"

"I'm sorry," I pleaded, rubbing my fingers against my temple. "But I had to do this."

"You promised, Raven. You promised and then I receive a visit from your mother only a few hours later with a note, a farewell note. I thought you loved me."

"I do, Hailey, more than you can ever know, but I have to do what's best for our people, and for us. Hailey, I'm making it safer in this world for us. When I have a more permanent home, I want you to join me. It's safe-."

"Are you insane?" her voice shrieked. "Never, Raven. You ended this, us, the moment you decided to leave. And guess what? No vamlure female is ever going to want you. You've disgraced our entire race. You've disgraced your family. Me. You're a liar, Raven. We were supposed to have forever, but you killed that the moment you left, and I haven't wasted a single thought on you since I read your stupid love note. If you loved me, you wouldn't have left me. Goodbye, Raven."

The call ended with a beep in my ear. That hadn't gone nearly as well as I'd hoped. Not even close. I didn't blame her for being ticked off at me, but I hadn't expected the raging storm that had doused me in shame. I'd never seen her this angry, and it tore at me, as did her words. I had disgraced my family, but I was doing it to better our world. And, was she right? Would no female want me? Sure, I lived on the surface. Other males did as well...but every one of them I could think of were single.

An ache grew in my chest, blooming out to the rest of my body as a tear slipped from my eye. Hailey had been my childhood best friend until we'd both realized we had strong feelings toward one another. We were never without the other, but when I started talking about leaving after the Great Reveal, she'd grown colder, more distant, pleading with me to change my mind. On some level, I'd known how that call would end, which was likely the reason I'd let Jezzi as close as I had. My subconscious knew I'd never be forgiven by the first girl I'd ever loved, but I couldn't make her happy and come back home. I could never live with myself by doing that.

If this call hadn't gone well, then the next one I had to make would be even worse. There was no point in making it besides to give them some relief that I was still alive. This would not end in my favor, and Hailey was right. If Dad disowned me, I'd never have a female, not even a human. I couldn't protect her without having a House to retreat to if the situation up here turned to the worst.

"Hello? Who is this?" my mother's familiar voice asked, likely not comfortable receiving a call from an unknown number. The unknown always made her anxiety grow worse.

"Mama, it's Raven."

"Raven," she breathed, relief spilling from her mouth with the sound of my name. "Oh Raven, where are you? What've you done? Come home now before your father makes his final decision on your fate. There's still time."

My gut twisted. I'd been right. I hated it, but I'd been right.

"I'm on the surface, Mama," I confessed. A soft whimper passed through the phone and another tear fell. "I'm sorry I left, but I had to. Someone has to make this world safe for our people again."

"Come home, Raven, and stop this stupidity," she pleaded through tiny gasps, and I could almost see the tears streaming down her pale cheeks. "Come home before you can't."

Those words choked me. "Mama, I can't. I'm an Elite. They let me in, and I've been promoted to a Captain. They respect me and I'm proving our people can be trusted. I'm making progress for our people."

Commotion in the background interrupted my pleadings before a new voice came on the line. "What are you thinking, you idiot?" my father's surly voice yelled into the phone, stunning me. He was a hard man, but he'd never spoken to me like this. "You get your sorry butt back home or I'm disowning you right now. Already we've lost four other good men to your fruitless cause."

More had followed me? I'd hoped they would, but I hadn't expected it. Four was better than none, but not according to my father.

"Dad, I'm doing this-."

"You're coming home!" he bellowed.

"No, I'm not," I countered, my voice rising with his. "Dad, I have friends here, from all supernatural categories. They respect me."

"They're using you. It's what they always do. They'll get the information they need from you to destroy us and you'll be the first one dead."

"No, it's not like that."

"It is like that. Now, are you coming home or will I be one son less?"

My throat closed off. I couldn't speak. This was the moment I'd feared would come.

"Raven?"

"I have to do this, Dad. Our people are dying. What do you see when you look in the mirror? I can tell you what I see: a slow, painful death. Maybe not for me, but for my children and their children. Weakness. Well, that was before I left. Now every time I look in the mirror, I see hope. My eyes have never been so bright. I've never felt so strong. I'd never created a shield over my body, not until a friend gave me his blood and we sparred with lion shifters. And we won. I have friends who are willing to give me their blood. They'd even be willing to give you blood if you'd let them."

"Never," Dad spat, sinking what little hope I had to the bottom of my soul. "If this is truly your choice, then so be it. You are hereby banished from the First House. Returning will mean your death. Do you understand?"

"Dad-." My voice caught in my throat, and I swallowed, but I didn't have a chance to continue.

"Goodbye, Raven. I hope your stupidity and useless dreams are worth it, worth this."

The call ended as abruptly as Hailey's had, and all I could do was stare across the room, a dark hollowness carving a hole in my chest, in my soul. The room could've been empty or having a party being thrown in it for all I noticed my surroundings. That was likely why I missed someone entering and sitting beside me until a hand pushed against my shoulder, drawing me out of my shocked state.

"I brought you cake," Avery announced, sliding a plate with a large slice of chocolate cake on it further toward me. The scent of chocolate assaulted my nose now that my senses were present, and with my initial shock vanishing, despair swamped me.

Tears rolled freely down my cheeks until I sobbed, my whole body shaking. For the next ten minutes, Avery held me as I released the tears of my anguished soul. They wouldn't listen to me, wouldn't give me a chance to try. Instead, they cast me out. If I was from a lower level family, no one would even care that I was gone, but being the lead family of the House...they could've given me more time.

But they hadn't, and they never would. What was done was done. I could never go home. Never marry. Never see my family again. All I could do was move on and do what I set out to do. If I didn't do that, then all of this was a waste. Losing everything would be for naught. I couldn't let that happen.

My tears slowed and stopped. Leaning away from Avery, I wiped my face dry and stared at the cake he'd brought.

"Thanks. Please don't tell anyone about this."

"I wouldn't dream of it."

My gaze locked on his still worried stare. "How'd you know?"

"General Davis called me. He said he ordered you to call home and wanted to give me a heads up in case you were upset after the call. Knowing what you told me when Smith wanted you to call home, I figured you could use a little pick me up when you were done. I take it the call went badly."

"About as well as I expected."

Avery sat quietly for a moment before jerking his thumb toward the cake. "Eat that. I had to sneak into the kitchen to get it, so you'd better not waste it. Then me and you are going for a ride."

"Where are we going?" I asked, digging the fork into the cake. Avery wasn't usually a rule breaker, so for him to have broken several to sneak me this cake, he had to have known how upset I'd be.

"Wherever we want. You're driving, so you decide."

"I'm what?" I asked, mouth full.

"You're driving. You've only driven the once, and you need to learn how before anyone will start to respect your new title. Or at least it'll help a bit more than them learning you can't drive. Plus, if something happens and you're the only one able to drive, like after an attack, I don't want to bleed to death before you drive me to a hospital at turtle pace."

He was right. We both knew it. And it would likely take my thoughts away from the conversations I'd had tonight. I'd need to deal with them, but not right now.

"Okay. By the way, why chocolate cake?"

Avery shrugged, a grin growing. "I don't know. Apparently it works for women, so why shouldn't food therapy work on a man?"

I stuffed another bite into my mouth. "It tastes good and it's food, so you won't hear me complain."

"Yeah, I didn't think so."

He gave me a few minutes to finish, and declined when I offered to share. After I'd cleaned the plate, he shoved it aside and placed a piece of paper on the table. It was a list of addresses I didn't know.

"We might also want to take a trip around to see these places and see what they look like. Jezzelle wanted to bring this to you, but I told her it was a bad time, so she gave the paper to me to give to you. We may not be able to see a whole lot or go inside, but at least if we can tell from the outside which ones we'll consider or not, we'll be ahead of the game and can take tours tomorrow."

I nodded. "Good thinking. Let's go see how overboard the ladies went with this project."

Chapter 17

Overboard was the wrong word, but I had no idea what a better, stronger word would be to use for the description of the girls' enthusiasm. Surely General Davis hadn't meant for them to search out houses that looked like they could be small castles in the ritziest part of town. Right? That seemed to me to be a huge waste of money, but I did have to admit that they were nice houses. More than nice.

At first, I was a mess, driving and trying to look at the homes and yards at the same time. Some of the houses we couldn't see from the road because they were set too far back and behind tall cement fences, if that was what such a thing could be called. Barriers were more like it. The wrought iron gates were imposing, as were the tall trees just inside the property that obscured even more than the fences did.

"And here's the last one," Avery announced as we rolled up to another obscured house. "I think we can see something if we get out. Here, pull over. That's street parking."

They had street parking on these narrow boulevards in this kind of neighborhood? Then again, it likely didn't matter as at this time of night we were about the only people driving around this area. I did as he directed and pulled over and we both climbed out of the truck. He'd let me choose what we drove, and since I'd only ever driven a truck, I chose it. Some of the vehicle basic needs were in different locations, but after Avery helped me figure out what was where, we were on our way. The large truck took up a good portion of the street, but I didn't pay it any heed when the house came into view past the iron gate.

House was an understatement, just like the women's taste who picked it out. It was by far a mansion. From here we could even see the circular driveway, multi car garage, and a fountain in the middle of the drive.

"Apparently it has a finished basement, a pool, a game room, and more square footage than we'd probably need," Avery mentioned, reading details off the paper.

"Does it list a price by chance?" He'd already stated there were no prices, but I had to be sure.

"Nope. You like this one, don't you? I can tell by the drool running down your chin." His belly laugh when I wiped my chin to find no drool whatsoever echoed off the cement barriers up and down the road. "I was kidding, Raven. It's just a saying. When you want something, you drool over it."

"I don't drool. But yes, I would like this one. Of course, I'll want to see inside it first."

"Why of course. It's never a good idea to buy a house sight unseen." Avery smirked at me. "The girls are going to appreciate that you liked at least one of their choices. But I have to ask, why this one?"

I shrugged. I had no idea. "It just feels right."

"Good enough for me. Okay, let's get back and go to bed. I'm sure we're going to have an early morning."

"Why's that?"

"Because you don't know what it means to sleep in most days. I swear, in some ways you're worse than Pike."

Grinning, we headed back to the truck and climbed in. "I'll take that as a compliment."

"You would."

It took far less time to reach Headquarters than I thought it would, which was another perk the place had going for it. Tomorrow I wanted to drive it again, but during rush hour so we'd know the longest time it would take, since inevitably, besides freak accidents, that would be the slowest progress. Not that we would always go between the two places, but it helped to have at least one constant.

The following four weeks turned into a pattern, with a few random items thrown in, like buying the mansion. Avery said he'd never seen a house deal close so fast. Other than that, we met as a team every morning to discuss updates on our current theories and to make new ones. The team was quickly becoming friends of sorts, at least the females were. The one a little out of place was Cole, mostly because of his much older age and rank. It was still difficult for me to feel like I should lead him instead of him leading me.

In the afternoons, I continued to get my butt handed to me by Captain Smith, but as the days progressed, I found I was less bruised and moving faster. I wasn't just lucky anymore, but I could hold my own for longer. My scrappiness was becoming productive scrappiness. After that first day, Smith was less surprised by my speed and strength, so when I was able to take him and pin him to the mat for the first time since our first spar, the time Cole had thrown me with his shield didn't count, I was a bit proud of myself. He even took me out to dinner as a reward, and we'd spent the whole meal talking about my new position and some tips he'd learned along the way.

We'd barely pulled into the parking garage when Jezzi sprinted over to us, meeting me at the driver's side since Bruce, who'd asked me to stop calling him Captain Smith, had allowed me to drive when I asked to do so. I still wasn't comfortable with it, so I wanted practice. He'd promised to work on getting me a real license.

"We have to go," she stated, breathless. "Dad wants to have dinner."

It was our code for when Luke Coye needed us. Looking down at my uniform, I groaned. At least she was in a pair of skinny jeans and a lacy pink top over a white shirt that exposed some of her mid-drift. This look was all her, and if I'd been interested in shifters, I would've been all over this boyfriend thing we had going on. Not only was she gorgeous, but she hadn't stopped kissing me, and I could get used to that, especially after being told by the only woman I'd ever loved that I'd never amount to anything. She was right, but Jezzi made me believe otherwise. There just weren't any feelings on my end.

"I need to change, and then we can go. Is something wrong? Is he okay?"

"He's all right, but he said it was urgent. I asked around and someone said you'd left, so I was just heading to find a car to make my way to you. Hurry. Change."

I didn't waste time, but raced inside, skipping the elevator to race two levels up to my floor, with Jezzi right behind me. When I entered my room, finding it empty, I didn't even tell her to stay outside. She wouldn't have, so why waste the breath? She also wasn't shy about staring as I stripped out of my shirt and dug in a dresser drawer for one that wouldn't link me to the Elite. Shirt in place, I kicked off my boots and unzipped the fly of my pants, meeting her gaze.

Jezzi arched a perfect brow at me. "Yeah?"

"Turn around."

"Really? You're going to be like that? We're on a time schedule, buddy."

"A time schedule that would proceed much faster if you turned around."

She smirked and folded her arms. "I'm a shifter, Raven. I see naked men all the time. I haven't seen anything on other men that you don't have...or do you?"

"Seriously?" I barked, ripping my pants off and pulling jeans into place, all while her eyes traveled over every inch of me. It made me glad I'd put the fresh shirt on so I wasn't just standing around in my boxers. I wasn't shy, but the way she always stared and made it clear she wanted more than what I was willing to offer, made my skin prickle, and not in the greatest way sometimes.

"You done already?" Jezzi purred, watching me stuff my feet into tennis shoes.

"I thought we were in a hurry." Grabbing the truck keys from the dresser where I'd set them down, I led the way back out of the room and down the hall to the stairs. There was still no sense in waiting for the elevator when it was easy to jog down the two flights.

She snorted, keeping pace with me. "Oh, I am, but I wouldn't have minded a few extra seconds to stare at you."

"Because I don't want you like that and it turns you on, or what?"

"Something like that, and you're built just like a shifter: all toned muscle."

"So, you only like me because I'm hot?"

"No, that's not the only reason," she confirmed as we barreled through the door into the garage, almost smacking two Elite on the other side. They started yelling at us, and one even started cussing, until they caught sight of my officer wrist band. Then they both went silent and raced through the door as fast as we'd exited it.

I threw the keys to Jezzi. "You drive. You know the way and you're better and faster at it."

"On it, Captain."

"Don't call me that anymore until we get back."

"Yes, Sir."

"Jezz."

She cackled at my warning, much like a coyote. I'd never seen a real one, an actual animal, but I knew enough. Research and television shows about the surface world were enlightening.

In minutes she had us barreling down the road, much like General Davis. When she spotted the gate, she slowed down to a reasonable speed. By now, the men at the gate were familiar with us, especially since I'd just driven back in with Bruce.

"Date night?" one of them asked, eyeing Jezzi with open interest.

"It's long overdue," I confirmed from the passenger's seat, a hint of steal in my voice. Apparently I was taking my girl out for a date, yet he had the nerve to eye her up in front of me? Taking Jezzi's hand, I nodded my head toward the exit. "Let's go."

"You betcha, babe." She grinned at me, leaving the gawking guard behind. "Is someone jealous?"

"No. I just don't like him trying to steal you away right in front of me." I winked at her and she grinned.

"You are jealous." She was quiet for a few minutes, biting her lip as she thought. "I should've already asked this, and you haven't said anything, but do you have a girlfriend?"

"I did." My mood plummeted. I tried not to think about the day I'd called home, but at least once a day I was reminded of it. Each time was less painful than the last, but there was always an ache in my heart.

"Did? What happened?" She shrugged. "If you don't mind me asking."

I was quiet for a few minutes, not really thinking, but watching the trees fly by in the darkness as the last light of the sun faded over the horizon. My favorite time of day. The time when I felt closest to home.

"I left," I murmured in a voice even I barely heard. "She begged me not to leave, to join the Elite on the surface, but I did anyway. When I called home a month ago, I spoke to her and she made it clear that we were through. I doubt she'd even consider forgiving me if I did come back after that call."

"I'm sorry." A second later her grim expression lifted with a bright smile. "How would your girlfriend feel if she knew you were kissing me while still dating her?"

My groan filled the cab as I wiped my hands over my face. "If you ever meet her, please don't tell her."

"Tell her that you were cheating?"

"Technically you kissed me the first few times."

"Yes, but you did kiss me."

"But I didn't mean anything by it."

She shook her head. "That's not how it works, Blood Drinker. You kissed me. You."

"I guess I always knew it would end when I called her."

We drove for another few miles before Jezzi squeezed my hand. "Something else is bothering you. Tell me."

"She was right about something. That's all."

"She let you go. She couldn't be all that right."

The truck rocked side to side on the dirt road, and I appreciated Jezzi not pushing and asking for details. Maybe a few months ago she would've, but she'd learned to respect my boundaries. Either that, or me being her superior had tamed her a bit. With a glance over to her, I changed my mind. It was definitely her respecting my boundaries. Or I was less fun to tease now.

We rode the rest of the way to her father's estate, because it was large enough to qualify in my mind, holding hands. She refused to let go, and I needed the comfort of her touch. Life wouldn't always be like this, and maybe someday I would meet a female willing to take me. Until then, I had to keep my mind focused. That wasn't what I was here for. I was here to make the world a safer place for my people. Finding a female willing to accept me for more than friendship, who wasn't a shifter, would be an added bonus.

It was pitch black outside the truck by the time we reached Luke's home. Most of the windows were dark, but a few had light spilling from them. When Jezzi cut the engine, she took her hand from mine, but didn't exit the truck, but stared at me expectantly.

"What?"

She rolled her eyes, an exasperated breath buzzing her full lips. "We're supposed to be dating. You need to come open the car door for me."

"Oh, yeah. Sorry, I forgot."

"That we're dating?"

"No, the car door." Winking at her, I grabbed for my door. "I can't forget that we're dating. You won't let me." Jezzi slapped at me as I leapt from the truck and rounded the front of the cab to open her door.

The moment her feet touched the ground, her arms snaked around my neck to pull me in for a kiss. It wasn't her normal, playful kind. This one had heat behind it as her lips slowly caressed mine. If I'd been able to think of her as more than just a beautiful shifter and friend, I could've gotten lost in that kiss.

"Whoever that girl is," Jezzi murmured, her lips brushing against mine as she spoke. "She's an idiot for giving you up." With another, more playful kiss, she closed the truck door and led the way across the grass, her hand in mine once again.

Luke met us at the front door like he had when I'd come over with General Davis. He grinned at our enjoined hands and smirked at me.

"Hello, son. Welcome back. I'm glad Jezzelle brought you along for dinner. I want to get to know my daughter's boyfriend a bit more." He held the door open and we entered, Jezzi giving her father a kiss on the cheek.

Once the door was closed, Luke led us back through the house to his study where he'd met with me the time before. A tray of cups with brown liquid inside sat on the table, and I could smell the chocolate from within as we entered the room. I may have already eaten dinner, but there was always room for hot chocolate.

"The weather is a bit nippy tonight, so I thought something warm and soothing was in order." Luke handed Jezzelle a mug, and then me. He sat on the same couch as last time with his own mug in hand, while Jezzi and I sat together on the other sofa, nice and comfortable with our thighs almost touching. If there was still a need for the act, I was sure her hand would be all over my leg the instant she sat down. As it was, her attention had already shifted focus.

"You said this was urgent. What have you heard?"

Taking a sip before answering, Luke met my steady gaze. "I'm not sure exactly which base it is that's next, not by name anyway. It's led by Major Dunkirk. That's what my 'friend' said, and they're expected to receive at least a dozen guests tomorrow night."

"Do you trust your 'friend'?" I asked, needing to be sure this information was correct before it left this room. Or as correct as possible.

"I trust him with my life, and with the life of my daughter. I'd even trust him with yours."

"Mine isn't the life that matters most." I squeezed Jezzi's hand, and Luke grinned at me.

"So, that's how this is?"

She snorted. "Not quite, but he needs the practice. Trust me."

Chuckling, Luke set his mug down and stared at us. "Well, I've told you my news, but, seeing as you're here for dinner, you'll need to stay a while longer, am I right?"

He was right, yes, but I needed to get this information back to General Davis as soon as possible so he could decide what to do with it. Then again, this was my mission, so maybe it was me who needed to make the decision. First, I needed to know where this base was located. There was no way I would call Davis from Luke's home, though.

"You're always right, Daddy," Jezzi snickered. "And I know just the thing to keep us busy for about an hour."

When she grinned at me, I wanted to run. Long and fast.

Chapter 18

An hour's game of Twister was not what I'd had in mind when Jezzi had stated she knew what to do to spend our time with Luke. However, I wasn't complaining. It was liberating to stretch that much, even if Jezzi intentionally rubbed herself against me more than was necessary. She'd enjoyed it, but I found myself shaking my head more often than not. Her antics gave Luke quite the chuckle as he sat calling out body parts and colors the whole time. When Jezzi managed to position herself underneath me the one and only time I couldn't avoid it, I was sure my face was beet red when she made sure to place herself in all the right places to press against me. I may not have been interested in her physically, but the move certainly awoke me to the fact this was way too intimate, especially in front of her father. How had she been comfortable with that?

Coyote. They were both coyotes and she was playing me. That was why.

A little over an hour later, I was more than ready to leave. While we'd played, I'd tried to devise a plan to take to Davis in case he asked for one. If not, I was in the clear. However, with Jezzi distracting me, I was left with half a plan, but half was better than none. While she careened down the road back toward the base singing at the top of her lungs to some song I'd never heard on the radio, I retreated inside myself to think and stare out the window.

"You okay?" she asked when she was forced to slow down as we entered the light traffic of the late evening. "You've been awfully quiet. I didn't step too far over your boundaries, did I? I know you don't feel anything toward me, which is why I thought it was okay. Plus, if anyone happened to stop by, they'd think we really were into one another."

"No, it's fine. You didn't do anything wrong. I'm just thinking about what your dad told us."

"You want to go to this base, don't you?"

I shrugged. "If it's not too far. If we can be there when it's attacked, maybe I can smell the creatures again and we can verify if the attack on me was just a fluke or if I really can smell them. Also, it would allow us to be first on the scene to gather more evidence."

"I suppose that's true. Maybe whoever it was behind these attacks heard that you can smell the creatures and changed their chemical."

"If it's even a chemical." I sighed and leaned heavier on the door. "Sometimes I wonder what they were thinking putting me in charge of this team. I'm still a kid."

"You're young, just like most of us, but you think differently than we do. That counts, and it's likely one of the main reasons they chose you. However, your downfall is letting people walk all over you and not standing up for yourself. You've got to fix that, Raven. You're strong, you're smart, and you're not going to hurt any of us. Quit letting them treat you like crap, and you know who I'm talking about. And when you call this Major Dunkirk, you don't let him walk all over you either. You stand up for yourself because if you don't, no one else will. We can try to convince him you're worth putting his trust in, but he won't believe it until you show him, so you show that man you have a backbone."

I had to admit, that was the best pep talk I'd ever received. She was right. I'd been letting some of the officers talk about me behind my back, well, they made sure their whispers carried to my table at lunch as they "tried" to keep their conversation to themselves. I hadn't wanted to cause a problem, so I'd stayed silent. It was coming back to bite me, and she was right, I had to stand up to Major Dunkirk, especially if we were able to travel to his base.

"Pike is going to be there too," Jezzi added before I could speak my thoughts. "They'll want to look to him for leadership and direction instead of you. Make sure they know you're the one to deal with. If you let them deal with Pike, they won't respect you."

"How did you become so inciteful?" I snickered, trying to lighten the mood in the cab. "I didn't realize there was so much wonderful knowledge inside of you."

"What? You thought I was only good looks? That's shallow, Raven."

"Nah," I responded, my grin widening. "It's not your good looks I was thinking about. I saw you take down that badger shifter yesterday in training. He's a monster and aggressive, and you didn't even break a sweat. You beat the crap out of him. With all that physical prowess and your observation, you're a force to be reckoned with."

Instead of her normal, snarky grin, she turned to me with a small smile. "You mean that?"

"Of course I do. I said it."

"That's honestly the nicest thing anyone's ever said to me."

"Well, I meant every word."

Jezzelle took her time climbing out of the truck while I raced ahead up to General Davis's office. I wasn't sure if he was in or if he'd gone home. It was late, so I was shocked to find him still in his office. Was the man's wife okay with his late hours? She had to be, but at this rate, the two never saw one another.

"Raven, come in," he directed when he saw me standing beside Fay's desk, staring at him, unsure if I should knock or call to him. He didn't seem the kind to startle easy, but I didn't want to be the cause of surprising him. People usually didn't take kindly to being surprised or snuck up on. "What can I do for you?"

Closing the door after I entered, I sat in my same spot. When Davis glanced at the closed door and my face, he set his pen down, giving me his full attention. He knew this was important, and I tried to be as formal and serious as possible. I wanted him to take me seriously, like Jezzi and I had spoken about in the car. This man already did, but I needed the practice.

"Luke Coye called Jezzelle, so we went over to his place tonight."

"I see. What did he have to say?"

"There's an attack scheduled. He didn't say who his source was but that he trusted the information was correct. I believe him."

Davis nodded, his eyebrows drawn low and his body rigid. "Did he say which base?"

"The one under the command of Major Dunkirk."

"He's practically next door. Five hours west. Well, northwest."

"I want to take my team to his base to meet the attack. It may be the only chance we have to access one of the creatures before it's destroyed, compromised, or refused to be sent to us. It could help us determine a source for the creature's oddities. Plus, it couldn't hurt to test my sense of smell and give Major Dunkirk six more Elite at his disposal."

I wasn't sure what I expected, but it wasn't for General Davis to grab a sticky note, write something on it, and hand it over to me. "Here's Dunkirk's cell phone number. Call him. Tell him what's happening and that you'll be there tomorrow morning. Since we don't know what time the attack will happen, I want you all there early, so make sure your team is well rested and gone before sunrise."

"Yes, Sir."

He wanted me to call Dunkirk? This had better go well. First impressions were everything.

Leaving Davis's office, I crossed the hall to the conference room. This room and I didn't have the greatest track record, so I prayed this call would go better than the last I'd made in here. Taking a deep breath, I dialed the phone number I'd been given and tried not to shake or stutter when a man answered after the third ring.

"Dunkirk."

"Major, this is Captain Cartana under the leadership of General Davis." It was still odd referring to myself as a captain. "I'm on one of the teams he's directed to find out who's behind the attacks on our bases and our governor."

"Okay." His voice sounded perturbed, like I was annoying him and all he wanted to do was hang up, so I spoke faster.

"We've heard through our sources that there will be an attack on your base tomorrow. General Davis would like my team to be there when the attack happens, so you should expect us mid-morning."

"Davis doesn't think I can do my job?" the man growled, and I wished I'd had the foresight to ask what category this man was from.

"He knows you can do your job. He also knows that having a few more hands available to keep an eye out wouldn't hurt, especially when what we really want to do is study the bodies after the attack to see if anything has been missed in the other attacks. We don't want to step on your toes, but do the opposite. It's our goal to assist you, not get in your way or push you out of the way."

The other end was silent for a moment before Dunkirk spoke again. "I've never heard of you, Captain."

"I was promoted a few weeks ago, Sir."

"Trying to show off already, then, I see."

What was wrong with this man?

"No, Sir. My goal is to save lives. It always has been and always will be. Whether those lives are civilian or Elite, I don't discriminate. If I need to bring my team to your base to learn more about these creatures to save lives, that's what I'll do. You don't have to like it, but I need to be there to gather information. If you feel like I'm stepping on your toes, that's not my intent."

"I see. Well, as it appears, I have no choice in the matter, I'll be expecting your team in the morning. Don't get in my way, Captain. You won't like it." He ended the call before I could respond, and I stared at the phone wondering what it was I'd said that set him off.

I was leaving the room the same time Davis was closing up his office. He met me in the hall and grinned at my frown and furrowed brow.

"Didn't go well, did it?"

Davis found this funny? "Not really. I'm pretty sure he doesn't like me."

"He's a warlock with a chip on his shoulder. I guarantee the moment he sets eyes on you, he's going to despise you even more."

I stifled my groan. Barely.

"Don't worry," Davis chuckled, leading the way down the hallway toward the elevator. "You'll have Cole there to keep the peace."

The elevator doors closed and I took a quick breath before speaking again. "Sir, I know Cole can help me and that he'll defend me, but I need to do this on my own as well. If I can't gain his respect, or attempt it, he never will respect me. Neither will his people."

"So, you don't want Cole to go with you?" He arched his brow in interest, like he thought what I said amusing.

"No, that's not what I mean. While I want Cole there, I want to make sure he knows it's clear that I'm in charge. I don't want him to come to my rescue. Do you think that's disrespectful? Will I offend him if I mention that?"

Davis shook his head as the elevator dinged and opened to reveal the parking garage. "No, I think he'll respect you for it, and you'll be clear about what you want instead of leaving a gray area. Make sure your whole team knows, that way you don't single anyone out. Good luck tomorrow, Captain. I expect you to keep me updated."

"Yes, Sir."

He exited the elevator, leaving me to breathe a deep sigh of relief. This would work. It had to work. If the information was wrong, I was in trouble. If I couldn't smell the creatures, something had changed. If we couldn't find anything weird about them, it would be a wasted trip and we'd be back to square one.

The elevator doors opened again, and I blinked a few times as Avery entered and stared at me like I wasn't feeling well. I probably wasn't since I hadn't punched the button for my floor and I hadn't realized the elevator was even moving. I'd been too much in my head. Closing my eyes, I let my head fall back against the stainless steel.

"You okay?" Avery's voice was laced with humor, yet also held a hint of worry, like he was concerned I was finally losing my mind.

"Yeah. We need to leave here by four o'clock tomorrow morning."

He groaned and a thud announced he'd let his head fall back, mimicking my pose, except he was less gentle with his head. "You hate me, don't you?"

"Four o'clock. Not a second later," I chuckled, pulling out my phone to text the team about the mission while I explained it to Avery. By the time we reached our room, everyone had responded that they'd be ready. I figured Jezzelle had already warned Felix that we would be leaving, she just wouldn't know when.

Crawling into bed, I closed my eyes and prayed I wouldn't dream about grumpy warlocks, disgusting Wights, and anything that involved Twister.

Chapter 19

I insisted on driving for the first two hours of the trip, wanting the practice while few people were out on the road, and because it was dark and easier for me to see. Cole sat up front with me, giving directions when needed while Kara sat between us and the other three dozed in the back seat. They'd need their energy, so I let them sleep. Kara was likely too uncomfortable, or she was busy thinking about our trip. Either way, her eyes were often unfocused when I looked over at her, and she didn't look around much, just stared out the windshield. No one awake spoke unless necessary. Turned out I was about the only morning-ish person on the team. Everyone else was grumpy and non-functional.

When I was ready for a break, we pulled over at a fast food restaurant and grabbed breakfast inside while taking a bathroom break. After returning to the truck, Cole and I switched places so I was navigating and he was driving. This time, Kara leaned over and rested her head on my shoulder and closed her eyes, falling asleep in seconds.

"So, what's the plan when we arrive?" Avery asked a few hours later, his question punctuated with a large yawn.

"How long until we arrive?" Cole asked, jerking his thumb toward his phone which we were using as a GPS.

"Ten minutes." I breathed out a sharp breath. "All right, everyone, wake up."

"What's going on?" Jezzi murmured when Avery pushed on her shoulder where she was curled against Felix's side. "We there yet?"

"Nope, but Raven's going to be giving us some direction. We're ready, boss," Avery snickered, and I wanted to punch him. That would have to wait. There were bigger irritations to handle first.

Turning in my seat, I surveyed the truck's occupants. "First and foremost, if Major Dunkirk or any of his people want to speak to the person in charge, remember, that's me."

Avery tapped Cole on the shoulder and stage whispered, "I think he's talking about you."

"I think you're right," Cole responded with an equally dramatic whisper and chuckle.

"Mostly," I corrected, "but they could come to any of you. It's doubtful Dunkirk will like me considering what I am. Anyway, always direct them to me. Second, we don't know what we're dealing with besides that it's a dozen creatures. It could be anything, so keep your eyes and ears open. If something seems off or feels weird, it probably is. Next, the first thing I want is for two teams to scope the building from top to bottom searching for any possible entrances or weaknesses in security. If Dunkirk is smart, he'll have added to his security detail."

"Dunkirk isn't known for his brains, but his brawn," Cole interrupted. "Some of us still aren't sure how he managed a leadership position like that besides bribing someone. Don't expect him to change anything, which means we need to be on our guard at all times."

My eyes narrowed on Cole. "Just who is Dunkirk and how do you know so much about him?"

The warlock chuckled and cast me a wicked stare. "You don't think the Elite have only been around for six months, do you? Trust me, we've been around for far longer than that, only no one knew about it."

"Like Area 51?" Jezzi asked, her exhaustion melting away in an instant, replaced by hyped up energy as she leaned her head between Kara and Cole's seats.

"Young lady, Area 51 is a myth. The Elite, on the other hand, are very much real and we've been working to keep the Threats at bay long before now, only on a much quieter scale. Both sides didn't want to draw any attention. I've known Dunkirk from the beginning. He's managed to weasel his way up to the top, but besides being unqualified for the position, he's harmless."

"Being unqualified for a position like that doesn't sound harmless," Felix muttered, and I had to agree, but I kept it to myself to finish off our mini meeting.

"If you see anything suspicious, report it to me right away. I don't care if Dunkirk likes me or not, we have a job to do, and when the creatures are dead, don't let anyone near them. Kara will be there to take samples. If we can manage it, we'll take one of them back to our labs to let the other teams take a look and see if there's something we may have missed."

"We won't miss anything," Kara promised with a cheeky grin. "I plan to be as thorough as I've ever been."

"Good. Any questions?"

Avery grunted. "Yeah, will they be serving breakfast when we get there?"

"We just ate," Jezzi retorted, making Avery snort.

"Girl, that was forever ago. You've been sleeping the whole trip so you have no idea how long we've been on the road. I'm starving."

"You're always starving."

I left the two of them alone to bicker back and forth while I turned forward again to give Cole the final instructions for our route. This base was shockingly in the middle of nowhere, and Cole had to explain that it was one of the first bases built, long before the Great Reveal, and most of it was underground. I wasn't sure if that was comforting, or if it made this more of a trap.

The building alone was massive, and my jaw dropped when we pulled through the dense trees into a large clearing. Large was an understatement. Four helicopter pads sat off to the far right with the main building in the center of the field with two smaller warehouse type structures off to the left. The base itself looked like an overly large, fancy office building. Every floor had glass windows with a balcony. Whoever designed this must have done it to hide what the base really was, but unless that glass was unbreakable, they'd made it the perfect target for attack.

"Please explain why someone would go through the trouble of coming all the way out here to attack this," Jezzi murmured, once again planting her face between the two front seats. "It's out in the middle of nowhere for starters, and there really isn't anything here. I guess if you're just looking to kill, that's fine, but why here and why now?"

"We'll find out soon enough," Cole murmured. "Dunkirk was supposed to have gated this field off months ago. He was given the budget to do it."

"So, basically it's an unprotected area," I murmured, staring around us for danger in the morning light. "Those helos could be tampered with by anyone. Where are the Elite? I don't see a soul out here."

Cole ran a hand through his graying hair. "He probably has cameras everywhere and thinks they're foolproof and has a few trainees watching them at all hours of the day. Those can be tampered with and they have blind spots. If the right person knew of those blind spots, anything could attack. Raven, if I were you, I'd bring this up to Dunkirk."

"But, Cole, I'm not his superior. He doesn't have to listen to me."

"No, but you've been sent here to keep this place safe and to stop an attack we know to be coming. Tell him, and then report that you did to General Davis. Log it all in a report. Paperwork may not save lives, but it may in the future if we document everything that happens here today."

Closing my eyes, I sunk deeper into the truck seat. I'd never asked for this, never wanted it. I wanted to help people, but taking on a Major was never in the plans. But, it didn't look like I had any other choice.

Kara took my hand and squeezed it. "We won't let anyone get hurt or killed if we can help it, okay? Don't worry about the Major. We'll do our jobs and he can be background noise."

"Do me a favor," I told her, my chuckle lacking real humor, "if he gives us trouble and he's a coffee drinker, separate the water from the rest of his drink, will you? Leave him coffee bits."

She snickered. "You're cruel, and I like it."

Avery laughed from the back. "I think she could manage to do that with any of his drinks of choice."

"I totally could." Kara nudged my arm. "He's going to be furious when I do, though."

"That's fine. Tell him it was an order, and you had to obey it."

"He's going to kill you."

"Let him try."

Jezzi reached up between us and squeezed my shoulder. "That's the attitude, Captain. You give him what he deals."

Taking a deep breath, I watched the building grow larger as we drew closer. On the outside it appeared like a random office building in the middle of the forest, but the inside would be far more advanced and secured than a normal office building, or so I hoped. If the inside was as lacking in security as the field, then I wouldn't be sleeping if we stayed the night, or we'd be staying together and sleeping in shifts. Even our base had a fence and guarded gate.

Cole drove the truck around the base toward one of the warehouses, which turned out to be the entrance to an underground parking garage. Again, it was unguarded and the doors were left open. Several more comments about the lack of actual security floated through the car, and I was beginning to see why this would be a great base to attack. The whole place would be slaughtered before they even knew what hit them.

Once parked, we climbed from the truck, grabbed our bags from the bed, and strode toward the marked tunnel to the Headquarters. Even the tunnel had little security as there was no locked door or even a gate that needed to be opened from somewhere secure.

"Who designed this place?" Felix grumbled as we hiked through the well lit tunnel. "If we have to stay the night, I think it's safer to sleep in a locked truck."

"I second that," Jezzi muttered.

The hairs on my neck were standing on end by the time we reached the tunnel's end and a doorway leading to a set of stairs. Again, they were unguarded, and I wanted nothing more than to turn around, but I couldn't. People's lives were at stake, and even more so in this base. Just because it was built in the middle of a forest didn't mean it wasn't open to attack.

At the top of the stairs, I opened a metal door and led us into a small, metal plated room that showed the first traces of security. That security was five Elite soldiers, one of who had his hands on his hips with the Major stripe on his wristband. This had to be Dunkirk, and the glower he gave me the moment our eyes met only grew harder as hate lifted his lips into a silent snarl. When the rest of my team entered behind me, Dunkirk's eyes landed on Cole. While they studied one another, I took another sweep over the over-powered Major. His highlighted brown hair was shaved around his head and cropped close on top, and spiky from its coarseness. He was built more like a heavyweight champion than most warlocks I'd seen, which made sense that Cole said he was more brawn than brains. One look at him and this place and I could believe it.

"Cole, I didn't realize you were coming. A Captain Cartana called and said he was bringing his team. Care to explain what this is all about?" Dunkirk crossed his arms over his chest, the look of annoyance on his face rubbing me the wrong way. I clearly stood front and center while Cole stood in the rear. Of course, I also had purple eyes, so Dunkirk knew exactly what I was and he didn't like me already.

"Major Eric Dunkirk, I'd like to introduce you to Captain Raven Cartana. You'll work with him directly." Cole either pointed or stared at me because Dunkirk's eyes shifted to me a second later and the irritation switched to disgust in the next second.

"Explain this, Captain." He spat my title out like it was the grossest word he'd ever had to say. "How are you leading a team with a Major on it? You're only a child."

"A child who happens to be leading a team with a Major on it," I countered. "Apparently I'm brilliant, a force to be reckoned with, and I can smell these creatures no one else can. I guess you'd say that makes me a big deal." I shrugged. Where was this snarkiness coming from? It wasn't my norm, but I didn't like this man one bit. "Major, I have a concern. I let you know there was going to be an attack today and yet your security is lacking. Are you trying to invite trouble into your base?"

He took a few steps forward until he stood right in front of me. It was a relief to find the two of us were nearly matched in height. Nearly, but I still had an inch on him, though he by far had more muscle. I needed to work on building more as I trained with weapons.

"I don't know who you are-."

"Raven Cartana, Captain, Vamlure, Elite. That's the start of the list. Listen, Major, there have been half a dozen attacks on Elite in the last month alone, and as a survivor of one of those attacks, I can tell you that these creatures aren't to be trifled with. From the reports I read, the attacks have grown more intense and deadly. Do you have more security than what I've not seen thus far?"

"I will not be told how to run my base by a baby Blood Drinker," he seethed in my face. The men standing behind him stiffened, obviously having no idea what a vamlure was before this moment.

Swallowing my rising temper, I closed the distance between us, leaving our noses an inch apart. "I was given orders to help protect this base at all costs, including my life, and I'd gladly give it up for anyone here. I don't understand why you just don't care. But, no matter what you think of me and I think of you, I have orders from General Davis, and I will follow those orders."

"And you'll stay out of my way," he growled, leaning closer.

"I'll do my job."

Turning his attention from me, Dunkirk sneered at Cole. "So, do you like being under the direction of our enemy?"

"Get to know him before you cast judgement," Cole directed, his voice frigid. "There's far more to Raven than what you see before you. He's right in calling out your lack of security. This is no time for your ego to get in the way, Eric. Lives are at stake."

"You think I don't know that?" he seethed. "We're lacking in personnel right now. Half my teams are out helping surrounding cities because of an uptick in Threat attacks."

"Then stop arguing with me and let us help you," I interrupted, bringing his attention back to me. "Use my team to help support your security instead of counting us as the enemy."

"Do what you feel you need to do, but stay out of my way." Dunkirk spun on his heel and marched from the room. The moment he was gone, I breathed easier, sucking air into my lungs to steady my racing heart.

"Did anyone else want to wet their pants when Raven stood up to Dunkirk?" Avery whispered behind me, his voice not reaching much farther than our group. Confused, I turned and arched a brow at him, making him grin. "My friend, remind me not to be on your bad side. You scared the crap out of me and I wasn't even staring at your eyes. I think the only reason Dunkirk left was because he didn't want to publicly wet himself."

Shaking my head, I murmured, "That may be true, but be respectful. He already doesn't like us."

"Yes, Captain." Avery didn't appear the least bit chastised as he continued to grin.

Shaking my head, I addressed the four men left in the room. "Can we enter?"

"Of course, Sir. We'll need to see your ID, then you can go anywhere you wish."

One by one we handed over our ID's to one of the guards. Each wore a sword on their back and knives on their hips. While I waited, I noticed three monitors built into a side wall which showed the entrance of the warehouse, the entrance to the tunnel, and right on the other side of the door we'd entered. They'd be able to see danger coming, but how well could they stop it? And if danger was disguised, they'd never see it before the disaster struck.

"Thank you," I told them as Jezzi led the way into the Headquarters.

Ceiling to floor windows lined every wall on this level. It appeared more like a fancy office building than an Elite Headquarters on this level even on the inside, which was what I'd feared when I'd seen the style of the structure. Plants, small fountains, and chic decor hanging from the ceiling littered the space, and two sets of stairs took up the center of the room. One led up to the next landing while the other extended to the floor below. An elevator dinged off to the right and a pair of Elite warriors stepped off, full of smiles and laughter. Neither carried weapons. We'd only just arrived but each of us wore a knife or small axe. Felix even carried her favorite sword on her back. While I could easily defend myself with a sword against her now, I still preferred smaller blades, and my teeth.

"Is it just me, or is this place too cheery for an impending attack?" Jezzelle muttered, eyeing the pair as they sat down on a black and white striped couch near an outer glass wall.

"Much too cheery," Felix confirmed. "Has Dunkirk even told them about it? Or does he think it's a rumor?"

"There's one way to find out," I muttered. "Felix, Jezzelle, go talk to them and find out. Warn them if they know nothing about it. Cole and Kara, start at the top of the building and work your way down. Look for anything suspicious or security issues, large issues, and talk to those you meet along the way. Avery and I will start at the lowest level and work our way up. We'll meet in the middle. If the Major, and by that I mean Dunkirk, has an issue, send him to me. I'm not in a good mood and I could use an excuse to blow off some steam."

"Aye, aye, Captain," Jezzi teased with a mock salute before she and Felix crossed to the happy pair. The rest of use moved to the elevator, taking it up first to drop off Cole and Kara.

"Be careful," Cole warned as he stepped off the elevator. "My gut is telling me there's something wrong here."

I gave a sharp nod. "So is mine. Let's find our monsters."

Chapter 20

The lowest level, Avery and I soon found out, was used for storage. Two men were on duty to make sure everything in the lockers and storage rooms wasn't tampered with. After warning them about an inevitable attack, we moved up a floor to the armory.

Major Dunkirk's security may have been lacking, but his armory wasn't. Weapons of the best quality hung on walls, in cases, and on racks in rows throughout the large, single room. They were sorted by type and by quality. Half a dozen Elite roamed the room, likely making sure nothing was removed without their knowledge. I wasn't sure if these weapons had to be checked out or purchased, but one look at a pair of thin swords had me itching to make them mine.

"That pair just came in," one of the men said from right behind me. "If you want to purchase them, I can guarantee it'll cost you."

So, we would have to buy them. I'd have to think about it. If we survived today, I'd likely purchase them if the price was right. After letting the man know about the threat, with Avery spreading the word to the others, we moved up a level.

This one was comprised of one long hallway with doors on either side. We knocked on each door, only finding a few occupied. Bedrooms. After delivering the same message as before, we headed back to the elevator.

My phone rang as the elevator door opened to another long hallway lined with more doors. More bedrooms or offices. If we didn't need to warn everyone we saw about the attack, I'd skip this floor and continue going up to a more interesting level. But the ringing cell phone in my back pocket distracted me as we stepped from the elevator.

"Hey, Cole. Find something?" I asked as a door further up the hallway opened and Major Dunkirk and another soldier stepped out. He took one look at us and they hustled in the other direction. It took everything in me not to growl.

"Yeah, and it's not good. We just found Dunkirk's body in his office. Part of it's been eaten. I think it's-."

"Ghoul," I murmured as the scent hit me in the face. "They're ghouls."

Avery's eyes widened. "Umm..." Turning to stare back down the hallway, the snow leopard shifter pulled the axe from the hook on his belt. "I guess we have a Major's head to remove."

"What's going on?" Cole asked when I was quiet for too long.

"We found Dunkirk's ghoul." I turned to Avery. "Can you smell him?"

"No, can you?"

I ignored his question. "Avery can't smell him. These things are already in the building. They could be anyone. Stay alert and keep your weapons out. Call Jezzi and Felix. We're going after Dunkirk's killer and another one."

"Be careful. Call me when the deed is done."

It would figure that Dunkirk would be the first one dead, or at least one of the first ones. Ironic even. Though I didn't like the man, I didn't like that he'd suffered a gruesome death. Ghoul deaths weren't painless as they started eating their victims to kill them. The very idea twisted my gut.

"Keep an eye out for anyone. You see movement, let me know so I can verify human or ghoul," I warned Avery as we strode down the hall after our quarry.

We were reaching the door they'd escaped when Avery slowed. "I may not smell them, but I'm picking up the scent of fresh blood."

"Yeah, me too. It's likely the female soldier with Dunkirk." I nodded toward the door. "Check it out. I'll watch the hall and sniff for more."

I took a deep breath as he opened the door and quickly closed it after a peek inside. He swallowed twice before nodding. "Yup, it's her."

"You okay?"

"If I don't ever see something as disgusting as what they left behind, it'll be too soon."

I hadn't thought about that when sending him in there. "I'm sorry. I should've-."

"No." He shook his head and nodded down the hallway. "We have to hurry or they'll slaughter someone else. We don't need a higher body count."

I took the hint. Letting him sniff out fresh blood, I kept track of the ghouls' progress. Voices reached us as we entered the floor's recreational area, complete with couches, snack bar, and a big screen TV currently playing a Western I'd never seen before. Dunkirck stood behind a male soldier while the female had her eyes set on another, who she was currently making her way toward.

"I've got her," Avery murmured before leaving my side to track the female across the room.

Dunkirk's ghoul noticed him and glared over at me as I approached, pulling a knife from the sheath on my thigh. "Hey there. I've never met a ghoul before, but I have to say, you smell pretty nasty."

"What're you talking about?" Dunkirk's victim asked, staring at my raised weapon before swinging his gaze to the ghoul and then over to Avery and the female. "What's going on?"

"Ghouls have infiltrated the base." I kept my eyes on Dunkirk's ghoul. He could strike in either direction, and the soldier wasn't armed, or he hadn't pulled his weapon yet. "Major Pike just found Major Dunkirk's body upstairs and that woman's body is down the hall where that ghoul left her."

"Are you serious?" The other man didn't waste a second but leapt over the couch away from the ghoul to where a sword rested on a counter, far too out of reach from the couch.

The female lunged around the couch, but Avery tackled her from behind. While I wanted to keep an eye on that fight, mine was beginning. One look at my exposed knife and the ghoul I faced off against turned on the easier of the two of us. Or, so we both thought. I didn't have time to react fast enough as the ghoul grasped the man's head and his lips pulled back to expose sharp, pointed teeth. But the man had a surprise of his own. He shoved a small dagger into the ghoul's head, making it pull away and scream as it tried to rip the blade out. I didn't give it time as I dove, tackling it to the ground and killing it the only way it would die: I sliced its head off. In seconds, the ghoul's body shifted shape to its humanoid, gooey form.

Silence encompassed the room, meaning the other fight had also ended.

"Avery?" I whispered, still straddling the ghoul's body to keep it down, even though it was headless. My brain was still processing what had happened.

"We're all right. You?"

"We're fine. The two of you soldiers, keep an eye on these bodies. Don't let anyone near them and don't touch them yourselves."

"What if someone wants to come in here?" the one nearest me asked, and I rolled my eyes at him.

"If they listen to you tell them to leave, then they're safe. If they don't, assume they're a ghoul and take their head off. Tell them it's Captain Cartana's orders."

"Yes, Sir."

Pulling myself up, I pulled out my phone and called Cole. "Two dead."

"Two more here," he confirmed. "We can't smell them, but they'll attack us just the same. Felix killed one on the floor below us. Keep working your way up. Hopefully those you warned will be on alert."

"Good luck." Ending the call, I skipped the elevator to climb the staircase at the opposite end of the long hallway. It was faster, and quieter.

The sight that met my eyes at the top of the stairs to the next floor made my heart stutter and a sharp pain twisted my gut. This was a large rec room, or it had been until the four ghouls occupying it had left a dozen bodies behind. We found them mid feast on those they'd last killed, and it took every ounce of will power I had not to puke at the sight of one human eating another, even though my brain was fully aware that it was a ghoul eating a human.

Avery made a soft sound of disgust, but it was enough to draw the ghouls' attention. How I wished now that I'd bought those swords. Left with only knives, I drew the one on my other hip and waited. With the enemy closing in, Avery gripped his axe tighter and waited. Timing would be everything.

"Think we can do this?" Avery asked, eyeing the pair closest to him.

"We'll find out soon enough."

They attacked at once. I didn't hesitate. The first one to reach me found my knife buried deep in the soft part of his shoulder and my teeth sinking into the other as he cried out from the pain of the knife wound. My venom streamed into him, and a second later I ripped my teeth and blade free to take on the next ghoul, who was ready for me. I wasn't sure if my venom would kill the first, but I had to hope it would. It killed everything else.

I wasn't quite ready for the next ghoul to throw an uppercut my way and took the blow to my jaw. My head flew back, as did my body, smacking into the wall behind me. Avery cried out, but I didn't lose focus. I had my own problems to deal with at the moment. There was no way to help him if I got myself killed. This ghoul was a better fighter, older perhaps, and had faster reflexes and smarter fighting moves. We parried blows and he never let me even come close to landing a strike with a weapon.

One of his buddies screamed, distracting him. It was my opening and I took it, burying the blade in his throat and slicing with the other. A sickening squelch was the last sound he made before his head came off. Without taking a break, I searched for Avery. He had one ghoul lying on the ground with its head half cut off and the other was facing off with him. Well, kind of facing off. They stood on opposite sides of a pool table, mimicking one another's movements.

The ghoul on the ground was already healing, so I completed severing its neck before sneaking around behind the other to take it out. Avery caught sight of me behind the ghoul and hopped on top of the pool table to reach the ghoul. It stumbled backward, not expecting this move, and met me, or rather, my blade as it slashed through its neck. Seconds later it laid in a heap on the floor with its buddies.

"What happened?" Blood coated one of Avery's arms and he winced when I grabbed his arm.

"It's fine. Well, not really."

He strode toward the nearest wall, which happened to have a first aid kit hanging on it. Somehow he was able to manage lifting it off the wall and opening it without my help and with the use of only one arm. Grabbing some gauze inside, he wiped his arm down revealing several large gouges where the ghoul had bitten him.

"Okay, is this deadly? Like, am I going to die from this bite?" His voice was panicked, and I tried to remember all I knew about ghouls.

"No, not unless we allow the wound to become infected. This is going to hurt, but I need to clean that and wrap it so we can keep searching. I wish we could secure this room, but we'll have to deal with the secure bodies we have."

Minutes later, Avery's arm was disinfected and wrapped up. He'd almost punched me twice when I used disinfectant on the wound, but I'd managed to avoid them. While I worked on Avery's arm, I called Cole and reported our find. Between what they'd found, we'd found, and the girls, we were nearly to our one dozen.

"Can you fight?" I asked Avery, eyeing the bandaged arm.

"I have to. Lives depend on me, so I'll do what I can. You wouldn't stop, so neither will I." He cocked his head at me and grinned. “Do you realize that you have blood on your face?”

While the ghoul hadn’t tasted nearly as disgusting as the Wight, mostly because it was in actual human form, its blood tasted like death. Until now, I hadn’t given it much thought, especially to the fact I’d swallowed a bit of it. Thankfully ghouls weren’t Magic Users of any kind. They fit under the Others category, making their blood harmless to me.

Wiping what blood I could from my face, I led the way back to the stairwell and up to the next floor. The next two levels were clear of ghouls, but the third level up was chaos. Rows of cubicles divided the area and screams echoed around as those in the room realized five ghouls were attacking them. The nearest ghoul raced at me, and I once again didn't think but acted on instinct. With a healthy dose of venom in his neck, the ghoul dropped.

More yells across the room ended the bloodshed as Cole, Felix, and Jezzi entered the fight, slaying the last of the ghouls in the room. Several of the local Elite were dead, and even more injured. Chairs lay tipped over behind desks and several of the cubicle walls were smashed and broken down.

"Who wants to tell me what happened here?" I yelled across the room, my deep voice carrying over the shocked silence and one man's puking.

One of the warriors nearest to me drew his sword. "Get back," he yelled, and I could only stare at him. Why was he threatening me?

"What are you doing?" I asked him, and after a second, Avery barked a laugh and slapped a hand on my back.

"Raven, you've got more blood on your face. You should probably wipe that up or every Elite on this base is going to think you're a ghoul who just had a meal."

"And that's funny?" I asked over my shoulder, sobering him.

"Well, not really, but considering what just happened and what we've been through, I do find it a bit humorous, in a dark, sick, if I don't laugh I'll cry kind of way."

That was understandable. This wasn't my first battle, but it certainly was the most extensive and brutal. Too many had been killed. Far too many, and most could've been prevented if the Elite had been properly warned about an attack.

"Here," Jezzi crossed the room to hand me a wet towelette from this level's First Aid kit. "Never mind, let me. I can see where the blood is so you don't miss any."

I let her clean my face, including wiping the towelette over my lips. No matter how many chemicals it tasted of, it still tasted far better than the blood in my mouth. Sooner than later I'd need to find something to suck on or eat to rid my mouth of the flavor of ghoul blood. With her job complete, Jezzi backed up and I surveyed the room again.

"I asked what happened. Who's in charge?"

"Dennis," one of the men stated, pointing to a body in the middle of the main aisle, "but he's dead."

"And he didn't have someone to take over if he died?"

The man shrugged. "This is only my first week here, Sir."

That was no excuse, but it would do for now. "What's your name?"

"Kenny."

"Congratulations, Kenny, you've been promoted to his position. Now, what happened?"

While he spoke, I strode through the room, eyeing video feeds from various stations and piles of paperwork strewn over the room.

"A few members of Paula's team entered the room, but they weren't actually her team. The next thing we knew, they attacked and started biting and eating people. That's when you showed up. How many are there?"

"We've killed six on lower levels."

"The rest of us killed seven, and that doesn't count these five. That's well over a dozen." Jezzi's eyes narrowed. "Though, our source did say about a dozen. I suppose that leaves leeway for more or less."

"Do you think there's more?" Felix inquired, studying one of the ghoul bodies that was already turning back to its natural form. She prodded it with her foot and lifted her lip in disgust.

"There may be." I ran a hand through my hair. "Felix, Jezzi, take three Elite each from this room and comb the building level by level. Move the bodies to one central location. I don't care where, I just want them together. Where's Kara?"

Felix pointed to the ceiling. "We killed two on the floor above and she's starting to take samples."

"Avery, will you go watch her back?" I looked to his arm and grinned. "Maybe she can do a better job as nurse than I did."

He rolled his eyes and started toward the stairs. "I can guarantee it."

Felix chose her three Elite and left, heading downstairs while Jezzi took her three upstairs. One of Jezzi's shook his head, his face pale and refused to leave, but one look into her narrowed gaze and he followed the others to the elevator at a hustle. Yes, they'd been attacked, but it wasn't any worse than what the rest of us had been facing.

"I want to know how they got in," I told Kenny. "How do I work this equipment? Or can you do it?"

"I can help." He sat at one of the large monitors and pushed a chair out beside it so I could sit down with Cole standing behind us, looking over my shoulder. "What do you want to see?"

"Did anyone arrive after we did?" I pulled on my lower lip as I watched him scroll through the footage. The answer became a clear yes when a jeep pulled into the warehouse and down into the parking garage. Six people climbed out and headed toward the tunnel and the guards at the little room let them come right inside. "They didn't need to show ID?"

"They're one of the teams here."

"Yet, you don't think your teams can be compromised out there? Because these guys obviously did."

"You sure it was them?" Kenny stared at the screen and shook his head. "You don't have proof of that. We've been monitoring the cameras."

"And your cameras monitor every angle of the building? There's no blind spots?"

"Well, sure there is-."

"Then it's quite possible these people are ghouls. Does this place have an area large enough where all of those remaining can meet as a group?"

Kenny scoffed. "You see the ghouls here, and as you can smell, they don't have a scent. Any other ghouls left in the base can fit in and attack us if we're herded together."

"I smell them," I bit out. "And I can promise that no ghoul is going to want to attack a group as large as the one I hope we still have in this building. Now, get on the intercom and tell everyone to meet in that area on my orders."

"And you are?"

"Captain Raven Cartana. And you can tell them that if they don't go, they'll be considered a ghoul and killed on sight."

While I stepped away, Kenny made the announcement. Cole joined me as I stared at the dead around us. My temper was simmering, and it wouldn't take much to set it off.

"Care to tell me what I'm doing wrong or missing?"

He didn't snap back at me, even though I rightly deserved it. "No, I'm here for support. If I feel that we could be using our resources better, I'll suggest it. As it is, you're doing fine. This is a tough situation, lots of death and bloodshed. For your first official mission, you’ve done well."

"But I could've done better." I rubbed my forehead. "I should've come straight here and made an announcement that an attack was coming instead of going floor to floor."

"Yes, you could have, but Major Dunkirk was still alive and would've likely thwarted any larger effort than we gave. Don't look back. We don't have time for that yet. You can learn from hindsight when this is all over. Be in the moment. Fix what you can now."

My shoulders slumped as I released a deep breath. Letting my mind go through all of the events, I turned back to Kenny. "I want you to reach out to each of the teams who aren't here. If you can't reach them, note it and give the names of each to me. Those you can contact, make them do a head count of their team. After you're done and you've given me a count, go back through the feed and do facial recognition against those who don't respond and see if any of them entered the building within the last twenty four hours. Let me know what you find as soon as possible, and if you need help, I'll assign it to you."

"Yes, Sir." Kenny scrambled to do as I asked, and I nodded toward the elevator.

"I guess we'd better go join the crowd upstairs so we can make sure no ghouls are there and everyone can be on the same page."

Cole grunted and followed me. "Keep your nose on patrol. We don't know what else we might find."

Chapter 21

Hours later, I fell onto the mattress in some random, unused room and closed my eyes. My body ached in every way possible, both from fighting the ghouls and directing those that remained. Cole had let me take leadership of the whole base, only offering advice when I requested it or when I wasn't available. Since I could smell the ghouls and I'd been leading the attack on them, not one of the Elite left alive questioned my orders. It shocked me, but I was glad not to have to waste time arguing.

Thoroughly exhausted, I'd been sure I'd crash the moment my head hit the pillow and sleep until morning, which was a few hours away, but every time I closed my eyes, images of today sprang to my memory. Gruesome sights I never wished to relive flooded me and I rolled onto my back to stare at the ceiling. Avery's soft breathing from the room's other bed made me want to groan. I was glad he was resting, but I wasn't sure how he could sleep. Of course, he'd been down here for two hours already. His body may have taken that long to drain of energy. I wouldn't know how long it took his mind to calm until he woke up.

I wasn't sure how long I laid still until sleep took me, but it wasn't long afterward before nightmares of people eating other people broke through my relaxed sleep. When someone grabbed my shoulders and shook them, waking me, I pulled my lips back on instinct, showing off my lengthened canines. With my mouth full of venom, I met Avery's wide eyes. We both stared at one another, unable to speak for several seconds.

"You were screaming," he murmured. "I didn't want you to suffer with that nightmare anymore."

"I almost bit you."

He shrugged. "Lesson learned: throw a pillow at you to wake you up. Scoot over. Neither one of us is going to get any sleep with you yelling like that, and my mother is a firm believer that when you're upset, physical contact with others helps calm you. That being said, I'm a shifter, and that's usually how things work in the feline family. You can call me 'Mother' again if you want to, but I'm looking out for my best friend." Avery laid down beside me and was quiet for several minutes as we both stared at the ceiling again. "Plus, after what I saw today, I don't want to be alone either. I'm sure we'll grow used to this, but the first time..."

"Yeah, I know."

Eventually we both calmed, but the moment I closed my eyes, the doorknob creaked as it turned. Avery tensed and my hand went to the knife strapped against my thigh. Everyone was still armed. It would be a while before those left here were comfortable again to go unarmed.

"You awake?" Jezzelle asked through the crack between the door and its frame and my head fell back to the pillow.

"I am now that you gave me a heart attack," Avery mumbled. "Come on in. It'll be a slumber party."

When Jezzi stuck her head inside the room, she caught sight of me and Avery in my bed and grinned wide. "I see that. Who knew it would take me seeing the two of you spooning to make my day?"

"We aren't spooning," I grumbled, growing cranky, but she snorted.

"You will be when I tell you to scoot over so I can lay beside you. Raven, you can be the big and little spoon, how's that?"

"Does that mean I have to be in the middle?" I mumbled, my mouth barely opening.

"Yup," Avery chuckled, rolling to his side. "Come on, buddy. Cuddle your girl, and so help me, if either of you push me out of bed, I'll lay on top of you."

Jezzi crawled up the foot of the bed and laid facing the wall, her body fitting against mine almost perfectly. That she didn't make a single comment about it showed how deeply upset she still was about today. With my friends on either side of me, I finally drifted off to sleep.

During the large meeting the day before, I'd called General Davis with an update, and he'd promised to send reinforcements as soon as possible. Those new Elite and a General Cliant arrived just after sunup. I was still sipping from a mug of hot apple cider when they arrived. Cole met them downstairs and escorted them to the security room where I sat watching the footage Kenny had pulled up for me. It was of the first missing team arriving the night before we'd arrived. If that hadn't been a red flag for Major Dunkirk, I didn't know what would be.

General Cliant wasn't nearly as tall or broad as Dunkirk had been. In fact, he was far shorter than I was, but when I smelled wolverine on him as he approached, my lips almost twitched with a smile. He may be smaller, but he was fierce. I'd make sure to stay on his good side.

"You're Raven Cartana?" he asked, holding out a hand for me to shake, so I complied.

"Yes, Sir. General Davis said you'd be taking over and we were free to leave after you arrived."

He nodded and stared around the room. "Yes. Those in positions above General Davis and I have decided to shut this place down. It's seen plenty of upgrades, just not in security or other necessary systems. The only upgrades have been in the decoration of this place. We'll likely clean it up and sell the building. I hear you're taking the ghoul bodies back with you."

"Yes." I swallowed hard, trying to forget the feel of skin giving way under my knife as I slit the throats of the creatures. My taste buds would forever remember the taste of them. "We took samples already, but we want to run more tests on them."

"All right. Then, consider yourselves free to go whenever you wish. I'm not kicking you out. I just don't want you to feel like you have to stay if you want to leave."

"Thank you, Sir. I'll gather my team, and if there's nothing else we're needed for, we'll be on our way."

Cliant nodded. "I'm impressed with your team, and Major Pike has expressed to me that this was your first mission. That makes it even more impressive."

I shook my head. "It's not impressive. People died that I could've kept alive if I'd handled the whole thing differently."

"You'll find that happens quite often. We learn from our mistakes, but every situation is different. Someone will always die, whether it's you, a member of your team, or the person trying to kill you. Don't ever second guess yourself when you did your best. It's all any one of us can expect of ourselves. Expecting even more than that will lead you down a bad road. Good luck."

Within the hour, we were on our way, the bodies of half the ghouls loaded into the truck bed and our belongings tucked up front with us. It was a tight fit, but we managed it. I drove again, needing something to do besides think about the last few days. No one slept this time, even though every eye in the truck had dark circles and deep wrinkles around them. Even Cole was quiet, and his hair was disheveled from a night of tossing and turning.

"Find anything interesting?" I asked Kara, who again sat in the middle seat of the front bench. Her usual smile was gone.

"No. Not yet, but I'm just starting. When we get back to my lab, I'll be able to give you more."

"Please tell me we're going on a less intense mission next time around," Felix ground out from the back. "Or a vacation. That was brutal, and I've seen a lot of things I never want to see again. I've never been on a mission like that."

My hands squeezed the leather steering wheel as aggravation gripped me. "And if we don't find the person responsible, I fear we're going to see a whole lot more in the coming weeks."

"Please don't say that," she murmured, her voice trembling. "I don't want to bury any more friends and colleagues."

"Then let's find the creep doing this." After a deep breath, I addressed her once again. "However, in the meantime, we do have a new mission, and it could be relaxing depending on how you look at it."

"What is it?" she asked, her voice less curious and more wary.

"General Davis told me last night that the purchase of the house has completed and we can begin moving in once we return. I guess that means today, though we should likely work on ordering furniture first."

"Can we order that today?" Jezzi asked, leaning forward again. It was becoming a habit. Next time, she rode shot gun.

"Sure, why not. I get final say, though," I warned, but the mood in the car had lifted with the promise of a new place and furniture shopping. Hoping I wouldn't regret this, I listened as the girls discussed styles, colors, and textures for couches, chairs, tables, and far more that I could've cared less about. As long as I had my basement bedroom and a bed, I'd be happy. "Don't forget a mini fridge for me," I added when they started making an actual list of items to purchase and have delivered.

"Adding that to the list now," Felix responded. She'd been given the job of scribe, which I didn't envy her. Trying to write in a truck with a good driver was bad enough, but with me driving...if she could read her list when we parked, I'd give her a medal.

The drive back to our Headquarters seemed far faster than our trip to the other base, and when we pulled up to the gate, the guard stared at each of us like we'd been dragged behind the truck instead of riding in it. He opened his mouth to question us, but I glared at him, having lost my patience with questions late in the evening. While the girls purchased our house items, I wanted to sleep, but Davis had already made it clear that I was to go to his office first thing upon arrival.

Parking the truck, I climbed out with everyone else. A team from Kara's old unit was already waiting to take the ghouls' bodies inside, and since they had that all under control, I trudged toward the building. It was best not to keep General Davis waiting. Avery had joined the girls' planning session when they'd brought up the house's floor plan and decided an actual game room was in order. He'd had plenty to add into the conversation then, and while I walked ahead of them, I shook my head over the debate of whether to buy a foosball table or an air hockey table. I didn't care either way, having decided more about my living space. What I wanted was a workout and sparring area in the basement, and an office. Whatever I could fit down there where I wouldn't need to go up into the sunlight would be great.

Kay lifted her gaze to me with a smile that twitched and fell when she took in my appearance. Sure, I looked like crap with bruises and scrapes I didn't remember receiving, but the others looked worse. Avery's arm was already beginning to heal, and no infection had taken hold. Some prayers over this trip were answered.

"Is he in?" I asked Fay when she continued to stare, and she nodded, dropping her gaze to inform Davis that I was waiting.

When he opened his door, he took one look at me and grimaced. "Please tell me the other guy looks worse."

"Considering they're dead, yeah, they look worse."

"Glad to see you still have a sense of humor after yesterday, Raven. Comc on in."

I wasn't sure it was a sense of humor or a sense of sarcasm, but I followed Davis into his office and took my usual place. Instead of sitting behind the desk, he sat in the chair beside me.

"I hear you aren't happy with how this mission went, but I'd still like to congratulate you on a mission well accomplished. You brought your whole team back alive. That's a start." He snatched a manila folder on the desk that was in reaching distance and opened it up. "Last night before he went to bed, Cole sent me an email reporting what you'd found, just as I asked you to do as well. Both of your reports match several details, and the ones I find most disturbing are that Dunkirk was so callous about security and that he treated you with disrespect based on your age and species. You were there under my orders, which he should've respected, as well as the knowledge that we'd obtained information leading to the attack. With that being said, I'm happy to hear how you responded and stood up to him. He needed that."

"He's also dead, Sir."

"I don't believe in the adage not to speak ill of the dead. He's dead for a reason, and he could've prevented his own demise by heeding our warning. The Elite deaths are on him, not you."

"Yes, Sir."

"What can you tell me about the creatures? Have you been able to identify a cause for their scentless and senseless states?"

I shrugged. "We're moving as fast as we can, I promise. Kara is already taking the creatures to her lab and working with her former team to evaluate the situation. When she finds something, I'm her first call, and you'll be my first. I can tell you that I'm still the only person who can smell them. I'm still not sure why. I also know that my venom works on ghouls."

"Well, that's good to know, I suppose. Now, what do you need from me?"

Leaning back in my chair, I studied his office while I thought. I'd hate to be stuck in this drab office every day, but I supposed since it was colorless with no wall decor, Davis liked it this way. It fit him. All business.

"The team wants to move into the house as soon as we can. They're already choosing furniture. Is it okay for us to purchase some?"

Davis chuckled. "Of course. You have the credit card I gave you when you became Captain and team lead. All purchases should be made on that card and reconciled monthly like you've been directed. Don't go too crazy, but make that place appear normal and like someone actually lives there."

"I think the girls are managing that okay, with Avery's help."

"I can believe it." Davis reached into the folder again and produced a small, rectangular card. "Cole also believes you deserve this now, too. As an Elite, you'll need it."

When he handed over a driver's license, I almost fell out of the chair. "This is for me? I thought I had to take classes and pass a test." That was what Avery explained he'd had to do to gain a license, and Jezzi had confirmed it with her own stories of Driver's Ed.

"For most, yes, but you're a special case, and apparently you're a good driver. I'll still want you to learn how to drive a manual and not just an automatic, but for now, that will do. Now, go help your team pick out furniture and go take a look at the house. Here's the keys." Davis handed over a key ring with several keys attached, one for each of us. "Security systems will be added to it over the next few weeks, but you might want to have Cole start working his magic now. Good luck, and have fun. You deserve this break."

I took the license and strode out of the office and downstairs to meet up with the rest of my team and show Avery my new "go anywhere" card as he liked to call it. Now I'd be able to take any vehicle out without needing someone else in the car. Not that I planned on going many places alone. We had more work to do, just not as bloody.

The girls and Avery did a good job choosing furniture. At least common area furniture. We each chose our bedroom sets, and I ordered office supplies and furnishings for the larger, vacant room on the opposite side of the basement from my living space. The men took the third floor while the women were happy with the second. Everyone having their own space while sharing common areas was easy as the house was so large we rarely ran into one another after we moved in the second week back.

One night after we'd just sat down for dinner, a local police chief called my cell phone to ask for help dealing with a group of ogres destroying a bar. I'd never seen a bar fight consisting of ogres, but when we arrived, my jaw fell. They'd completely destroyed the place...and all because one had called the other one ugly. To me, they were both hideous, but after we'd managed to capture them alive, I didn't want to antagonize any of them by making that comment aloud. This time, no one died, not even a bystander. They'd fled in time.

Another night we were called out to help with a domestic dispute between a pair of goose shifters. I'd laughed when I'd received the call, but when we arrived, I understood why it was us handling this particular case. Geese were testy, and they made their presence known. We left that scene with a few scrapes.

After two weeks of hearing nothing about another attack and Kara no closer to determining the source of the oddities, I wasn't the only one growing frustrated. She'd found traces of an odd substance in their noses, but the team was still trying to pinpoint exactly what it was. We weren't the only team to consider a chemical agent now, but at least one stayed with the theory that it was an Other who could do this. After what I'd seen, I wasn't so convinced.

I was in the middle of changing into my pajama pants two days into our third week when Jezzi burst through the door, her eyes wild, phone in hand. Her breathing was erratic, and even I could hear it beat in her chest.

"What's wrong?"

"Dad. He called. Said he needs us now. It's an emergency. Raven, I've never heard him sound so frantic."

Whipping my Elite uniform back on, not caring that Jezzi was still watching, I called Cole and told him where we were going. Everyone else had taken the night off and were out on the town or at the Headquarters. I'd decided to watch a movie, which I rarely did anymore since moving to the surface, and I hadn't been aware Jezzi was even home. She was in no shape to drive this time, making me glad for the license now tucked into my wallet. I'd been fearing another report, but since the perpetrator hadn't been caught, we all knew it was coming. There was no preparing for it.

I wasn't sure where to drive, but Jezzi pulled herself together enough to give directions, and I raced with our new truck through the city and into the forest surrounding it, going as fast as I dared. I was more comfortable behind the wheel, but not by much.

After what felt like eternity, and too many times reminding myself to breathe, Jezzelle's childhood home came into view. Like the last time I was here, several lights were on, but even before we climbed out, my gut twisted.

"Jezz, something seems off."

"Something is off." She retorted. "Dad wasn't himself. Something's wrong."

When Luke didn't greet us at the door, pinpricks passed over my skin as the hair on my arms stood on end. Jezzelle led the way into the house, and when she called and Luke didn't answer, my breathing grew rapid.

"Jezzi, I need you to stay here," I told her in the kitchen. "Keep an eye out, but stay here. Please."

"Rave-."

"Stay. That's an order."

She glared at me, and I hated it, but I needed her to listen to me. If Luke was anywhere, he'd be in the study. If he was in trouble, I wanted to meet it head on without Jezzelle near the fight. Her mind would be too clouded to think properly, let alone fight an assailant with her father near or involved. I'd do the same to any of the others, except maybe Cole.

I smelled the blood before I even reached the study. Grabbing the knife at my thigh, I entered, watching for trouble, but when I found Luke's body face down on the floor, I sucked in a sharp breath. Reaching him after verifying no one else was in the room, I checked his heart and pulse. Nothing. He was dead. My breath caught. How could I tell Jezzi we were too late? That this likely had to do with him digging into our problems? I was guilty. He was dead because of me.

Taking a deep breath, I retraced my steps to the kitchen where she was watching out the windows, keeping an eye on the grounds. The moment she turned and caught sight of my face, she knew. Bursting into tears, she screamed and her legs buckled underneath her. I barely caught her body before she landed on the tile floor where I held her tight, shock and guilt erasing any other emotions.

All I knew for sure was that someone was going to die for killing Luke Coye.

Chapter 22

"Where is he? I want to see him." Jezzelle's sobs had dwindled down to quiet sniffles as her shock wore away to reality. "Were his guards with him?"

"Not that I saw."

"How'd he die?"

Lifting her up so she stood beside me, I brushed my thumbs under her eyes to wipe away the lingering tears. "To be honest, I don't know. I saw him lying on the floor, and I checked for life, but I didn't see a cause of death. Jezzi, I'm so sorry. I should've driven faster."

I hung my head, too many regrets stealing any more words from my lips. She cupped my cheek with a hand and stepped closer, letting me hold her as another bout of soft tears trickled down her face and her body shook. Her sorrow consumed me.

"I swear to you," I whispered against her hair, "I swear that I will find his killer and I will end them."

"Not if I beat you to it." I'd never heard her voice so cold, but I shook my head.

"No, Jezzi. Come on, I'll take you to your father and then I need to call Major Davis. This is about our mission. It has to be. And I'm so sorry for that. It's my fault." My voice broke, and a single tear leaked from my eye to dampen the hand she held to my cheek.

"I'm scared," she confided. "I'm scared that when I see him, it'll all be too real."

"I won't leave you, Jezzi. I promise. If you aren't ready, that's okay. I'll call Davis now."

She nodded. "We need to check the video too." Swallowing hard, she stepped away from me. "No, I need to see him. Then we can do all of that. Don't leave me."

"I won't."

Hand in hand, we made our way to the study. Jezzi's hand squeezed mine right before we stepped through the room's threshold. My hand lingered on the knife's hilt, ready to pull it if trouble had returned and showed itself, but the room was as quiet as when I'd arrived the last time.

Holding a hand over her mouth with more tears flowing, Jezzelle crossed to her father, who lay beside the coffee table. I followed on her heels, searching for any signs of a struggle or attack. The scent of blood surrounded us, which meant he'd been hurt somehow, but there wasn't any blood to be seen.

Since he lay face down, I pulled out my phone and snapped pictures of the area before turning him over to search for the cause of death on the other side of his body. Within a second, my eyes zeroed in on four bloody gouges on his neck while Jezzi searched his torso. I tapped her arm and pointed, my stomach knotting.

"Here."

A soft gasp escaped her as she covered her mouth, her words muffled. "Vampire? A vampire killed him."

"No," I corrected. "No, his body is still full of blood. A vampire would've drained him dry."

"But what could've..."

Her eyes popped to mine, and for a brief half a second betrayal stared back at me before she hid the emotion. It was too late, I'd seen it and my heart shattered. One of my best friends, someone I trusted with more than my life, with my heart, had just thought I'd killed her father. How could she even think that? Okay, I'd been the person to find him, alone, but didn't she know me better than that?

A combination of rage and agony fought inside my chest as I turned away, clenching my jaw. "You know I could never kill him, Jezzi. I could never do that to you."

She crawled to me, wrapping her arms around my neck. "I know. I'm so sorry I even thought it, Raven. It was wrong, so wrong. Forgive me."

I wanted to slap myself. Her father was dead, and she was looking for someone to blame. I just happened to be the closest person with the ability we saw here to kill him. But it didn't make sense why a vamlure would be behind this. However, that didn't mean I had to be a jerk.

"There's nothing to forgive." I held her tighter. "The signs were there. Your brain jumped to the first plausible conclusion."

"But it wasn't you. There wasn't time, and you've been with me since he called."

"You mentioned a video. Where's the security footage?"

She stood, and I joined her, both of us wiping stray tears from her face. "This way." Leading me further into the house, we stayed on alert. When we reached a doorway on the second floor, Jezzi stopped, a soft moan proceeding more distressing news. "The security detail is dead."

I peered around her shoulder to find two men on the floor, both with puncture marks to their necks. Whoever was doing this knew where to go in the house. It certainly wasn't me.

"Is that the feed?"

We strode into the small room and maneuvered around the dead bodies to the computer monitor. Within seconds, Jezzi had the video of the study backed up to an hour before, and we watched it until the screen turned to static. Every camera she tried did the same thing.

"Someone messed with the footage," she grumbled. "It must have been when they killed Sals and Torque. Come on. There's a second system in here."

"Your dad was either highly prepared or extremely paranoid," I muttered when she set a hand on the base of a brass table lamp and a wall panel opened up, allowing us into a further high tech room with even more security systems in place.

"Paranoid. We're the shifter version of the mafia, surely Davis explained that."

"He did, but it's one thing to hear it and another thing to see it. What can you tell me?"

She backed the feed up again and scanned through until her father entered the study, talking on his cell phone. "This was when he called me." We watched the sped up version until a figure entered the room, then Jezzi slowed it to real time. I gripped her shoulder, and she reached back to hold my hand as we watched the attack unfold.

A figure dressed in all black with a black cloak and hood approached from the door we always entered as Luke ran fingers through his hair. Either his hearing wasn't up to par or the person was beyond silent. It leapt at Luke, burying its teeth in his neck, or from our angle with the hood in place and from our knowledge of how he'd died, that was what was happening. When Luke fell to the ground, the person raced from the room toward where the two men lay just outside this cubbyhole.

"It is a vamlure, isn't it?" Jezzi breathed, her breathing erratic.

"I...I don't know," I replied as honest as I could. "It could be, but something just seems...off about the person. I can't explain it, but something about them being a vamlure doesn't sit right, and not because I'm trying to protect my people. There's just something wrong about this in my gut."

"I trust your gut, Raven, just like I trust you." She patted my hand. "That was awful. I kinda want to be sick."

"Do what you need."

She shook her head. "Nope, I have to be strong. Just as long as I don't have to watch that again, I'll hold it together."

"Good. Then back it up to a few minutes before the killer enters the room."

We watched as Luke called Jezzi again and moved to sit on the couch to write a note and then stand up to pace. My eyes narrowed as I stared at the piece of paper. The killer hadn't bothered with it after killing him, which meant he wasn't concerned by it, or he hadn't known it was there.

"Stop the feed," I directed. "Go back to when he's writing."

Jezzi paused the feed as Luke wrote on screen. "What is that?"

"I don't know, but I'm going to go find out. You don't have to come."

"There's a crazy person going around biting people in this house. I'm coming."

I didn't blame her one bit, but if we ran into that person, I'd be the one to bite. Hard.

Back in the study, I maneuvered around Luke's body to sit on the couch where he'd sat to write. In front of me was a small piece of torn paper shoved mostly under a novel, a Western by the look of the cover. I'd never heard of the title, but skipping that irrelevant detail, I tugged the paper out and stared at the letters written on it.

"St. Louis," I breathed. "He knew something was going to happen, that he was in danger, so he left us a note just in case. That has to be what this is, right?"

"I think so." Jezzi sounded as anxious as I did. "You do realize how huge St. Louis is, right? You won't find anything there until it attacks, especially not if we couldn't find ghouls until they attacked in a base a thousand times smaller, likely more. And it was in the middle of nowhere. This is a city."

My phone was out and ringing General Davis in a heartbeat. He didn't pick up, and my heart leapt to my throat. Dialing again, I waited. Four rings later and he answered.

"What?"

It was likely he was home since he sounded a bit perturbed. Echoes of a TV filled the background, as well as laughing. Children? Was he really a family man? Shoving those thoughts aside, I got down to business.

"Luke Coye called Jezzelle about an emergency. We came over here as fast as possible, but we were too late. He's dead, General."

"What?" Davis bellowed, silencing the laughter around him. "Please tell me you're joking."

"No, Sir. I wish I were, but I'd never do that. He's dead. From what we can tell from the security video feed...it was a vamlure, or something like it. That's the assumption since the killer came up from behind and bit him and he dropped." I ran the video through my memory again, picking up on more details. "It's a woman. It has to be. Even with the cloak you can see she's slender. Too narrow of shoulders and light curves. It's the body of a female."

"That's more than we had. Okay, I'll reach out to one of the other teams and have them meet you there. They can sweep the house and gather evidence. You've done well. Since his daughter is on your team, I'm handing this one off to another."

I nodded, even though he couldn't see me. "Yes, that's understandable, and we have a different lead to follow. Before he died, Luke wrote St. Louis on a small piece of paper."

"That could be anything," Davis argued, but I cut him off.

"It was right before he died. Minutes. After Jezzi's call and before he died. That man knew something wasn't right and wanted us to find that note so we knew where to go. General, something bad is going down, and I need to take my team to the fight."

Davis groaned, and I could picture him in my mind running a hand through his hair. "I'll reach out to the commander of the St. Louis base. He's more willing to bend than Dunkirk, but for the sake of time and the situation, it's best if I do this. I'll let him know that I'm sending your team and Bruce Smith's team. The two of you can duke it out over who's on point. When the other team shows up, you and Jezzelle get your butts back to your house. It's a solid twelve hour drive to St. Louis and if this is going down, it'll be soon. Gosh, that base is massive. What would they send against it?"

While we'd spoken, I'd stood and walked the room. Studying the landscape out the window, my eyes rose to the nearly full moon. "Werewolves," I breathed, my chest constricting. "General, tomorrow night is the full moon. It has to be werewolves."

"My gosh." His airy voice broke in disbelief. "I hope you're wrong. That would be a massacre, not just with the base, but all over the city. Let me call General Kapen right away. No, I have to call in the other team first. Stay put, don't touch anything else."

"We won't," I murmured and the call ended. Turning around to face an even paler Jezzelle, I took a deep breath. "You heard all that?"

"Werewolves," she stated, her head bobbing up and down. "Oh my gosh. It'll be a slaughter, on both sides."

"Not if we can help it." I rubbed my temples. "And by we, I mean the rest of us. Not you." She opened her mouth to argue, but I silenced her with a look. "No Jezz. You're too emotionally involved, and your father was the pack leader. Where's your mother?"

"She's dead," Jezzi breathed.

"That makes you alpha female, right?" She nodded. "Then you need to stay here and be with your pack. You can still be an Elite and lead them, I'm sure. I can work with you on that, but I can't let you come on this one. Your pack needs you alive, I need you alive and not making stupid, emotion driven decisions. I'll be doing enough of that for the both of us. Please, don't argue with me about this."

"I won't." Her solemn response confirmed her words. She wouldn't argue. "No, I need time to think and decide what my future will be now. I've always known a day like this would come, but I never expected it to be now, or anytime soon."

"Come here." I held out my arms and she came to me, letting me hold her for the length of time she needed. In the end, we found our way to the kitchen where I fixed her a small sandwich and a cup of hot chocolate. From what I understood, most women liked chocolate when they were upset, and it was the only chocolate I could find.

When the new team showed up, we directed them where to go, and they promised to only touch what they needed, and that they'd leave the rest of the house alone. I doubted it, and I could tell by Jezzi's face that she was thinking the same thing, but we'd been given an order. Once the new team was set, Jezzi and I left.

I'd texted the rest of the team to go home and start packing a bag while we'd eaten. When we pulled into the driveway, Felix was already standing on the front porch. The truck had barely stopped before Felix had the passenger door open and was helping Jezzi from the cab and giving her a long, tight hug. Her reassuring words were lost on me as Cole made his way out of the house to me.

"Connor Davis called and told me what happened. I'm so sorry. I know you'd grown to like Luke."

I shook Cole's outstretched hand of support. "It was less that I'd grown to like him as much as I care for his daughter and I don't want to see her hurting. And Cole, it looks like it's a vamlure doing the killing, but my gut says it's not."

"Then follow your gut, but be willing to accept the truth if it is."

"I am, but I'm almost positive it's not a vamlure."

"Trust your gut." He patted my shoulder and watched the girl's approach, Felix's arm around Jezzi's shoulder. "What's the plan?"

"Jezzi and Kara stay here," I announced. "Jezz and I have already talked about it, and I need Kara working every second she has on the ghoul bodies and on the bodies they're bringing back from Luke's home. Whatever answers she can give us before we reach St. Louis will help us find our killer and combat them. She can't do that out in the field until we've been attacked. Also, Smith's team is joining us, so it won't be only four of us going into this alone."

"Good. Let's go finish packing and start on our way. We've got a long way to go, and not a lot of time."

"Raven, can I have a minute?" Jezzelle asked when our group moved toward the house. I waved them on and held back to talk to her. Jezzi's fingers twisted in a nervous action I'd never seen from her.

"What is it?"

"I did a lot of thinking on our way back from my house."

"You were quiet, and I didn't want to disturb you. Are you okay?" I wanted to slap myself. Of course she wasn't okay. Her dad was dead.

"No, but I will be, and that's what I want to talk to you about. You're right, my pack needs me, and right now, I don't think I could handle both pack alpha duties and Elite responsibilities. I need to choose, and I'm choosing my pack. It wasn't an easy decision to come to, and I hope you understand."

"Jezz, of all the people here, I understand the most. Your friends and family need you. Your pack needs you there to lead them while my people need me here. I do understand. But, I'll miss you."

"You'll miss my kisses," she snickered, the first real sign of humor she'd shown since she'd come to my room hours ago.

"Yes, I will." Leaning in, I placed my lips to hers in a hard, desperate kiss. I took the lead, nipping at her lips until she opened her mouth and allowed my tongue to twist around hers. When she tried to deepen the kiss further, I ended it, not wanting to take it further than I should have. Already I'd gone too far, and I wouldn't play her.

"I thought you didn't like me like that," she slurred, leaning her body into mine.

"I don't."

She chuckled, running her thumb across my swollen lower lip. "Then I was right, you just like to kiss."

"Be safe, Jezzi. I'll call you when I'm back if you aren't here. Know that you can come to me any time. For anything. You'll always be one of my greatest and most trusted friends."

“You too. I’m sorry that I doubted you.” She leaned in and placed a gentle kiss against my lips. “I guess I like to kiss too. Be safe. I can’t lose anyone else.”

We walked toward the open front door. “I don’t plan on dying. I plan on killing anyone who stands between me and the mastermind behind this. Then, I plan on killing them.”

Chapter 23

The trip to St. Louis was the longest journey of my life. I couldn't sleep, waiting and wondering what we'd find. I'd never seen a werewolf before, not a real one anyway. All I could picture were Hollywood versions, and I knew not to trust those to be accurate, unless one of the creators of the movies had actually met a werewolf before the Great Reveal and lived to tell about it.

When the city drew closer on the horizon, I shuddered. This was going to be a disaster. With so many freeways intersecting on one location, how would we ever be able to know in which direction the attack would come? Even this early in the morning, making our way through the city was a nightmare, and it was after the evening rush hour should've ended. Had word gotten out of an impending attack and people were trying to escape it? I would've.

"Would it be faster if we parked and walked?" Felix grumbled from the back as we continued trudging along with the stop and go traffic. "I'm feeling a bit nauseous and we could definitely walk faster than we're driving."

"We're probably the only ones wanting into this city, too," Avery commented. "Now, how did they all find out?"

"Easy," Cole grumbled from his place at the wheel. "Davis calls Kapen, Kapen tells his base, they all tell their families, those families tell their friends so that they're safe too, those people tell their family and friends, and the cycle continues until we have this. People want out to escape, others want in to get home and grab their families after a night shift or other reasons they were out of town. They should all just stay home and leave the roads clear for us, but they're panicking and not thinking."

"Can't say that I blame them," I muttered, staring out my window.

Over an hour later, and deeper into the city, Cole growled and pulled the truck over into a space with a parking meter beside it. "This is as far as I'm driving in this crap. We only need to go another three blocks anyway. Grab your things, and don't bother with the meter. If the city wants to ticket us, I'm ready to fight them."

Climbing from the truck, we grabbed our bags, slung them on shoulders and backs, and started the hike up the street. Felix had been right. We were moving much faster than the cars we strode past. They looked at us like we were crazy until they noticed our uniforms. More car doors slammed shut behind us, signaling that Smith's team of two filled SUVs had finally caught up to us after being separated by a few cars, and they'd parked and were following.

"I wondered how long it would take you to give up so we could get in our daily steps," Smith called from half a block back.

"Too long," Cole called back. "This is insanity."

"We'd better make sure to start moving people inside before nightfall." Smith's team caught up to us and we all started walking again, our destination growing closer.

Every so often I caught a glimpse of the large arch that I'd seen on our drive into the city. Apparently it was one of the things the city was known for, even though I'd never heard of it. That wasn't too shocking, though. While we walked, I kept watch for anything suspicious. We could guess the attack would come from werewolves tonight, but before then, anything was free game. If the killer had chosen a city this big, and if Luke had been so panicked and become worth someone taking the risk to kill, this venture would be far more massive and catastrophic an undertaking. He or she was now showing their force and what they were capable of doing.

It was easier to gain access to this base than I thought, but General Kapen was one of the men to greet us, and he knew most of Smith's team personally, and Major Pike vouched for those of us on his team. They were under too much of a time crunch to be picky with the Elite coming in, except to verify we were living and not monsters. I cringed when I saw bowls of raw meat sitting around, ready to attract creatures who fed off dead flesh, like the ghouls. Swallowing hard, I turned my attention back on General Kapen, who was leading us to a set of elevators off to the right.

"I can't believe this is happening," he was telling Pike and Smith.

"You'd better believe it," Smith grumbled. "Every attack has escalated. It was only a matter of time before they worked up to something this size."

"I wish they hadn't." Kapen rubbed his face, and Smith caught my gaze and smirked.

"By the way, General, Cole and I aren't in charge of our people. I want to introduce you to Captain Raven Cartana. He's the lead of his team, which includes Cole, and I've decided to let him speak for all of us. Since he's about the only person who can smell these creatures, we trust what he decides to do when he smells them."

General Kapen stared at me. "Him? The purple-eyed kid?"

"Yes, that's the one." Cole chuckled at Kapen's slack-jawed stare when he turned to the Major.

"He's a kid."

"He's a Captain, and like Bruce said, he can smell the creatures. We haven't found anyone else who can."

"And that doesn't sound suspicious?" Kapen questioned Pike with an arched brow as the elevator dinged its arrival.

"What floor are we going to?" Smith asked, waving his team off.

"Seven."

"Meet us up there," Smith directed at his team and the rest of mine, which was only Avery and Felix. Meanwhile, I joined Pike, Kapen, and Smith on the elevator. Smith waited until the doors closed before turning a hard stare on Kapen. "Let's be clear about this: we trust Raven with our lives. He's the one who discovered the Wight about to attack our governor the first time, which was how we first found out about these creatures. He almost died that day, and I don't believe anyone who is helping in such a cause as the deaths these creatures have left behind would continually run head on into the fight against them."

"I agree," Cole threw in, nudging my arm. "He's young, but he has more brains than half our soldiers. There's a reason why Connor Davis and I agreed to promote him to a Captain with his own team."

Breathing out a deep sigh, Kapen rubbed his neck. "I'll take your word for it. It's been a long day here, boys, so I'm a bit tense and questioning everything. We've got a plan. Now we just have to hope it works with minimal casualties."

"We'll do everything we can to prevent a massive death count," I murmured. "That's why we're here. We know the risks, and we're ready to face them."

Kapen nodded. "Then let's do this."

When the elevator opened, he led us down a hall to the largest conference room I'd ever seen in my life. Half the long table was already filled with men and women of different species. I waited for their reactions to me as my scent drifted through the room. Heads lifted to us as Kapen directed where we should sit. Of course I'd be placed across from a stern looking witch who openly glared at me.

"What's he doing here?" she snapped, turning her glare on Kapen.

"He's leading the group General Connor Davis sent down to us."

"He's a vamlure, a Blood Drinker."

"We know that," Cole announced as he and Smith sat on either side of me. "We know what he is and we also know who he is. By that, I've learned to trust this vamlure with my life and I know he'd never hurt me."

"Then he's bewitched you."

"In the best possible way. He's my friend, and the best young warrior I've had the pleasure of working with in a long time. Oh, and he's punctual. Show me another sixteen-year-old who's always on time and willing to lose his life to save another and I'll gladly make him an officer as well."

The witch shook her head, still not happy with Cole's answer. "It isn't safe to have a Blood Drinker among us when this battle starts. You won't know when he'll go crazy with the need for blood."

Smith snorted as the rest of our team joined us, and he pointed to Avery. "I've seen Captain Cartana bite into that kid in the middle of a mission, and it wasn't for fun. Raven needed the blood, and you know what, Avery Clark let him, and Raven only took the three swallows he said he would. He has control, and a rule he only takes from those who are willing."

Our witchy friend turned her attention on Avery, who sat three chairs down from me. "And you were willing?"

He stared her straight in the eyes without blinking, his voice steady. "Absolutely. Raven's my best friend. I'd give him every drop of blood I have if he needed it, but I also know he'd never take it. He only takes what he needs or what you're able to safely give. If you can't trust him, then trust that we trust him."

She didn't argue with that, and the rest of the table filled up quickly, leaving a few of Smith's team to stand against one wall to listen. Kapen sat at the head of the table and pressed a button that allowed for the center of the black glass to vanish, and in its place was a city map that focused on roads and larger buildings. I'd never seen technology like this, and my fingers itched to request some to have at my disposal. Avery's small gasp announced I wasn't the only one thinking this.

"Our plan is simple, which is how I like it," Kapen announced, standing and leaning over the table, a laser pointer in hand. He directed the red light to a building near the center of the map we were staring at. "This is our location. We know they have to come in from the outside. There are no tunnels leading in and out of here. Our hope is to stop them from even making it into the building. We want pairs of Elite on the streets, watching and waiting. When they see something, they'll report it in and backup will be sent to them. Since we want a two block perimeter, the time for help to arrive will be short."

"They'll have to be on foot," Smith muttered, "unless you plan to blockade the surrounding streets and not let anyone use those two blocks in their escape routes."

"We plan for them to be on foot, and as you know, shifters travel quite quickly."

"Are you accounting for civilians being on the streets when this goes down?" I asked. "Considering what we think is coming, it might be best to put out some sort of warning for everyone to be locked inside for the night."

"We're working on it."

A man across from me raised his hand. "Now, someone said werewolves..."

"It's a guess," I stated. "Tonight is a full moon. It would only make sense, but, knowing that this battle has escalated above the others, I would expect more than just werewolves. Since most Elite can't sense or smell them, this is going to be a long night full of surprises."

"And death," the man stated. "Lots of death."

Nodding, I stared at the city map. "Hopefully more on their side than ours."

"You've pulled all your teams in?" Cole asked Kapen, who bobbed his head.

"Yes. We're at full strength."

"Good. We'll need every person we can get to help us."

For the next few hours, we determined who would be stationed where, and which teams would go to their assistance should they need it. It wasn't a foolproof plan, but it was the best we could come up with on short notice with an unknown enemy. Or enemies. I still wasn't convinced that our only attacker tonight would be werewolves.

"Let's think about this," I murmured when Kapen moved to close the meeting. "Most of the attacks thus far have been by various different species of Threats. What if those were just the test runs for each species and this is the main event? If that's the case, then I'd expect to see those other species involved in this."

"I'm gonna puke," Avery muttered. "That actually makes sense. So then how are we going to know if ghouls show up. We couldn't tell by looking at them what they are."

"A code word," I stated. "They don't have our minds, just our bodies. If you're unsure, ask for the code word. Only an Elite would know it, but we'd need to make sure that everyone knew the word."

"We'll get on that," the man who asked about werewolves stated.

Kapen set balled fists on his hips and addressed the room. "If no one else has any concerns that can't wait, we'll adjourn to prepare. Since not all the creatures are limited to a full moon, I suggest we take our places sooner than later. All the gear and equipment your team will require, Captain Cartana, is on the third floor. Take what you need."

"Thank you."

We stood and headed straight for the third floor where we outfitted ourselves with more weapons and communication equipment. A quick trip to the cafeteria was next before we strode back onto the street. The congestion of cars had only grown worse, and the sound of car horns was about the only sound that could be heard for miles.

"Who else thinks this is a bad omen?" I asked, staring at the people packed in their cars. "It's a werewolf and ghoul smorgasbord."

"And this is only a small sector of the city," Smith murmured. "The monsters will have to enter the city first. The ghouls I'm not as fearful of since they only kill. It's the werewolves that concern me. They'll make new ones."

My throat tightened, making it impossible to swallow. I didn't need to be able to do math well to know the amount of werewolves that a crowd like this could create. We'd be overrun in no time.

Pulling out my phone, I sent Jezzelle a quick text to let her know we made it and a plan was set. To give her a smile, I added a kissy face emoji. If I died, her last memories of me would be positive. There was no use calling home. They wouldn't care.

"Texting the girlfriend a final farewell?" Cole asked with little humor. "Good idea."

"No, just letting her know we made it and so far so good. I don't want her to know how bad this is going to be."

Cole slapped me on the back and moved in the direction of the street we were supposed to monitor as Smith moved back into the building. "She already knows, kid. Trust me, she knows. Now focus and make that nose work overtime. It may be the difference between our life and death today."

I didn't want to tell him that whoever had planned this was a genius. With all the exhaust in the air and no breeze to blow it away, I could barely smell Cole as he walked a few steps ahead of me. We were so dead.

Chapter 24

The closer the sun drew to the horizon, the more my nerves were on edge. At any time, I expected a random person on the street to jump out at me, sharp teeth lunging for my throat before I could smell them. As the sun kissed the horizon, a voice came over the piece in my ear.

"We've got strange activity in fourth sector. Three and five, keep an eye out."

Cole grunted before responding, both of our eyes scanning the area. "This is sector three. Define strange."

Crickets.

"Sector four, come in." When no one responded again, Cole nudged me. "Your call."

Taking a deep breath, I spoke into the communication device. "This is Captain Cartana. Sector four back up, go check it out and report what the strange activity is. Everyone else, be on alert. Base, lock down until further notice."

"Sector four back up on our way," a female voice stated seconds before a male voice announced, "Base locked down."

"Who was on sector four duty?" Cole asked, searching around us. The cars had thinned out some, but the roads were still clogged. "This is insane."

My temper was simmering below the surface. He was right. Striding over to the nearest car, a family of five, I knocked on the passenger window until the wife lowered it. "You have two choices: Get out and make a run for it or find a building and hide. Escaping in a car is no longer an option. You won't make it and you need to be as far from here as possible. And go in the direction you're coming."

"My parents are at home-."

"Then call them and tell them to start walking because you won't make it. This is going down now. Get out."

While I spoke to the woman, Cole got on the com link. "Sectors not seeing any Threat activity, get people out of their cars and inside or have them walk out. It may not be the safest option, but those closest to the base are likely going to die. Have any Magic Users you find protect those nearest to them. Tell shifters to shift and run. Belongings mean nothing anymore."

And that was the crux of this whole issue. The shifters should've been on foot and running long before this instead of trying to pack their cars full and drive out. Their pack would help them. It was anyone without a pack that needed the help, and those who couldn't shift to a faster form who needed their cars.

Going car to car, I smelled the occupants and gave orders. Within minutes the street was clearing out of people as shifters of all kinds made a run for it. Magic users, humans, and Others raced on foot when they could. Those who couldn't run away entered the nearest buildings to find shelter.

The moment the sun dipped under the horizon, the light of day withdrew with it. An eerie calm followed before a deep howl cut through the twilight air as the moon rose. We'd been right.

Werewolves.

"Sector four back up. What's your status?"

"Ghouls. Six. Half the team is dead."

Crap.

"Don't forget the code word, people. And remember to be specific."

Seconds later, "Zone seven," a woman shrieked. "Back up requested. Werewolves. Four."

Bigger crap.

"Everybody inside!" I yelled up the street. "Get in a building and be silent!"

Screams broke out halfway up the next block and people scattered as disjointed and crumbling bodies attacked. The dilapidated bodies grabbed the people closest to them and stabbed knives, metal shanks, and anything else they could find into those people who couldn't escape fast enough.

"Zombies?" I breathed.

"No, undead," Cole corrected, reaching for a woman near him who'd fallen. He helped her up while I braced myself for the first creature to reach me. "Zombies bite. Undead just kill. These have been raised by a necromancer."

Using the com link, I stated, "Sector three requesting backup. Herd of at least a dozen undead. Civilians caught in the middle of the fight."

"Backup on its way," Avery spoke over the link. He, Felix, and Smith's team were our backup, which was beyond comforting as the first of the undead reached us and I sent my knife into its head.

"Kill it like a ghoul, boy," Cole yelled when the undead swiped at me, not the least bit affected. "And I doubt your venom will work. These aren't normal bodies. They're dead, just reanimated."

So, take its head off. Retrieving my blade, I aimed for the thing's throat, but it moved too fast out of the way. For being a brainless, dead creature, it was quite agile.

"Any other ways to kill it?" I yelled back to Cole, who was now facing two undead while a third wanted to join his fight and a second moved around me.

"Yeah, kill the necromancer. He has to be close."

Speaking into the com link, I avoided a swipe from the second undead. "Sector three requesting beta backup unit to search out a necromancer near our sector."

The first undead raked his fingernails across my arm when I didn't dodge fast enough, drawing droplets of blood. My control snapped. Reaching for my other abilities, I strengthened the purple shield over my skin and drew on my strength. In a second, I grabbed the undead by the face, threw him to the ground, and crushed his skull as I shoved it into the sidewalk. The second undead to attack me couldn't run away fast enough before he met a similar end.

Cole's sword had decapitated four undead by the time I finished with my two, and backup had arrived to finish off the rest. Avery whistled at the damage I'd done to my two, his axe held at the ready.

"Wow, I have to say that was some roar and head crushing. Remind me not to make you angry."

I opened my mouth to make a snide reply when more howls ripped through the night, as well as more screams, this time much closer...only the screams were coming in the completely wrong direction.

"Sector five, wights. Need backup."

"Sector eight, undead and ghouls."

"Sector four, nine werewolves, no ten. That guy just got bit. Run!"

"This is Captain Cartana," I spoke with as much calm as I could muster with the reports coming in. "All beta backup units, help the nearest sector to you. Elite, hold your ground. We must-."

Windows shattered in the building above us, raining glass around us as four large, furry bodies fell with the cascading shards. Only, they'd jumped on purpose, their red, fiery eyes locking on their targets: us.

"Wolves!" Felix shouted, raising the crossbow she carried to her shoulder. She released the silver bolt, hitting the first werewolf in the chest. When his body hit the ground, he didn't stand up. The others did, however.

One wolf, the largest in the group, grabbed the closest car and chucked it over his head in our direction. We scattered. Half the team ran up the next street for cover while Cole, myself, and half of the others ducked behind a building in the other direction. By now, screams were coming from everywhere, and not only human sounding cries, but explosions, metal screeches, and roars of the multitude of creatures attacking. And they weren't only attacking us. Anything that moved was free game.

"Any ideas?" I yelled to Cole. "I'm all out."

"Stay alive. That's the only one coming to me," he shot back.

"Wights," Fennel, one of Smith's bobcat shifters called, staring up the street behind us.

Sure enough, a horde of Wights was creeping up behind us at a pace faster than I thought was possible for the creatures. We turned to face them as a stream of hot hair smoothed over my neck. Pivoting on my heel, I turned to find a werewolf less than ten feet from us. Behind me, the team screamed as they attacked, and the werewolf roared.

I prepared for its attack, his eyes hard on me, but when he lunged, he dove to my left.

"Cole!" I screamed, throwing myself at the monster to stop his attack. We went down in a heap of arms and legs, both Cole and I fighting the creature with our silver laced weapons. Its claws fought to tear us apart, but we avoided them until the wolf grew still, my knife sticking out of his chest.

Breathing deep, I stepped away, lightheaded. "We did it."

"Not quite," Cole grunted, turning my attention on him.

Blood coated his torso, but it was the jagged bite mark on his arm that drew my attention and all time stopped. All emotion drained from me. My world ended again.

"No. Please, no."

Cole doubled over, pain gripping him tight as skin along his shoulders tore and fur began to sprout out of it. He gasped for air, standing back up, eyes black with a fiery center.

"Kid-."

"No."

He reached for me, wiping away the tears I hadn't known were falling. "Kid, I'm sorry."

My arms wrapped around him when another wave of pain struck. The fighting continued around us, but I was oblivious to it. Cole and I both knew the end of this situation, and I couldn't do it.

"Kid, I'm more human still than beast," he spoke in my ear. "I need your help."

"Anything," I cried, my voice more broken than words.

"Don't let me turn into one of them. Don't let me kill anyone. Please."

"I can't, Cole," I wept, holding the one man who was more father to me than mine had ever been. "I can't."

"You have to." His legs gave out causing his full weight to crash down on me and we fell to the ground where he gritted his teeth, more skin stretching and splitting. "There isn't any more time. If I change, you'll have one more wolf to fight. Kid, I'm already dead. Save yourself and your team. Save me."

Our eyes met, and he shoved the hilt of his knife into my hands.

"Raven, my body is too weak to do it."

Sobs tore up my throat. "I was never on time until I met you. The first day you gave me a time frame was the first day I ever cared about being somewhere when I needed to be," I confessed. "I didn't want to disappoint you."

"And you never have. Never. I love you, kid."

His eyes pleaded with me in a way words never could before he cried out. Fingers gripped my arm, the nails digging into my flesh as they elongated into claws. Cole's scream morphed into a low howl of agony and my heart couldn't bear it.

"I love you too, Cole. I'm so sorry."

The knife plunged deep into his chest, between two ribs and into his heart. Cole's body stiffened, new pain replacing the agony of the shift. Pulling the blade free, I let blood flood from the wound to pool around us. As his life faded, Cole's lips lifted into a soft smile as his hand fought to hold mine. I gripped him tight, never wanting to let go.

"Don't you ever give up, and don't you ever tolerate anyone disrespecting you or your kind. Fight, Raven. You fight, and you find the person responsible." Every word was a battle for Cole to speak, and each was more difficult. "Get out." His voice choked in his throat as the last of his breath left him.

"Cole?"

I shook him.

"Cole?"

His eyes continued to stare at me, but there was no life behind them. I stared down at our connected hands, his Major's band a stark contrast to his skin. Gripping it, I pulled it off. It opened a little, allowing me to slip it over my empty wrist where it retightened. Until this was over, until I found the person responsible, I'd wear his tag as a reminder that I still had work to do.

Red crossed my vision as the world came crashing back, quite literally, around me. Wreckage from the building above cascaded to the ground.

"Raven, get out of there!" Avery yelled from behind me before his arms circled my torso to drag me away. We raced across the street to the overhang of another business where I looked up to find another building smashing into the one I'd stood under. What was going on?

"Warlocks are panicking," Avery spoke. "Ours and civilians. Everyone's fighting. This place is going to tear itself apart."

"Where's Smith?"

"I don't know. I got separated from him. There're monsters everywhere and spells being cast left and right. It's chaos."

Reaching for my ear, I found my earpiece gone.

"Here, use mine," Avery spoke, handing it over.

Chaos was right. Reports were coming in too fast. The whole city was literally falling apart as Threats attacked, magic users retaliated, and the rest tried to flee.

Somehow I felt the buzz of my phone. Staring down, I answered right away when General Davis's name popped up.

"Sir-."

"I'm getting reports from Kapen at the base. Raven, get your people out of there. He's being ordered to have his Magic Users bring the city down."

"They've already started," I yelled over the crashing of a building somewhere else in the city. Dirt and falling debris rained around us.

"Get out."

"How?"

"There's a helo at the base. Kapen's using it to escape to bring us sensitive information. Raven I need you alive. You're the only person we know who can smell and sense these creatures and I need to know why. Get to that helo."

"Sir, the others-."

"I'll call Smith and Pike."

"Pike's dead." The words cut through me having to say them out loud, and my voice broke. "He's dead. Call Smith."

"I will," Davis said, his voice deep. "Get you and any of your team you can out, but don't go looking for more."

"Yes, Sir."

Ending the call, I shoved the phone in my pocket. The dirt in the air made breathing almost impossible, and seeing around us even more so.

Buildings fell everywhere, and not as one piece, but magic tore them apart, sending chunks flying into the war zones.

"We have to go," I announced to Avery, taking his hand. "Don't let go."

Chapter 25

As a shifter, Avery had a better sense of direction, so when I told him where we were headed and he announced we were going the wrong way, I let him lead. Thankfully I'd only taken us a block out of the way. However, that block had taken us ten minutes to maneuver through. Heading back was worse.

By the time we reached the base, we'd torn off sections of our shirts to breathe through since there was no clean air around us and the dust was making us cough. We had to hide from a pack of Wights once. We'd never be able to take out all eight and live to tell about it.

Kapen waited with his guards at the main door, ready to let us in when we arrived, and as a group of a dozen Elite, we raced to the roof, bypassing the elevator for a safer route. After that, everything was a blur. I'd never ridden in a helicopter, and I vowed I never would again. I clung to Avery for most of the trip, not caring where we were heading. My heart ached, and that was all that mattered. It also kept me from looking out the window to see how high we were in the sky. I'd never thought I'd be afraid of heights, but apparently I was, or at least afraid of flying.

"Hey, we're on the ground," Avery murmured some time later. I lifted my head and stared out the windows as the machine powered down. The scenery wasn't familiar by any means, especially since we were in a random field surrounded by forest.

"Where are we?"

"Home," he murmured. "Well, as close as they could take us. Davis has a ride waiting."

General Davis didn't just have a ride waiting. Davis himself was waiting with it. Two SUV's idled on the field's edge. Kapen climbed into the back of one, and Avery and I were ushered into the one Davis rode inside. Two Elite sat in the backseat and another two up front while Davis sat beside me with Avery on my other side.

"Let's go," Davis ordered the driver. "We need to get these two medical attention."

We looked like crap. In fact, we probably looked like death warmed over. My breathing was ragged and my body ached like I'd been put through a meat grinder. I'd been relying on Avery, but he was likely in a similar condition, making me feel that much worse.

The SUV bumped and jostled as we left the field and found ourselves on a narrow, tree lined road. No one spoke for several minutes until we hit a paved highway and were able to speak easier and hear the person speaking.

"What happened down there?" Davis asked in a kind, fatherly voice I'd never heard from him, and it caused my chest to tighten and ache.

"I killed Cole," I blurted, a single sob breaking from my body before I could swallow it. "I thought the werewolf was going to lunge at me, but it didn't, and it bit Cole. We killed it, and then he begged me to kill him. I did."

"You did the right thing." Davis's voice continued to soften. The stern general had taken a step back, and in that moment, he reminded me a bit of Cole, which was both painful and welcome. "He wouldn't have wanted to change, to kill you and anyone else. I'm sorry. Now, Avery, give me a report from the beginning."

Davis likely had the idea that I couldn't do it, and he was right. I was a mess. But, I promised Cole in my heart, that I'd mourn for him until the sun rose. Then, I'd pull myself together and fight. Fight for him and for everyone else we lost, and I feared that number included Bruce Smith, Felix, Fennel, and Cage as well. And Luke Coye. Whoever caused the deaths of so many I cared for was going to die.

When we reached the base, Avery and I were directed to the medical unit while Kapen was taken upstairs with the briefcase I only now noticed was cuffed to his wrist. What was so important that it needed that much protection? Besides that, six Elite joined him. We'd had to leave all but two of his guards in St. Louis.

After a quick, cursory exam, I was given clean, blue scrubs and ordered to shower. Once clean and dressed, the nurse performed a more in-depth exam in which she bandaged my wounds and searched for anything I might've missed telling her about. My breathing was of the most concern for her, so after a dose of an injection that I didn't care to remember what it was, and an inhaler, I was given a couple pills for pain and told to rest.

A half hour later, Fay found me laying on the bed, still unable to sleep. In her hand was a vial of blood. When my eyes widened, she held up a hand.

"Don't worry. It's not mine. The general said you can't have magic blood, so I found a shifter willing to donate. General Davis thought you might need some."

"Thank you." I reached for the vial and downed the contents.

When she stepped out, Avery stepped in, a light smile on his face. "I was just coming to offer up some of mine."

My head dropped to the pillow. "I don't need your blood, Avery, but I could use the company."

"Same." The bed was small, but we made do, laying close together, no longer concerned about personal space. He was as much a brother to me as any of my real brothers. Maybe even more.

"Will they even bother looking for our team?" I stared at the white tiled ceiling, glad the lights were off.

"I don't know. Maybe. We failed, didn't we?"

"Big time, but I don't think anything we could've done would have stopped it. We were too far outnumbered in that chaos. Whoever is behind this knew what they were doing."

"It's going to cause mass panic everywhere," Avery murmured. "Gosh, this is a mess."

"We have to find out who's behind this. If Kara doesn't have any answers by now, then I'm going to request we bring in someone else to help her. It shouldn't be that hard to determine what's causing this."

Avery stiffened. "Speaking of Kara, I asked the nurse if she could send her down here so we could regroup, and she said no one has seen Kara since we left. She claimed a family emergency and disappeared."

"What?" I cried, sitting up. "Who did she tell? It certainly wasn't me."

"Well, apparently she didn't want to bother you."

Images of a large, mahogany stained study with a man writing a note on a small scrap of paper ran before my eyes. A figure in a dark cloak. Someone who had access to vamlure venom who might not have it otherwise...

"I need to take a look at the recordings from Luke's house. Now."

The floor was a lot closer than I thought, or I was that exhausted because my knees buckled and hit the tile hard. Wincing, I stood as Avery rounded the bed.

"Slow down. What's wrong?"

"I think I'm crazy, but I'm pretty sure the person who killed Luke Coye was Kara."

Avery's eyes bugged out and his face paled. "No. How? Why?"

"I don't know, but I knew there was something weird and familiar about the person who killed Luke, and why else can't she give us answers? I don't know why, but I plan to find out."

"Should we tell Davis?"

"We'll call him on the way over to Luke's place. And Jezzi. She'll need to meet us there."

We didn't have our uniforms here, but the scrubs fit fine. I wasn't planning on fighting, so I wouldn't need an official uniform. However, we did stop by the training level and borrow a few weapons. In the garage, Avery grabbed the keys to a jeep and climbed inside, speeding way faster than I'd seen from him yet.

The sky wasn't even tinged with light yet. This had to be the longest night ever. However, I wasn't ready to face the day yet, so if it stayed dark for a few more hours, I'd enjoy it. Facing reality would be easier in the dark.

As we drove, I dialed General Davis.

"Raven, what do you need? Fay said she gave you some blood."

"She did," I told him, taking a deep breath. "I wanted to tell you that Avery and I are on our way to Luke Coye's house. There's something about that security feed that's bothering me."

"You really don't know how to stay put, do you?" he grumbled. "I suppose I don't blame you. What can I do? Who do you need?"

I wanted to tell him who I needed, but the lack of those people were the reason he was asking in the first place.

"I need to know what you know about Kara."

"Kara? Let me dig out her file. I'll call you back in a few minutes with any information I can find. Can I have a hint of what I'm looking for?"

"Any reason pointing to why she'd be the one behind this."

Davis's voice hardened. "You're joking. Tell me you're joking."

"I wish I was. She disappeared right after we left. She hasn't found a single thing to point us toward what chemical could be used or what's even in it. And the person who killed Luke was certainly not a vamlure. The bite and attack were all wrong. General, she has samples of my venom. If she can create a chemical that can remove a creature's scent, then she can certainly use her power to recreate my venom."

He took a deep breath. "Watch that feed again. Find everything you can from it. I'll dig in her file to find what I can about why she'd do this. I'll have another team search for her. We'll find her, and if she's done it, she'll pay. I promise you that, Raven."

"Thank you, Sir."

My next call was Jezzelle, but she didn't answer. Not that I actually expected her to, but she'd been worried about me, so I figured she would. Although, this early in the morning, she was probably still sleeping. I wished I was.

"I'll try again when we arrive if the door's locked," I muttered.

Avery moaned, guiding the truck down the dirt lane at much higher speeds than anyone I'd ridden with yet had. "I'm hoping Luke was like everyone else and has a spare key under the front porch mat. Either that or our people didn't lock the house. If not, and she doesn't answer, I claim the back seat to sleep. You can take up here."

Our fears were quieted when we arrive and most of the lower level lights were on. "I hope that's not because of Jezzi," I muttered. "If she's back here with a killer still on the loose, I'm going to smack some sense into her."

We crossed the yard, and sure enough the main door was unlocked. The second I stepped inside, a sense of unease struck. Not again. I didn't need to find more dead bodies. Turning to Avery, I pressed a finger to my lips. He gave his head a slight jerk and followed me inside, both of us pulling our weapons.

When voices sounded up ahead in the kitchen, I turned to Avery, and found him with his phone in hand. He twisted his wrist to show me he was recording. Well, that was something I never would've thought to do.

"Quit stalling. Where is that extra security video feed you showed Raven?" Kara asked someone, making my heart skip. She was here. I clung to my knives with a tighter grip.

"I don't know what you're talking about," Jezzelle countered, and I fought to breathe.

"Oh, I think you do."

Jezzi's cruel laughter covered up our steps as we reached the corner that would open up to the kitchen. I wasn't ready to bust around it, but eased my face around to take in the scene. Neither woman had their back to us, but from her angle, Jezzi would be able to see us before Kara if we scooted into the room.

"You really did kill my father, didn't you? Why? Because he was digging into what you were doing?"

"Something like that. To be honest, I was helping to feed him information, send you all to the places I needed. Who knew I'd be so lucky as to gain access to Raven's venom. Too bad my attempt to frame him was thwarted. That would have been fun to watch."

Jezzi scoffed at her. "Why are you doing this?"

A syringe appeared in Kara's hand, the clear liquid glittering off the kitchen lights. If I had any guesses, I would say it was more manufactured venom.

"What? A girl can't decide that it's time for the supernaturals to reign, for the strong ones to rule and conquer? For too long the humans ruled, and we had to hide and pretend to be their disgusting species. Now we have a chance to grow and use them like they use us, and we're being held back. I just showed the world that humans and weak supernaturals are nothing."

Narrowing her eyes, Jezzi took a step back. "What did you do?"

"I destroyed St. Louis," Kara responded with a cackle.

Jezzi's hand flew to her mouth as she gasped for air. "Raven? Avery?"

"The city's in ruins, coyote. There's no one surviving in there. Sorry to tell you, but your boyfriend's dead."

Avery nudged me, our cue to enter the show. I stepped around the corner, followed by Avery and his phone. Jezzi stared at us, making Kara spin to find me sneaking up on her, my teeth bared and dripping with venom. Her eyes grew huge and her mouth popped open.

"I'm not dead," I seethed. "But you killed some amazing people, and I'm going to make sure you pay."

"How?" Kara whimpered, stepping back, not even realizing she was backing herself up to Jezzi until the coyote shifter lunged forward.

My heart stopped when Kara attempted to stab Jezzelle with the syringe as they fought for dominance. Then they stilled, and a breath later, Kara fell to the floor, the needle stuffed into her throat. Jezzi was breathing heavy, and when I lunged at her, she squeaked until my arms wrapped around her body.

"Are you all right?" I pleaded, holding her close. "Please tell me you're all right."

She held me in return, and seconds later, Avery's arms encircled us both. We stood like that for several minutes before he suggested we find somewhere to sit down and call General Davis. Staring down at Kara's unblinking gaze, I agreed.

Days later, we still hadn't figured out what had caused Kara to go off the deep end. General Davis had sent a team the moment I'd called him, and Avery had emailed a copy of the video he'd taken so Davis could view it. Jezzelle had officially given her notice that she was quitting, and she moved her belongings back to her father's house. As much as I tried to talk her out of it, she wanted to stay there. It was where she grew up and where she held her happy and sad memories of him. I couldn't argue with that.

The situation in St. Louis had been contained after hours of mayhem. Thousands of civilians had been killed, as well as Threats and Elite. By some miracle, Captain Smith, Felix, and two others on Smith's team had found a safe place to hide and had managed to escape. Cage and Fennel weren't lucky enough to make it out alive. The bobcats hadn't survived the Wights. The moment I saw Smith and Felix, I'd hugged them both for far longer than was appropriate, but they'd allowed it.

A memorial service for the fallen was held a week later, and General Davis asked me to say a few words as one of the commanding officers at the devastation in St. Louis. I'd barely made it through, especially since I was a leader, and I'd run, yet Davis had been right. Of anyone, I needed to survive, and I was glad I had, otherwise Jezzi may have also been dead and Kara would have continued to kill.

The day after the memorial was my first official day back to work. I'd been given the week off to relax, heal, and mourn. Going back to the mansion with only Avery at first had been difficult. When Felix had returned, it had felt somewhat more normal. There was still too much pain sometimes, and the three of us would fall asleep watching movies in the living room on the large couches, not ready to face the world yet.

Fay greeted me as usual with her normal smile, but a sad edge framed her eyes. It would be a long time before people would stop looking at me like that. Davis called me in and I closed the door, taking my customary seat.

"Honestly, how are you?" he asked, skipping small talk.

"Surviving."

"Are you ready to go back to normal duties?"

I nodded, breathing out a long stream of air. "Yes, I think so. I'm not sure it'll ever get better if I don't go back to work. This is what I do."

"Good. You're low on team members. Have you thought about who will replace the ones you lost?"

Shaking my head, I ran a thumb along Cole's band. I'd tried to give it to Davis, but he'd told me to keep it. I hadn't had the courage to take it off yet. For now, it served as a reminder for all that I'd promised Cole I'd do.

"Do you mind if I give you a list of suggestions this time?" Davis slid a paper across the desk, and I took it. None of the names were familiar, so I'd need to look them up.

"You're keeping me as Captain and team lead?" I asked him. "I failed. St. Louis was a huge failure."

"Yes, it was, but it wasn't your fault. In the end, you stopped the criminal. That's what counts. Think on those names. I want a minimum of three. If you want someone not on the list, you know what to do."

That was my dismissal. Another chapter was about to begin. Another team.

While my heart broke for the ones we'd lost, I would always remember them. I'd remember the promises. I wouldn't tolerate those who chose evil over good or those who looked down on me for being a vamlure.

Standing, I turned to General Davis. "How can I put someone in for a promotion?"

"You'll tell me about it. Who? And what position?"

"Avery. He's my second in command, and I think he'll do well as a Lieutenant."

Chapter 26

Nine years later...

"Hello, Fay," I greeted the woman behind the desk. "Connor wanted to see me."

"Go right on in," she instructed, flashing me a smile meant to lure in men, but we both knew I wouldn't be affected by it. More than one female had tried to grab hold of my heartstrings, and none had yet succeeded. Avery was convinced that was why I'd grown grumpy. I wasn't grumpy. Just determined and work oriented. There was a difference.

"Raven, come on in." General Connor Davis stood and shook my hand before we both sat back down. "The Interviews are in an hour. Have you thought about coming this year?"

"Nope."

"Do you mind explaining why not?"

I shrugged, staring around his new office. Four years ago, Headquarters had been moved into a newer, more high security building. The old base had become the new city college. Though I missed the old building, the high-tech security now available made the change worth it.

"Apparently I have a bad attitude."

"You and Luella are still butting heads, I see."

"She's a good Elite, but our personalities are polar opposite."

Connor grinned. "I warned you."

"You also didn't give me a choice but to take her."

"And I'm not giving you a choice but to come to the Interviews this year. You don't have to choose a trainee, but I want you to consider it. Come on. Let's head down together so I know you make it."

Stifling a groan, I followed Connor from the office. Five years ago, he'd told me to start calling him by name. It had been weird at first, and his name rolling off my tongue was odd, but I'd done as I was told. Now it was normal.

In the new parking garage, he climbed into his sporty car and I strode to my truck. I still loved the larger vehicles, and since I'd been coming from a personal trip to the store, I'd driven my truck instead of the team's SUV.

Pulling into the parking lot behind the Interview building, I spotted Avery and his little red sports car that my truck could run over and crush. He laughed when I pulled in the lot after Connor.

"So, he finally wrangled you into this, I see. Glad I won't have to suffer alone. Actually, if you're here, can I go home then?"

"Nope. We're going to suffer together."

We greeted several of the other Elite who were looking for a trainee, and I recognized one face more than the others. Felix grinned at me and strode over, giving me a hug. She was still one of the few females who dared to touch me. Though I rarely saw Jezzi these days, she always greeted me with a hug and a kiss. It was still platonic, but it was our tradition.

"How are you, Captain?" she laughed, tousling my hair.

"I'll be better when I can go home. How are you? How's the new team?"

She chuckled, leading the way toward the back of the building. "It's good. When Bruce retired and named me as his successor, I have to say I was a bit shocked, but I'm liking the new opportunity. How's my replacement?"

"We're still working out our differences," I muttered, making Avery chuckle.

"That's putting it mildly."

Felix's belly laugh had me grinning wide. "I wish I was there to see that."

Once inside, we took our places around the edges of the room. I hadn't been in this building since my own Interview, and the memories that flooded me were bittersweet. Unlike before, Connor personally went to escort each of the students to the building.

One by one he brought the students in and directed them to stand on a taped X. Some of them were a waste of time to Interview, but the law stated they all had to be here. They were either too scared or had no fighting ability at all.

When a young man came in who appeared to be able to hold his own, Avery perked up. The kid was smart, but human. When he answered some technological questions better than half the room could answer, I was impressed.

Avery bumped my arm. "I'm thinking he can work on that new security system we're trying to install."

After a moment of thought, I nodded my approval. In the end, Avery was given permission to train the boy, Lee. Like was normal now, Avery led Lee out the back door. They'd go grab his belongings and take them to the mansion.

While Connor went to escort his next victim, I lost interest and ran our last mission over in my head, trying to find how we could've done it better. We'd succeeded and it had been one of our easiest missions, but there was always something to learn.

A metallic scent drifted through the door when Connor returned, piquing my interest. I'd run into a few of my kind in the last couple years, and that scent was now familiar. What I wasn't expecting was the young female who followed Connor into the building. Long dark hair framed her face, and her curves were simple, but perfect. Green eyes stared around the room, and that concerned me. A knot tightened in my stomach. Her eyes were all wrong, unless she was a late bloomer. I'd been early, but at about twenty, she was late. However, the metallic scent didn't lie: she was close to needing her First Blood, and I made another promise to myself: when that time came, it would be my blood she drank.

Author's Note

As most authors will tell you, it's hard to pick your favorite book. It's like picking your favorite kid (or niece or nephew in my case). However, I have to say that this was one of my favorite books to write. I absolutely love Raven, but also all of his team. If you've read the First Blood trilogy, I hope you've enjoyed this look into the past. If this is your first novel in the First Blood world, then I hope you've enjoyed it enough to read the trilogy. Even more is to come in this world! I'm not ready to give it up just yet. More details are to come on those projects, so stay tuned! The best way to do this is by following me at any of the sites below.

Follow me on social media!
Facebook: http://facebook.com/heatherkarnauthor
Facebook Fan Group: facebook.com/groups/theweregalchronicles
Website: http://heatherkarn.com
Newsletter: http://eepurl.com/cdBPKP

Also, please feel free to leave a review on Amazon or Goodreads. I'd love to hear from you and what you thought of the book!

Continue for a sneak peek of "First Blood" and "Perfect Scents".

SNEAK PEEK

First Blood

The First Blood Series, Book 1

By: Heather Karn

Chapter 1

Ten years ago, life as humans knew it had been normal. Only humans existed, and the fairy tales, myths, and legends parents told their children were just that. Stories. Or so we'd thought. Those beliefs ended the day the President of the United States had called a special press conference to be shared worldwide. He'd announced that he was a lion shifter, the Alpha of the lion shifter pride in his home state of New Mexico, and explained how every creature out of stories was indeed real. Okay, most were real. The more popular ones anyway. Then he proceeded to shift on screen. I'd been almost eleven at the time, and though I didn't understand the significance of the event then, I did as time passed.

Everything changed overnight. Humans soon found themselves in the minority to supernatural creatures. There were several different categories created, with every species placed under a specific one. There were Shifters, Magic Users, Blood Drinkers, and Others. Others consisted of creatures who didn't necessarily fit into a category of their own because they were so different. Vampires, werewolves, and other creatures classified as the Threats went on a killing spree, and they didn't limit their victims exclusively to humans. In a matter of days, martial law was in place with a curfew to keep innocent civilians safe, and the Elite squads were put in place.

The Elite were the best of the best. The best fighters, thinkers, and blenders. Basically, the best spies, assassins, and bodyguards the government could hire. And everyone in my class at school wanted to join the Elite program a year later when it was created. Now, every high school graduate was required to enroll in college so they could not only continue their advanced education to find jobs, but also to learn all about the supernatural and gain fighting skills. At the end of the final semester of their Junior year, they took their Interview, which decided whether they could join the Elite as a trainee or if they finished college as usual. Failing the interview was easy. Passing was nearly impossible.

My forehead smacked against the wooden desk I sat at, emitting a dull thud that echoed around the classroom. I wasn't the only one to react in such a way. Several sighs and muffled groans, with a few other heads colliding with desktops, were the communal response to our professor's announcement seconds before. Even with my eyes closed, I was sure I heard soft sobbing from the Koala shifter in the back row. Her family had moved to the United States three weeks ago, right on time for Elite Interviews, which Professor Heldon had just announced were moving from two weeks away to tomorrow morning.

"At least now you have less time to worry over the Interviews," Professor Heldon, a warlock, chuckled after giving up trying to call the class back to order. His statement earned him a few glares from myself and several fellow students. "Unless of course you've procrastinated studying. I've warned you all year not to put off studying for the Interview. It's too late now to cram if you have procrastinated, and I urge you all not to pull an all-nighter to make up for the time you've missed. Study what you can. Leave the rest to fate. Maybe this will be a lesson to you. Now get out of here. Oh, and I want you all in your seats at ten minutes before eight tomorrow morning."

He had to yell the last part as students ducked out of the classroom as quick as they could and nearly ran down the hall to the cafeteria, library, or training rooms. Since I didn't feel like being mowed over by the rest of my classmates, I stayed seated until the majority had filed out. Only Lee, my twin brother, and our friend Oscar, and a girl named Kellie remained.

"Well, what's the plan?" Oscar asked in his usual loud voice, securing his backpack over his shoulder. "I vote lunch. I'm starving."

"You're always starving." Lee rolled his eyes, which were a stunning shade of emerald green that always seemed to sparkle, and motioned to the bag our friend carried. "We all know that bag is pretty much all food anyway."

Oscar shrugged, his long, wavy dark blond hair swaying with the movement. "Yeah, but that's my emergency stash. Come on, let's grab some real food."

Wiping my hands up and down my face, I moaned and settled back in my seat. "You guys go ahead. I'll catch you later."

"Let me guess, you're heading to the training rooms," Lee snickered, guessing accurately as he slid into the desk next to me. I glared at him in return.

"We both know I still can't fight well enough to even beat a racoon shifter, and that's when they aren't being shady critters. Being the smartest person in the whole class doesn't mean anything if I can't defend myself against an enemy. There's no way they'll accept anyone into the Elite program who can't fight, especially a human."

"You really think you can learn the skills needed to kill a werewolf, vampire, or other monster equally as powerful and deadly in the next twelve hours when you haven't been able to learn them in the last nine months? The last nine years even?" Oscar asked, a hint of annoyance touching his voice. It was the same old argument between us. We'd spent hours in the training rooms, him trying to teach me all he could about hand to hand combat. The lean, muscular build and fighting instincts from his panther shifter genes made fighting come easy and natural to him. Being human, I had no instincts like that to rely on. Neither did Lee, but even he excelled in physical training. I was the one who excelled in the classroom. And only the classroom.

"I'm going to try," I growled at Oscar between clenched teeth, grabbing my purse and phone before marching toward the door, following Kellie out into the hallway. She was a tiny girl, a rabbit shifter. Unlike most rabbits, she was an only child, her mother and siblings having been killed by a fox shifter when Kellie was young. Only she and her father had managed to escape the attack.

"Hey, Koda," Lee called from behind me, his trotting footfalls growing louder as he approached. "Koda, slow down."

"What?" I snapped, glaring over my shoulder at him.

"Easy, killer," he warned, raising his hands in surrender as he slowed to a walk beside me. "I was going to ask if you wanted some company. I could use the extra training time, just like you."

"No, you want to help me because you know I can't fight."

"Yes, and training helps me de-stress. Let's go."

Lee led the way out of the classroom building toward the much larger training grounds. The grounds held several fields that were sectioned off with fencing so that different classes could meet outside at once. Some were open areas while others were specifically made for certain weapons, like the archery range. A large building sat off to one side, and it was filled with various sized rooms for class and individual practicing. These were mostly used during the winter months since we had snow on the ground at least half of the year. I liked the private rooms over the smaller fenced in areas. There were fewer people to watch me be thrown around like a rag doll or crushed into the floor. I'd faced a young troll once my freshman year, and I hadn't been able to walk right for a week without tipping over from my dizziness. It was my lucky day that only my classmates had witnessed that disaster since the troll couldn't go outside into the sun.

"Some birthday we're going to have tomorrow," Lee snorted, closing the training room door behind us while I flipped the lights on. A window set high in the opposite wall allowed the sun inside to give us a bit more light to fill the large room.

After tossing my purse, phone, and jacket into a corner, I took my place on the practice mat, facing Lee. "The morning will be crappy, but I'm sure we'll have a great afternoon celebrating your success as an Elite trainee."

We both lifted our fists in a defensive stance, ready for the other to attack while he shook his head at me. "You'll be celebrating too. Once they figure out how much information you have stored up in that brain of yours, they'll want you. You're worth the extra physical training they'll need to put you through just for that."

"I wish." I feinted a strike at him, which he dodged with a counterstrike, and a second later I found myself flat on my back, staring up at the ceiling as a disappointed Lee stepped into view.

"Girl, if you do this tomorrow, I will personally smack you upside the head. You're better than this, even for a warm up." He held his hand out and helped me back up to my feet. We took our positions again, and this time I focused harder.

"Then let's not talk about our birthday."

He gave a sharp nod. "Deal. Focus."

It was often hard to remember the two of us, though we called ourselves twins, weren't even related by blood. My mom and his mom had delivered us on the same day, at the same hospital. Mine had died that day, but in some fluke had managed to arrange with Lee's parents that they would adopt me and raise me with Lee. I couldn't thank any of them enough, even my late mother, for allowing me to grow up with a family. I wouldn't have made it this far without Lee at my side.

Two hundred and forty pounds of muscle slammed into me, knocking me to the floor. Before Lee could deliver the kick he aimed at my ribs, I focused. That kick would drive the air from my lungs and make me useless for the next ten minutes. That wasn't going to happen today. I swept my leg around, knocking his feet out from under him. He regained his footing before me, but he didn't take advantage of my defenselessness like others would have, like whoever tested me tomorrow.

The moment I was back on two legs, he attacked. Some protective instinct buried deep inside had me blocking his right hook before I even thought about what I was doing. However, it failed to offer any defense against the left uppercut Lee aimed at my jaw, and as my teeth clacked together, I kicked out, missing my target. A flailing fish would cause more damage than I was as I found myself laying on my back again, this time of my own doing. Unlike last time, Lee didn't let me stand before attacking, and I barely rolled out of the way of the punch meant to knock my lights out.

We practiced for hours on hand to hand combat, knives, swords, and other weapons. Both of us were proficient enough with guns so we didn't bother with them, and the college president preferred we use other weapons. Most Elite didn't use guns anyway since several species of Threats had to have body parts removed to kill them. By the time Lee announced we needed to head home, we were both covered in sweat, and my skin was littered with bruises.

The cool air of the approaching evening chilled my sweaty skin and I regretted my decision to not put on my jacket, but only for a second. There was no way I would be tugging my coat over my sweat soaked clothes. Just the thought of that grossness made me cringe. I hadn't planned on training when I left the house this morning or I would have brought clean clothes to change into. Neither had my brother, but that didn't stop him from being comfortable. Lee had removed his shirt during our training session, and now he carried it in his hand so every female we passed had a clear view of his toned chest and abs. He wasn't as fit as most of the shifter males, but he was built well enough for a human to turn a female head his way.

Me, on the other hand, I was invisible in his shadow, and that was where I liked to be. For now, anyway. One day I'd make a name for myself. If I couldn't make the Elite, there were still several other programs I could apply for my Senior year. My detailed brain and impeccable memory would land me a good job...somewhere.

Before our Freshman year of college, our parents had bought a house near campus so that Lee and I could save money on housing. Plus, with our four younger siblings all planning to attend this university, they'd get their money out of the place. Oscar lived with us, as did another Junior, Clara, a petite hedge witch whose magic to grow plants was as weak as the healing potions she concocted. Even my bruises would be too much for her potions to heal. She was the most peaceful person I'd ever met. There was no way she'd be chosen as an Elite, and she was happy with that.

Both Oscar and Clara were home by the time we arrived. It was easy to tell. Oscar had the TV volume cranked up watching a sports game and the scent of dinner cooking told where Clara was hiding. Instead of heading to the kitchen to say hi as I usually did, I jogged up the stairs to the bathroom and locked myself inside. Without bothering to check on my bruised body, I stripped and showered. The warm water did wonders to loosen my sore and achy muscles. I should've thought about how I'd be feeling tomorrow before agreeing to spar with Lee. Maybe I'd ask Clara for some of her muscle relaxing creams tonight in hopes they'd work their limited wonders so I could move properly in the morning. Clean and smelling fresh, I ventured downstairs just as Clara was setting a pot of soup on the table. Lee followed close behind me, also fresh and clean.

"Is everyone ready for tomorrow?" Oscar asked as we all dug into the soup. It was Clara's specialty, homemade potato soup, and usually it was my favorite, but not tonight. My stomach turned. Couldn't he have waited until my food was digested before he brought that subject up?

"Let's face it, I might as well show up in a dress and heels for all the good it'll do me," Clara giggled, tucking strands of her long, black hair behind her ear as the rest shimmered in the dim light hanging above the small round table we were eating at. "I'm never going to be Elite material. They shouldn't even bother Interviewing me. It'll be a waste of their time, and mine."

"Yeah, but you know the rules," Oscar laughed. "They have to test you."

She shrugged. "And I'll fail. I have no qualms about that. What about you two? Are you ready?"

Lee groaned. "Between me and Koda we have the perfect candidate. She's smarter than any person I know and can remember every word in our textbooks, but she can't fight. Meanwhile, I can't remember what I ate for breakfast, but I can lay someone flat in thirty seconds. However, I don't think that's going to help either one of us tomorrow."

"Not likely," I mumbled before stuffing another spoonful of soup into my mouth. "I'll do my best. That's all I can say."

Clara drug a slice of bread through her soup. "Well, if you both fail tomorrow, we can have birthday cake and ice cream."

"What if we pass? No cake?" Lee grumbled. "I'd think we'd deserve it for passing."

She blinked at him. "Well, I suppose you're right. I was thinking you might be too busy doing your new Elite duty to want to celebrate with us simpletons."

"Not if you keep cooking like this," Oscar groaned, rubbing his full belly. "Even if I somehow make the Elite, I won't be missing much of your cooking. I'll be here every night."

"Unless they transfer you to a new location," I pointed out. It had happened before, though they apparently tried to keep most of their trainees close to the college for the first year, or until after graduation.

"Well, it's not like I want to be an Elite. I'd purposefully bomb the Interview tomorrow if there was a chance I wouldn't get in trouble for it. Then again, if I eat too much soup tonight because it tastes amazing, I could easily come up with a good reason for moving rather sluggish tomorrow."

We all laughed at Oscar's dramatic moan as he stuffed another bite of soup in his mouth, followed by half a slice of bread. The panther shifter had a hefty appetite, but also a high metabolism. It wouldn't matter how much he ate tonight. By the time the Interviews came, he'd be hungry again, even after a breakfast with the same amount of food ingested.

The rest of dinner consisted of the boys talking about sports teams and me and Clara ignoring them. While the educational system had changed, with new classes being added on supernatural creatures and the Elite program, much of the world remained the same. Only now we knew who was a paranormal or supernatural creature and who was human. It made sense that most sports players were shifters of some kind and that witches and warlocks organized and participated in most of the world's talent shows.

The biggest difference in every day life were the ugly and dangerous creatures who now walked the streets openly with the rest of us. The old system of police officers was still in place for every day crimes and detective work on a simpler level while the Elite teams were called in when either the police couldn't handle the situation or a far more dangerous supernatural was causing havoc. Like a vampire, or even a necromancer. The thought made me shudder, reminding me of tomorrow's Interview. I had to pass so that I could help rid the world of those evils.

"Okay, well I'm going to go do some studying before bed," I announced, taking my bowl to the sink so Clara could wash it. I wasn't lazy. She loved cleaning, and if I ever washed my bowl, I heard about it for a month at every meal afterward, and then some.

"Koda, you already memorized every textbook we've been forced to read," Oscar groaned, pulling his large body off the chair. His dark blond hair fell into his face to cover his eyes and he pushed it back behind his ear. "Can't you take a break and not wear yourself out? Come watch a bit of TV."

I glanced from him to the living room. "Sorry, not interested. You know how much I love watching sports."

"Fine, you can watch whatever you want. I'll even settle for a chick-flick."

"Sorry, Oz, but tomorrow's a big day, and I don't want to waste what precious little time I have left watching something pointless. If anyone wants to study with me, I'll be in my room." With that, I turned and walked away, already knowing that none of them would join me. None of them believed in last minute cramming. I usually didn't, but tomorrow was the biggest day of our lives, and at least I'd be able to pass one part of the Interview.

Read more here: mybook.to/FirstBlood1

SNEAK PEEK

Perfect Scents

The Weregal Chronicles, Book 1

By: Heather Karn

Chapter 1

Growing up the one thing that always made people wary of me was my ability to smell...everything. I could tell them exact spices used in every meal, and how long garbage had been in a trash can just by getting a whiff of it from twenty feet away. That's why I always sat in the far corner of the high school lunchroom. If you think that milky, ketchup smell is bad from a few feet away, for me, it's just as bad from the other side of the room. The one smell that could rival it would be the boy's locker room, and I was more than grateful I never had a reason to go in there. I could deal with the gallons of perfume my female classmates put on after our gym hour.

If I had to have a special talent, time travel would have been preferred over an amazing sense of smell for several reasons. First, it would just be plain fun. A real life Dr. Who? Who wouldn't want that? Secondly, I'd get out of school and this stinky cafeteria sooner.

The third, and most important reason, would be that I could see my parents again. Dad was killed in a drunk driving accident two years ago coming home from a late night at the office. Gerry wasn't my real dad, but after marrying my mom, he'd adopted me. My biological father was nowhere in the picture. I didn't even know his name.

Mom died of cancer two months ago. A year after Dad died, Mom was diagnosed with breast cancer. We stayed in Michigan until it became apparent she wasn't going to make it. Then she moved us to West Virginia to be with her mom and sister. Now that Mom was gone, Gram and Aunt Gwen were my guardians. I liked it here most days, but today was one of the hard days, and on those days, I avoided as many people as possible.

The scent of sweaty teenage boy and spearmint gum told me I had a visitor before he arrived at my table, interrupting my quiet lunch.

"You know, Joey, you're always depressed," a whiny male voice above me stated, dragging me from the book I held, but wasn't reading. It was a front to keep people at bay. Today it wasn't working.

"Excuse me?" I was dumbfounded. Who was bold enough to tell me I was depressed? Closing my book, I tucked my long red hair behind my ears so he could see the glare in my green eyes when I looked up.

The dark haired boy stared down at me as if he hadn't said anything offensive. "Well, you're always sitting over here by yourself, and you don't smile or laugh. What's anyone supposed to think?"

"That I like to read, and I'm not a social butterfly."

"Yeah, I get that. What I don't get is why you avoid everyone. We don't bite. Half of us only want to be your friend, but it's like you don't want anyone near you. We all know about your mom and what you're doing here. It's no secret. We can help."

"It's Mitch, right?"

"Michael," he corrected, rolling his mocha brown eyes like I'd proven the point he'd been trying to make.

"Okay, Michael. Why do people think I have to let them into my business? What happens in my life isn't a free for all. When I decide I need friends, or that I need to talk to someone, I'll look you up. For now, I'd like to get back to my book, please." The words came out harsher than I'd anticipated, and I felt bad the moment they were said. I wasn't as upset with him as I was with the whole situation. He just happened to be the one who got the full taste of my ire.

Michael stalked away shaking his head. I turned back to my book while his words replayed in my mind. Before I could get too depressed about my state of life, the bell rang. Time for trig, history and Senior English. Then I would be free.

Mrs. Huckabee had been teaching English for almost forty years. She was a small woman with curly white hair and large, metal rimmed glasses. Technology was not her thing, so if she couldn't use it, neither could we. I liked her, though. She was feisty.

"All right class, today you get to pick your next essay assignment. The topic is mythical creatures and deities," Mrs. Huckabee explained, which was met with several groans from the class. She continued without acknowledging that she'd heard the moans. "I have a list of topics you can choose from that William will pass out for me. If the topic you want is not listed, discuss it with me and we'll see if it fits the criteria. Are there any questions?"

No one said anything as she finished and handed William, a short, stocky kid with the bluest hair I'd ever seen, the topic idea papers to hand out. He'd eaten French fries for lunch, and the smell of them clung to his skin and clothes, hiding his usual musky scent. He was a nice kid, though, and hung to himself a lot, like me.

As I read down the list of topics, my frown grew into a wider smile with each topic. There were Ancient Greek gods and goddesses, as well as Egyptian and Norse gods as well. There were more recent mythological creatures as well as events and places such as the city of Atlantis. At the bottom of the list, I came across a name I'd never heard of, which was odd because I knew every other creature, god and legend listed on the paper.

"Mrs. Huckabee?" I asked as she strode past me from talking to the girl who sat behind me, her apple cinnamon scent flowing with her. Oh and the smell of her three cats.

"Yes, Joette?" She refused to call me anything but my given name.

I pointed to the name on the list and asked, "What's a weregal?"

"You don't know what a weregal is?" Chrissa, a tall, blond girl who sat to my left in the next row of desks asked. "They're only the scariest and coolest thing around here."

"They live here?" I asked, looking between her and Mrs. Huckabee. "I thought we were doing mythical creatures, and you're telling me these things are alive?"

"You see, Joette," Mrs. Huckabee explained. "About a hundred and fifty years ago the first weregals were spotted out in the mountains and hollows. They seemed to have disappeared about twenty years ago. There hasn't been a sighting in years. In that time they've become more myth than reality."

"Yeah, but what are they exactly?"

"They're werecats. You know humans who can turn into cats. In this case, they turn into tigers," Chrissa explained, her eyes overflowing with excitement.

"I have an idea," Mrs. Huckabee announced, "Why don't you do your essay on the weregals, Joette? I believe the library has some newspaper articles about them. Many people around town also have information. I think you'll like this topic. I'd best write it down before I forget that's your topic." She made a mad dash to her desk before I could tell her I truly didn't want to write on this. There went all the fun of the essay right out the window.

When the last bell of the day rang, I packed up my books and followed the rest of my class out of the room and headed toward my locker. The school wasn't that large, so I was there within a minute. Chrissa's locker was right next to mine, and she had beaten me there. She usually did. I waited for her to put her books away and grab her backpack and coat before I moved to get into my locker. The aroma of Oreos and peanut butter wafted from her, making my stomach growl. That was an interesting combination.

"You are so lucky; you know that don't you?" Chrissa told me as she closed her locker and stepped out of the way so I could get into mine.

"Lucky? How so?"

She smiled showing her perfect, white, straight teeth that had me envious every time I saw them. Sure mine were straight, but they would never be that pearl white that she had. Her bubbly laugh was also a cause of envy. It could attract any guy's attention within earshot and cause them to trip over themselves to stare at her. And that's exactly what happened as she stood there smiling and laughing at me. I almost snorted out a laugh as two boys collided next to us in the hall. Chrissa didn't notice as her attention was all on me.

"Really, Joey? You get to write an essay on weregals. I mean, that's just pure awesomeness right there, girl."

"What part of it is awesome? I didn't even get to pick my own topic. At least you got something fun like the Egyptian gods." I'd been so jealous when she'd announced to Mrs. Huckabee that she wanted to write on that. I loved studying the Egyptian and Greek gods and would have traded her in a heartbeat, but I'd gotten stuck with stinkin' tiger people that didn't even exist like everyone here seemed to think they did. After all, we were studying myths and legends.

She reached in front of me to pull my locker shut as I grabbed out my bag and jacket. "Seriously, rumor has it that a weregal male is like the hottest piece of manliness you'll ever see in your life."

"It's not like I'm going to see one. I've got to read about them and write about what I read. Trust me, if I were going to see one and study it, I'd be a lot happier about this assignment."

She laughed again as we left the building together. As luck would have it, no guys were close enough to hear her laugh as lockers continued to slam shut. "Well if your research happens to have any pictures that show up, please let me know. I'd love to hang them on my wall and stare at them for hours."

Her gusty sigh made me chuckle. "I'll be sure to let you know."

"You and I should hang out sometime. I think we could have a lot of fun together." She slung an arm around my shoulders as we headed to the small student parking lot. It was a little awkward because Chrissa had almost six inches on my five feet.

I could see Gram waiting in her old, rusty car and wanted to cringe. Being seventeen and getting picked up from high school by your grandma in a piece of junk car like that was so not cool. Just another perk of living in paradise.

"Are you sure I won't be too boring for you? Some people find me too depressing to be around," I responded.

"Michael's an idiot," she said, stopping us at the edge of the parking lot. It didn't surprise me that she'd know about my conversation with him. By now everyone knew.

She took her arm away and gave me the first serious look I'd seen her wear. "We all know you just lost your mom. I can't imagine what that's like. You have every right to feel depressed about that. If wanting to be alone at lunch and reading a book is how you cope with it, then you go girl. Don't let that fool stop you. But if you want a friend, or just someone to talk to, I'm all ears. And don't worry, I won't say a thing. People around here already have too much to gossip about."

I stood there smiling like an idiot, not knowing what to say. Someone was actually talking to me without prying into my private life. That was a change.

"Thanks, Chrissa. I think it would be fun to hang out. Right now I have to go, though. Gram's waiting for me."

"Oh that's right, your grandma picks you up. Don't you have a car?"

"Nope. We had to sell Mom's after we moved here. Not that it would do me any good since I don't have a driver's license."

She stared at me for a moment as if my hair was changing from its natural red to William's blue before her eyes. "You're kidding right?" I shook my head. "You don't have a license?"

"I didn't need one. Before we moved here, I always used the city bus system, or I rode my bike. I'd be riding it now except Gram thinks that October is too cold to ride around outside."

"Ok, well that makes sense, I guess. Hey, do you want to work on our essays together?"

I had a hunch it was less about the essay and more about the weregals, but I was okay with that. "Sure. I was thinking about hitting up the library tomorrow morning to do some research. If they're open, that is. Did you want to meet me there?"

She thought about it for a second while nibbling on her thumbnail. "Sure. What time?"

"Depends on when they open, but I'm sure they're open by nine, so I was going to aim for that."

"Nine on a Saturday, are you crazy?"

"Some people think so."

She shook her head at me. "Okay, well call me when you find out if it's open and I'll be there. Man, you're crazy."

"Hey, you wanted to hang out," I reminded her, laughing as she shook her head.

"This does not count as hanging out."

"You said you wanted to work on our essays together. I want a head start."

"You just want to see if there are any pictures," she replied with a wink, implying that I was the one who wanted to stare at hot guys all day; whatever floated her boat.

I rolled my eyes at her. "I'll need your number."

She whipped out her cell phone. "If you give me your number I'll text you so you'll have mine."

My cheeks grew hot as I scuffed the toe of my shoe against the sidewalk. "I don't have a cell phone."

"No driver's license, car, or cell phone. Honey, we've got to fix this."

"Not my fault."

Chrissa took off her backpack and ripped a small piece of paper from a notepad and scribbled her phone number on it. As she handed it to me, she gave me an order of, "Don't lose it."

"Well, have a great night. I'll most likely see you tomorrow," she said and headed toward her car.

"Yeah, see you then."

With that, I crossed the parking lot toward Gram. She watched me approach with a curious expression on her face. My guess was that she was surprised I'd been talking to someone, and I'd let that someone put her arm around me. I was about to find out for sure because Gram never lets anything slide by without getting more information. She was one of the worst busybodies in town, but she kept our business to herself...most of the time.

I opened the door and got in with a sigh. When I pulled the door shut, it made a loud screeching that made me shudder every time I heard it. One of these days I'd remember to grab some WD-40 while I was at the store. And I'd need to get an air freshener. The car smelled old.

"New friend?" Gram asked as she waited for me to buckle up before turning on the car. Her bright blue eyes never left me as I fought the seat belt into place.

"I guess," was my reply. "We need more milk."

"I already stopped by the grocery store and grabbed some. I also got some apples and bananas, and a head of lettuce. Oh, and some oranges. You need to start eating better and lose some of that weight you've put on. I thought fruit might aid with that. And you need to start exercising again. I think that will help your mood."

Leave it to Gram to cut to the chase and be as blunt and honest as she wanted to be, even if it was offensive. Yes, I'd put on a few extra pounds since moving here, but I wasn't unhealthy or overweight. My old habit of running in the evenings had ended since Mom died, and I'd started eating a lot more junk food, all of which had been supplied by Aunt Gwen. She knew what a girl needed, and it wasn't health food.

Gram wasn't a health food nut, but she didn't eat as much junk food as Aunt Gwen and I did. She was barely taller than I was and as skinny as a twig. Mom had been built the same as Gram and me. Gram's hair was dark but had started to acquire some gray highlights. It looked good on her with her short, layered haircut. This was where we differed. I had Grandad's red hair, just like Mom did. Aunt Gwen, on the other hand, had Gram's dark hair.

Aunt Gwen was the complete opposite of Gram and me as far as body structure. She had Grandad's build, or at least that's what I was told. He'd died before I was born. Like him, Aunt Gwen was close to six feet with broad shoulders and strong upper body muscles. She wasn't overweight either, but she was a bit hefty. In more ways than one, she and Gram were complete opposites, and it made for some rather interesting discussions at home.

"Now who was that girl you were talking to?" Gram asked, steering us back on topic.

"Oh, that was Chrissa Larsen."

"Well, she seemed like a nice girl."

"Yeah, she is. Can we go now? Everyone's staring."

It was true. Anyone who was close enough to see inside the car, which was just about everyone, was watching. They probably wanted to know who owned the junk metal sitting in the parking lot, or if the car would even start. I knew it would, and it would blow out a cloud of blue-gray smoke behind it that would stink and linger in the air for several minutes. It made me wish Gram would just leave it running. She'd let me ride my bike to school for the first month and a half, but for the last few weeks, she'd argued it was too cold outside. I still thought it was nice, but I couldn't convince her of that. So now everyone got to see that I rode around in style.

Gram laughed as she started the car and pulled away. I kept my face down so I wouldn't meet anyone's eyes. Once we pulled out of the parking lot, I lifted my head.

"So what did this Chrissa want?" Gram prodded after I'd been silent for a few minutes. She didn't quite understand my need for quiet in the car after school.

"She wants to hang out sometime."

She smiled in response. I knew that would make her happy. "That's great. When?"

"We didn't set a time. Just sometime in the near future. She wants to work on our English essays together too."

The trees were going by at a steady pace, and so were the hills. It had taken me a while to get used to the constant ups and downs of the road, and for my ears to stop popping all the time. There was a mountain trail I could bike that was pretty flat and took me most of the way home from school. The popping wasn't too bad on my bike.

"Other than working on your essays, what are you going to do?" Gram asked with a wry smile. The local police department should have hired her to be an interrogator. She was relentless.

"If I had to guess, I assume she'll want to go shopping or to a movie or something like that. I'm not into shopping that much, but a movie would be nice." I sat silent for another minute or two. "Do you know if the library is open tomorrow?"

Gram turned off the highway onto our road, which led into a wooded hollow. If I was honest with myself, this part of the country was beautiful. The fall colors were at their peak. I'd never seen such bright hues.

"I think it's open from nine until noon. Why do you ask? Do you need a book?"

"I need to do some research for my English essay. We have to do one on mythical creatures, and Mrs. Huckabee assigned me the topic of weregals, or whatever they are. She said there are newspaper articles and other information in the library. It's not due until the end of November, but I wanted to get a head start."

It took me longer than it should have to realize that Gram was too quiet. Taking my eyes off the view out my window, I turned to look at her. Her usual smile was gone, replaced by a frown.

Read more here: https://www.amazon.com/dp/B01JBOI29G

Made in the
USA
Lexington, KY